Totally Bound Publishing books by Jayce Carter

Larkwood Academy

SILENCED

JAYCE CARTER

Silenced
ISBN # 978-1-80250-967-0
©Copyright Jayce Carter 2022
Cover Art by Kelly Martin ©Copyright July 2022
Interior text design by Claire Siemaszkiewicz
Totally Bound Publishing

SILENCED

Dedication

To the many hours of sleep I lose
because I'm writing porn.

Chapter One

Eyes forward – just ignore the werewolf.

I repeated that to myself as I quickened my steps. It wasn't hard to identify the shade who crouched over a trashcan, rifling through whatever he could find inside. Even if he hadn't been wearing the law-required bright yellow band on his wrist to identify himself, there was just something about shades that made it easy to spot them.

They had this *danger* in them, this bone-deep hesitation they provoked in normal humans when a shade crossed our paths. They had a feral quality to their movements and an emptiness in their eyes, as if everything that had been real about them had drained out when they'd become infected by source.

It meant that this shade, despite appearing young for the change—he couldn't have been older than eleven—could have torn me apart if he lost control.

Though, the fact he was out on the street, even identified, meant he had to have been a weaker specimen and on the proper medication to treat his affliction. Otherwise, he would have been properly secured at an academy.

"Don't stare, Hera," my friend Moa said.

"How can he be out on the streets?" I asked, keeping my voice low as we passed by the shade. "I thought we had groups to keep them out of sight."

Moa gave me a sharp look, one that reminded me just how different our lives were.

Moa wasn't privy to reality, to the danger shades posed. She got to live in ignorance, to pretend the world was a safe place while I watched as people were slaughtered by uncontrolled shades. Then again, her family ran a little consignment shop whereas my mother was a senator and headed the committee for shade control, and my father ran one of the largest pharmaceutical companies in the country.

I was Hera Weston, the only child of Zachary and Regina Weston, which meant I didn't have the luxury of not knowing.

Still, I played along, pretended I had no idea what her censure was for because there was no reason to have this fight again. A nonchalant sip of my water bottle helped to sell that. "What?"

"He's just trying to get some food. Do you have any idea how many shades are kicked out of their homes when they change? How many can't get hired after that?"

"They don't *change*. They're infected and they die," I countered, but kept walking so she couldn't give me another long winded, politically correct explanation about how they didn't really 'die.'

Moa was one of those who thought that shades were just altered, that they were still the people they'd been when human. It wasn't true, of course, and if she paid any attention to the news or in school, she'd have known that.

Source—a substance that leaked through invisible tears between our realm and the darkness—could infect some humans. When it happened, that infection caused mutations so dramatic that only a fool would consider the resulting shade to be the same person as the human they'd been. The infections seemed random, since the tears could be neither tracked nor stopped.

It was just part of life.

"Besides," I added, trying to offer the next words like an olive branch as we passed the shops that lined the outdoor mall, "that's why we have academies set up, to take care of them safely and determine how best to treat them."

"Those academies are prisons," Moa snapped, tugging my arm to stop us, drawing the same line in the sand we'd danced around for years. She faced off against me as if we were engaged in some battle instead of standing in front of a high couture boutique shop. "Kids are stolen from their parents and thrown into the institutes. They're often experimented on, drugged and who knows what else."

"You need to stop reading the tabloids. Have you ever even *been* to one?"

"No," she admitted softly. "Have you?"

"Yes. Two years ago, I went with my mother to see Jasmine Academy. I can promise you, *none* of what you're talking about was going on there. The shades were happy, healthy and unable to hurt themselves or others. Isn't that the goal?"

Moa shook her head. "You are naïve, Hera. Do you think places like that want people to know what's really going on? Do you think they're going to just show all the bad things they do when the VIPs come around? It's all a publicity stunt so people tell the government to keep sending them all the money they want. It's just about creating enough fear so we don't pay any attention to the atrocities they do there."

I sighed and let the conversation drop. I could argue with her all day—and I had before—but Moa had no idea about the real world. I wasn't angry with her about that—I envied her some of the time.

It would have been nice to fall asleep each night with no idea of what lurked in the shadows. I still remembered my first time seeing a fully changed werewolf, the horror as it had pulled at the silver chains wrapped around it, as it had roared. My mother had brought me with her, had worried when I'd become enamored with shades as so many teenagers did.

The power, the rebellion, the danger of something so powerful was intoxicating and most people went through a phase where they thought they could change them. Why we women felt the need to do that, to find fixer-uppers who we had to work on, I didn't understand anymore.

Not after witnessing the bone-deep terror at coming face-to-face with a shade that could rake its claws through my throat in a heartbeat. I'd realized that day that the world was far more dangerous than most people knew.

Moa still had that fascination because her parents were bleeding hearts who hadn't taught her better. She'd learn, eventually. Everyone did, because the world didn't let people keep their illusions for long.

So, instead of furthering that line of thought, I pointed at a kiosk up ahead. "Let's look at the necklaces up there."

Moa let out a long breath, as if reining in her own temper, as if *I* were the difficult one to deal with, then nodded. "Sure. Maybe we can get matching ones."

The selection wasn't great, but it offered the perfect distraction. We were only weeks away from the new academic year starting, and we hadn't gotten into the same schools.

Moa had gotten into a local state school, something that would work well enough for her to get the business degree she wanted so she could help and eventually take over her family's shop.

I, on the other hand, had the acceptance letter on my desk from one of the premiere colleges in the country. I'd had good grades, but the fact that the building had a 'Weston Wing,' and my last name was Weston had gotten me in. In fact, I hadn't even filled out an application. One call from my father and the doors had sprung open.

Moa had held the letter in her hands, staring as if it were the holy grail. Me? I'd tossed it to my desk because fuck that. Going across the country to some university sounded dreadful to me. It felt like another nail in the coffin of my future, the one my parents had laid out for me before I'd ever been born.

The right education, the right career, the right husband. It was all a path to the perfect little Weston life they wanted me to have. And I'd trudged along that path because what other choice did I have? Even now, at nineteen years old, I was stuck. An adult by age but a child by freedom.

An arm wrapped around my waist, spinning me before lips pressed to mine. Aaron swallowed down my startled gasp, then only laughed when I smacked his chest.

"Don't sneak up on me," I snapped.

He offered a crooked smile. "Don't stand there looking like you want a kiss then. You never know who might just take you up on it."

I shook my head, grinning at his playfulness.

The right spouse. That had my smile disappearing.

Aaron was that. The son of a business associate of my father's—our parents had basically planned the wedding when we were still toddling around the playground in diapers. I'd grown up knowing what was expected of me, had fallen into line before I'd gotten old enough to question it.

Besides, Aaron wasn't that bad. He was charming, handsome, rich. The sex was tolerable, and he never treated me badly. I didn't have butterflies, or head-over-heels nonsense, but I was pretty sure those things were only in cheesy books and movies.

In the real world, 'not bad' was the best a person could hope for.

"What are you looking at?" he asked as he tugged me against him.

"Necklaces," I explained. "Moa and I were going to get matching ones."

"What about me?"

"What about you?" Moa asked with a smile. She'd always liked Aaron, probably more than I ever had, but she'd been respectful of our relationship no matter what.

"Well, I mean, we've been running around together all this time. I should be part of the whole necklace thing, too."

I rolled my eyes. Aaron could be awfully clingy at time, but he wasn't wrong. He'd been friends with Moa and me, like some weird love triangle, for most of our lives.

"I'm not wearing two necklaces."

Moa reached out and picked up a small white paper that had hung on a hook. A silver charm dangled on it, and she held it out to me. "Why don't we do chains? Then we can pick the charm we want each of us to have, and we'll all have those matching charms wherever we go."

"That is cringingly sentimental, and I *love* it." Aaron snatched a charm from the wall of product. "Look, a bear—this one is perfect for me because I'm big and tough and super manly."

Moa smirked and grabbed a rat. "Or this one because you're constantly shoving cheese into your mouth and are rather annoying."

Aaron put a hand against his chest as if she'd struck him with her words. "Fine, you don't get a charm from me. Good job."

I laughed at their antics as I scanned the available options. What was for me? What would represent me enough that I'd want my two best friends to wear it?

Aaron settled on a racoon, which seemed fitting. He was hard to ignore, stayed up way too late and was rather entertaining. Moa chose a paintbrush, because of her love of art.

My gaze landed on one, and I knew it was perfect to represent me. A silver music note, something elegant and simple and so intertwined with who I was that it felt obvious.

I'd sung my entire life. In fact, my mother said I hadn't learned to speak sentences so much as verses. The headphones hanging around my neck were a testament to my love of music, to the fact I couldn't fathom a few hours without putting on the large earcups and disappearing into the sounds, into how they took away everything happening in my life I couldn't control.

Music made me feel as if I still had a hold of something, and singing was my way of putting my voice into a world that always felt too loud, to make a mark when the world didn't want to hear me.

"That's perfect." Aaron took all the charms and chains to the salesperson to pay for them, Moa now complaining.

Aaron or I always paid for things, since our parents were far better off than Moa's. What was a hundred bucks between friends?

After Aaron handed them over, we hooked the charms on the chains, then put them on. It was a surreal feeling, like an acknowledgment of how much our lives were about to change, with all of us going to different schools, on different paths of life that would take us different directions.

Aaron and I would come back together—we didn't have much choice there—but I wondered what would happen to Moa. Was this the end of our little group?

The three charms sat next to one another, cool against my warm skin, and I had a moment of wishing things wouldn't change.

Unfortunately, I had a feeling nothing could stop that from happening.

* * * *

"I need to get home," I complained to Aaron three hours later.

Moa had already abandoned us, since she was by far the most responsible. She'd taken off around ten, but Aaron hadn't been ready to turn in, and I was easily bribed with a caramel macchiato.

"I'm leaving tomorrow." Aaron's voice lost some of its humor.

"You're only going to be a few hours' drive away from me," I reminded him. "And we'll talk on the phone all the time."

"It won't be the same. Come on, Hera, can't you at least pretend you'll miss me?"

I blew out a breath, sick of that question. He hurled it a lot, and it had taken me a while to understand why.

In the end? I just didn't think I was an affectionate person, not like he was, not like he wanted me to be. He wanted someone who called in the morning because I just couldn't stand not hearing his voice. He wanted someone who couldn't imagine life without him.

And I tried, I really did. I set alarms on my phone to remind me to text or call him, and I did everything I could to play the part he wanted me to, even if I never felt it.

"I will miss you," I lied. "I just think you're being a bit dramatic. It isn't like we're never going to see each other. We can visit every weekend, and we'll have all summer together. But I *can* say you're going to have a miserable flight tomorrow if you don't get some sleep."

He let out a slow sigh, and the lines in his face, the ones put there because I wasn't living up to what he needed, hurt.

So I slid my arm around him, trying to be and do what he wanted. "I'm sorry," I offered. "I think I'm just nervous about the move, about how everything changes, you know?"

He nodded, but a shadow in his eyes said he probably recognized the change of subject when he saw it. "Yeah, I know. It'll be good, though. We'll get out of this town, out on our own. And, who knows? Maybe I can get my classes on the right days and split my time between your place and mine."

I smiled even as I cringed at the thought. I wanted my own space, my own life, and I wouldn't get that if Aaron was my shadow the whole time. Still, I'd upset him enough, so I nodded. "Yeah, that would be nice."

He nodded, as if it had been decided. "Why don't we—" A yawn broke his statement.

"That's it—you're exhausted, and you have a long day tomorrow. You should go home and get a few hours of sleep before you have to leave."

"No goodbye sex?" He lifted an eyebrow to pair with his smirk.

"That would defeat the whole purpose of going home to get sleep. Classes don't start for two weeks. What if I agree to fly out to you Monday? We'll spend a week together at your place, then I'll fly to mine. It'll give you a few days to get set up."

"Then we'll christen my new apartment?"

"Sure." I didn't have to fake a smile at that. Sex might not have been mind-blowing, but like most things, I had a feeling that pretty good was the best a person could hope for, and Aaron's enthusiasm went a long way.

He offered me a ride home, but I said no. If we did that, he'd talk me into ignoring the things about sleep. Besides, I'd driven myself, and I didn't want to leave my car.

Once Aaron left, I was able to sip my coffee in silence, a benefit as my headache hadn't gone away.

Over the past year, I'd gotten more headaches—stress, my father had told me. Getting ready to move out for the first time, to a place across the country—that was a big deal. I was preparing to leave everything I'd ever known, the people, the places, the familiarity of it all and branch out.

That would make anyone lose sleep.

It felt like something more, like something deeper, but when I couldn't figure it out, I chose the easy answer.

The crowds had thinned, now that it was past midnight. There were those celebrating and those mourning, all drunk and stumbling and far too loud. Their voices lacked harmony, grating on my nerves, making my head pound worse.

Still, I pushed through, crossing the large outdoor shopping area with lights strung everywhere, toward the parking lot. I had a spot up on the top level. My father leased it every year so when he came for dinner, he never had to worry about finding a spot. Since he rarely came, I happily used it.

I got into the elevator, my hand shaking, my head throbbing. When the doors shut, I closed my eyes and pulled in a breath, trying to ease that tension inside me, a reaction to panic being my only guess. These attacks had kept getting worse, and even the pills my father had given me hadn't done much to help. The only thing that seemed to help were my headphones drowning out the noise.

The elevator moved quickly, and I held the railing to keep myself steady as my stomach churned.

Relax. Deep breaths, nice and slow. I coaxed myself through it, as I had before, as my therapist had taught me. The idea I had anxiety annoyed me. I had *nothing* to be anxious about. It made me feel like every other rich kid who didn't realize their life was damn near perfect so they came up with pointless little problems and blew them out of proportion.

I hadn't ever been that person before, but it seemed I was now.

Still, I refused to let myself remain that way, so I forced my body to relax and grabbed two ibuprofens from my purse, swallowing them with my coffee even though taking pills with hot drinks wasn't the easiest thing to do.

By the time the doors to the elevator slid open, I'd mostly gathered my wits. My head still ached, but the world seemed sharper again and nothing spun. I told myself a good night's sleep would do the trick, that I was just up too late and dealing with Moa and Aaron had just been overwhelming.

I walked the large parking lot, toward the back where my car was. Many of the spots were filled because the floor was also used for residents who lived in the condos just across the small path. It meant the cars were all expensive, since it wasn't a cheap place to live.

I turned the corner and froze.

Three men stood there in dark hoodies, one with a slim-jim already inside the window of a car. Their faces all turned toward me at once, and the curl of one's lips made all that panic I'd had inside the elevator rush back into me.

This wasn't good…

Chapter Two

I took a step backward and clutched my purse as if that could keep me safe. "Sorry," I rushed out. "I was just looking for my car."

The man who had grinned took a step my way. "Not a problem, darlin'. What's your name?"

"Hera," I said without thinking about it, without realizing what a stupid idea it was to give him my name.

"Pretty name," one of the others said. "Now, I know this looks bad, but my friend here just locked himself out of his car."

Lie. Pain echoed through my temples when he spoke, and I knew instantly what he said was a lie. I didn't know how, but it was as if just hearing it scratched against my brain.

Not that I didn't already know they were lying. No one tried to break into their own car at midnight in a parking lot, and especially not the sort of person who owned that sports car, which had to cost well over a hundred grand. In fact, I doubted a slim-jim would even work on such a car.

It meant the men were not only liars, but not as high-class criminals as they thought.

"I was just leaving," I said, a tremble to my voice. "I won't say anything."

No vehicle was worth my safety.

I tried to walk to where I could see my car sitting. If I could just get inside, lock the doors, I could get out of here.

Except, when I started to walk, the men moved as well. I cursed my choice of heels, feeling like every girl in a horror movie. To be fair, I'd dressed for a nice night out with my friends, not to run from car thieves.

"Hold up there," the first man who had spoken said. "Just wanted to talk to you a minute."

"I need to get home," I answered, quickening my steps. I didn't need to reach for my keys since my car unlocked automatically when I got the key fob close enough to it. I could have tried to run for the elevator, but it was much farther away than my car.

I didn't run—between the heels and the fact my head had that almost dizzying feeling inside it again, I couldn't risk it—but I walked as quickly as I could, the click of my heels against the concrete floors seeming so much louder than they were, but still not as loud as the pounding of my heart.

When the steps behind me quickened to a run, I realized I didn't have a choice but to do the same. I only got a few steps before something wrapped around my arm, yanking me to a hard stop that almost knocked me off my feet.

"Hold up, darlin'," that first man said.

"Let me go," I snapped.

He only tightened his hand. "I don't think so. See, you already caught us, saw our faces, and I don't want to end up back in prison."

"I told you, I won't say anything. I just want to go home." My last words came out a plea, and I struggled not to give into full panic. All the true crime I'd watched came back to me, the cases that weren't ever solved, the women who just went missing with no idea what happened.

I thought about Aaron, about how I wouldn't make it to see him Monday, about Moa who would blame herself for going home early and leaving me. About my parents, about how they'd pour so much money into finding any trace of me and how they'd cry when they realized what had happened.

My throat hurt, a soreness that had started a year before, like I was constantly sick and I could never shake it. Except, instead of the nagging, dull pain, it had turned sharp. It bled down, into my chest, as if my lungs burned as well.

I swallowed to try to clear my head, to focus on the moment instead of what-ifs.

"You can't go home," the man said, not looking all that sorry as he said it. His friends walked up as well, as if they'd realized I was a far better target than the car.

One snatched my purse from me, then reached inside, taking out my wallet and the keys. "Shit, girl, you got a lot of cash in here. And credit cards? Daddy sure does take good care of his princess, doesn't he?" He laughed, tossing the car key to the man who had been working the lock of the first car.

That man hit the lock button twice, my car honking and flashing the lights in response. "Oh, fuck. Look at that, huh? Bet that thing is worth even more than the one we were trying to snatch."

It was, of course. "Take the car." I forced the words past that pain in my throat. "I won't tell anyone about it. Take the cash, too. Just let me go."

A soft whistle from the man who had my wallet. "Well, ain't it our lucky day? You got any idea who we have here? Fucking closest thing to royalty we got. This here is Hera Weston."

The name felt like a punch to my stomach, especially the way he said it.

"No shit," the man who had my arm said. "Well, between the wallet, the car and what her parents will give us for her, this is our lucky night, ain't it, darlin'?"

"He'll pay," I said. "Just don't hurt me, and he'll give you what you want."

The man with my arm smiled wider, and the coldness in it made my stomach churn, made me feel as if I wouldn't be able to keep in that feeling that had taken me over in the elevator, the one I'd fought against for months.

"Yeah, he will pay us, but see, people pay better when they realize they got something to lose." He used his free hand to drag his fingers down the side of my face in a sickening touch. "Plus, if you're going to stay with us until he pays, well, we get awfully bored. A girl like you, who has an ass like you got, oh I bet you can keep us well entertained."

And *that* got me. That threat stole the rest of my restraint. The shaking got worse, taking over me, making it impossible for me to even think. The burning in my throat increased until I would have sworn a fire raged inside my lungs, branching up toward my mouth, turning everything to ash.

I recalled the coffee in my hand and, without thinking, slammed it against the man who held my arm.

I suddenly regretted not carrying pepper spray like Aaron had told me to, regretted leaving myself defenseless.

The man who had me cursed, his grip loosening. His skin was pink where the coffee had hit, but it wasn't nearly hot enough to do the damage it needed it to.

"Bitch." The insult was joined by the swinging of his hand, and the impact of it against my cheek knocked me down.

I'd never been struck before, had no idea just how much it would hurt, how it would blank my thoughts for a moment, how catching myself against the concrete ground would be damn near impossible.

Weight settled on top of me, and it was the man who had held me before. He continued to insult me, but the words made no sense. Instead of hearing them, I saw…something. Images floating through me, as if his words were pictures instead of sounds.

I saw him in a dingy apartment, screaming at a woman. I saw him pounding his fist on an ATM at the words *'insufficient funds'* that ran across the screen. I saw anger and helplessness and a belief that the world had fucked him over so he deserved whatever he could take.

I didn't understand it, but it wasn't the images that had my full attention. Instead, it was the pain in my throat.

I opened my mouth and something came out. Not words, but a wail—terrible and wonderful and so familiar it almost made me weep.

It was like I'd sung my entire life but never sung the *right* song, and now I'd finally found my voice.

The man above me yanked his hands from me and used them to cover his ears. Still I didn't stop, didn't think I *could* stop.

Blood leaked from the man's ears, even as he held his hands over them. A glance to the side showed the other two doing the same.

One yelled something to the one over me.

Siren.

The word meant nothing to me, not at that moment, consumed as I was by the song I sang, by the power it filled me with.

The man above me let go of his ears and reached behind him. The other two fell, writhing on the floor, their anguished screams like their own addition to my music.

The man above me gripped my face with one of his hands, but he couldn't muffle my mouth, not entirely. I didn't realize that wasn't his plan, though, not until a flash of silver.

He ran a knife along the front of my throat. Before the pain hit me, my song stopped. A sickening gurgling replaced it, and the absence of that music made the burning in my lungs worse, as if whatever that had been was now trapped there, unable to escape.

"And here I thought we just had a fucking slut to deal with. Go figure that you're actually a filthy shade. Good thing I didn't stick my dick into you—who knows what I coulda caught."

Shade. The word hurt almost as much as my throat. I didn't shove at him, grasping instead at my throat, drenched in blood, as if I could hold it together.

"We can't ransom her now," one of the other men said, his words pained, blood trails down each side of his neck from his ears. "Fuck, she ain't even gonna survive that."

"Shades heal fast," the man above me spat. "And I plan to make her pay for what she did." He still had his hand on my face, digging his nails into my cheeks.

And with the same sense as before, I knew he was telling the truth.

The world darkened, my body growing heavy and cold. Blood loss? It had to be. Slitting a person's throat was the sort of thing they rarely came back from.

A roar echoed off the concrete of the walls, and for a moment, I frowned. Was that me?

No, that couldn't have been right. Just like I'd felt inside the men's voice, I felt that new sound. It was feral, wild, nothing like me.

The two men who were still conscious turned their heads toward the sound. The third was either knocked out or dead, because he hadn't moved since he'd hit the ground.

Fear skirted across their features, and the world faded out for a moment. The man on top of me was gone, though his screams still hit my ears. I blinked, then the other man was gone as well, as if something had plucked them both from existence.

Everything was blurry, hard to focus on. They'd been wrong, it seemed, about me being able to survive.

A face came into view, just for a moment. Unnatural purple eyes met mine, so bright they seemed to glow even in the dim parking garage. They stared down at me, so much rage contained there, etched into the lines between his dark eyebrows.

I should have been terrified of him. There was no way he was human, and after what I'd just gone through, I wasn't in a trusting mood.

However, I didn't fear him. It was probably due to the blood loss, to the fact I teetered on the edge of unconsciousness or death. It wasn't that I didn't think he'd hurt me so much as I didn't care.

The world dimmed around him, closing on his purple eyes, until even they went black.

It seemed I'd been right.

My world was about to change, and there wasn't a damn thing I could do about it.

Chapter Three

I dreamed while I slept, which was weird because I didn't normally dream.

Or rather, when I did, I never remembered them.

This time, though, it was as if my brain had decided that if it didn't keep going, it might slip away. I dreamed about my first kiss with Aaron, about the clumsy way he'd pressed his lips to mine despite having been almost arrogant before, as if he'd expected to carry the whole thing with just his charisma.

I dreamed about my graduation party, about how my parents had thrown it, how my mother had looked ready to cry and my father had pulled himself from his work long enough to attend.

I dreamed about Moa, how we'd met in the first grade when another kid had picked on her for the car her mother had dropped her off in, and how we'd become best friends when I'd stood up for her.

I wasn't a sentimental person, so what was it with the trip down Memory Lane?

Because you're dying.

Yeah, that sounds about right.

I wasn't sleeping, was I? A man had slit my throat. That wasn't the sort of thing a person could shake off with a little nap. Was this nothing more than my life flashing before my eyes?

Redness washed through the dream, like a tidal wave that covered everything, that made me scream out. I could feel it in my mouth, down my throat and in my lungs as I tried to breathe.

Eventually, even that part of the dream drifted away. At the end, it was just me, in the center of a stage, a single light shining on me and making everything outside that circle dark.

I opened my mouth to sing, the way I'd done all my life, to calm myself with the rhythm and the sound and the way the vibrations felt inside me.

Except…nothing came out. Even with my mouth open, even as I tried, no sound escaped.

Panic gripped me, and I bolted upright, blinking wildly as I came to.

I reached for my throat, finding rough lines there, like old scars. *How can I be healed already?*

I struggled to my feet, expecting to be slow, pained. I had none of that, though. I felt…great.

My heart raced, but otherwise, no aches, no pain in my throat, none in my face where that man had hit me. Nothing…

I turned to take in the room, to try to figure out where I was. It wasn't the hospital I'd expected. No white walls or beeping machines or tired nurses scurrying from problem to problem.

Instead, it was a plain room with beige walls, a stone floor and a single bed with a metal frame bolted to the wall.

In fact, there were a *lot* of bolts in the walls with hooks.

It looked a bit like a BDSM dungeon someone had painted a horrible color. Maybe that was part of their kink?

I shook my head, trying to stay on track instead of wandering off. It was easier to not deal with problems head-on, but right now felt like the time to focus.

I went to the door, ready to leave, when I realized…no handle.

What the fuck?

I pushed on the door, but it didn't so much as groan.

Which meant I was locked in.

And there went that panic again, creeping inside me, ready to take over.

Instead, I pounded my fist against the door. If I'd learned one thing from my mother, it was to call a manager when I couldn't figure something out.

No one responded right away, so I did it again, adding a kick for good measure.

Each time I struck the solid door, my heart sped a little more.

I recalled what had happened before the man had slit my throat, that noise that had left me, him calling me a siren, but none of that could be true. It made no sense. Shades changed by the age of fifteen at the latest—usually closer to twelve or so, when they hit puberty. I was nineteen—far past the age where that happened. So if I'd been attacked, hurt, and now survived?

Why was I locked in here?

I delivered one more hard kick to the door when heavy steps from the outside made me yank backward a moment before that door was swung open with such force, I would have been knocked off my feet had I remained in front of it.

The man who walked in made me gulp hard, especially as he stared down at me, his dark eyes full of hatred.

That was a look I wasn't used to. Fear, sometimes, when people realized who my parents were, envy of the things I had, a good bit of anger now and then, but never hatred.

"Don't bang on the fucking doors," the man snapped.

He wore a uniform that made him look like a cop—gray pants and a lighter gray button-up shirt. He had a belt with a ton of things I couldn't identify hooked to it, but I sure as hell recognized the pistol.

I opened my mouth to tell him I was sorry, to ask for answers, but it was my dream all over again. No sound came out. No voice, nothing. I tried again before my eyes widened at the realization that I couldn't speak.

Some of the man's anger slid away, but pity didn't replace it. Instead, amusement took the anger's place. "I was wondering if they'd silenced you with that cut. When we mute sirens, we do it with a bit more finesse, but it seems you ran into a few folks who didn't mind putting you in your place personally. It'll be a lot fucking easier to deal with you when you can't use your voice, huh?"

I frowned at the name again. *Siren*. What did that mean?

The guard's smile widened. "You had no idea, huh? Well, kid, you're a siren. A *shade*."

I shook my head. It couldn't be true. I knew what shades were, had seen what they could do, and I *wasn't* one. I was just me, not some infected husk. When people turned, when they became shades, they lost all of who they were. Sometimes they could fake it, but just one look at them and it was clear they weren't alive anymore, not who they were.

But I was still me. I hadn't changed, didn't feel like another person.

Still, even as I shook my head to deny it, he only chuckled. "Yeah, you are. You think we don't run tests here? Your source levels are through the roof, highest I've ever seen, especially from a new shade. As if that weren't enough, poured some vampire blood down your throat to save your life and it didn't kill you, so there's that proof, too."

The dream, the red that had gone through it had been blood? I recalled the horrible feeling of drowning, the copper taste that had filled my mouth, and I couldn't believe that had been actual blood.

No, worse than that. Not just blood, but infected blood from a vampire?

My stomach churned but I swallowed to keep everything down. I pointed at the door, a question there.

What now? When can I go home?

Still no pity on his face, he stared at me as if I were nothing, just a dog at the pound he knew wouldn't ever get adopted and he didn't give a damn. "You want to leave? Sorry, sugar, but that isn't happening. Shades don't leave — especially not level 1 shades. You better get used to your life now, because this is it. You're here until we find a use for you or until you die. Welcome to Larkwood Academy."

He left, the clicking of the door as it locked behind him telling me I had no way out.

The churning of my stomach worsened, and before I could do anything but rush for the toilet in the room, the one without the least bit of privacy, I threw up. My knees hit the stone floor as I hunched forward, heaving up everything in my stomach.

I opened my eyes when it seemed to have stopped, spitting a few times to get rid of the taste in my mouth, only to be met with red in the bowl.

Blood.

That solidified it if nothing else did, like a piece of proof I couldn't pretend fit in any other puzzle.

I'd swallowed down blood to heal — and it had healed me instead of driving me insane as vampire blood did to humans. I'd been tested and found positive for source. I was infected, changed and *maimed*.

I couldn't deny it anymore as I collapse to the stone floor, the wreckage that had been my life crumbling around me.

I was a shade.

Welcome to Larkwood Academy.

* * * *

I had no idea how long I spent inside that cell. It could have been hours or days. I'd gotten hungry, but fear had kept me from making noise again.

Eventually, that blasted door opened and a different man walked in, not the guard from earlier, not the face I'd seen before I'd passed out in the garage.

At least he lacked the same level of hatred as the last. He wasn't kind, but he wasn't openly hostile, either. He struck me as someone doing a job to the letter and uncaring about anything else. "Name?" he asked.

I opened my mouth, but nothing came out.

He lifted his head, annoyance on his face, until he spotted my throat. He pressed his lips together but nodded. "Right. Muted, huh? You know sign language yet?"

I shook my head.

"You'll need to learn it. Most of the staff knows some. Until then, I'll make sure a writing pad gets delivered to your room tonight."

I went to say thank you, but nothing came out.

How long would it take to get used to that? To remember that I couldn't speak? It almost felt depressing, as if when I finally accepted it, I'd lose an even bigger part of myself.

Then the rest of what he said hit me. A room? I went to speak, then pressed my lips together when it didn't work.

This time, his expression softened just a bit. "Okay, look, you got a question, you raise your hand and we'll do a bit of charades until you get your writing pad. My name is Guard Dwayne. I handle intakes here at Larkwood Academy, so consider this your orientation. I'll get you to your room, show you what you need to know, tell you the rules and get you settled in. You'll have today to get your feet under you but tomorrow you'll be expected to follow your schedule. Come on, this way. Stay close, and don't do anything stupid."

The idea of leaving that room was worth a nod. Not that I planned to do anything *stupid* anyway, but I had grown tired of staring at those same four walls with nothing but my own thoughts to keep me company.

We went down a hallway, and I realized that the mirror in the door was one way, so the guards could see into the room. My cheeks flushed at the fact I'd had to go to the bathroom, at the idea that someone might have been watching.

Still, it helped to drive home exactly what situation I was in...

Countless other doors sat on our way, and I tried to peek in a few as we passed, but all were empty.

I raised my hand, then gestured at the empty room and shrugged.

"Why aren't there more people? This is level 1 holding." When I didn't understand that, he sighed. "You are new, aren't you? All shades are put into categories based on their type, then personal source levels and finally personality. A level 4 shade is hardly a concern at all, barely stronger than a human. We do it so we have the proper security."

I patted my own chest.

"You? You're 1AW. Level 1 since sirens are considered some of the most dangerous. A because of your high source levels. W is for white, which is the probationary color you'll have for a few months until we determine where to place you."

I frowned at the information. *A 1A? Me?*

I'd tried to join self-defense once, and they'd kicked me out after the first class because they said I didn't have a 'fighting spirit'. What they meant was that they struggled finding people willing to spar with a girl who hadn't made it to five feet tall.

So the thought that I was considered dangerous, here, that I was put in the same ranking with the worst of the worst struck me as absurd.

Guard Dwayne cleared his throat, his eyebrow lifted, making me realize he'd taken a few steps and I'd fallen behind. I rushed forward, tucking my hands into the pockets of my sweats, curling my shoulders in.

He nodded and continued forward. "Larkwood Academy is one of the oldest ones in this country."

I raised my hand, and despite the sigh from him, he nodded at me. I pointed around and shrugged again.

"Where are we?" His ability to guess my question was impressive, but then again, if he'd done this for so long, he probably had a good idea of what people wanted to know. "We're in the desert of Southern California near Amboy—nothing around for miles. People feel safer when places like this are out of the way, far from their cities and homes."

I nodded. I'd known Larkwood was nearby, but not exactly where. It seemed instead of going to the East Coast for school, I was stuck here, only a matter of a couple hours from where I'd grown up... It seemed funny, but when I couldn't pinpoint why, I chalked it up to fear and stress.

I swallowed hard and kept on the guard's heels.

"They call these places academies because that's what they're supposed to be. You'll have classes that help you get control of your powers, where you learn the history of shades, all the legal shit you need to be aware of. In addition, you'll have work. What you do will depend on your skills, but we expect the shades here to earn their keep. For some it means manual labor, for others cleaning, cooking and sometimes other tasks. A telepath, for example, may have to help with interrogations if they're trusted enough. The better you show yourself, the better chance at good jobs. Warden Amanda Kaser runs this place, and trust me, you do *not* want to draw her attention or talk to her."

I nodded, even though he wasn't looking at me. We went through a door, the brightness through it telling me that we'd reached the outside.

Through it was a courtyard with people running around, men and women from around ten years old and up.

They wore normal clothing—other than the wristband—and might have been mistaken for any other grouping. Well, other than the large fences that encircled the area.

This sure as hell didn't feel like a school of some sort. Moa's words came back to me, when she'd said the academies were just prisons.

Jasmine Academy hadn't looked like this at all when I'd visited.

Still, this wasn't so bad. The people smiled, talked, laughed. There were guards at the outer edges, but they seemed at ease.

Nothing like the guard who had talked to me at first, when I'd banged on the door.

"This is the level 3 area," he explained. "Level 4 is through that gate over there, because level 4 shades rarely stay more than a month or two."

We crossed the courtyard, and I stayed close when the other people stared my way. They had a similar hesitation to the first guard, as if they knew there was something wrong with me.

They were shades, so I had no idea why they'd fear me.

Because I'm one too…

I still struggled to accept that, to believe it.

We reached a gate near the back, and Guard Dwayne lifted his wrist to a small metal device beside the latch. The device flashed green, and a click said it had unlocked. "You'll have a wristband after orientation. It'll show your designation and will be programed to open specific doors for you. That'll give you access to the things we approve you for. Behave yourself, and you'll get more freedom. Break the rules, and you'll find your world can get very small."

The walls of that room I'd woken up in told me he was right.

We passed the fence, and everything changed. Another courtyard sat, but where the last had games and laughter and furniture, this one was an open space with only a few people in it. Those there watched us closely, not speaking, not coming nearer. A running track rested on the outer edge, and one man ran laps on it, his gaze down, sweat soaking his shirt. They wore regular clothing as well, but they no longer looked like people who could have been anywhere. The guards who watched over them were less relaxed and carried obvious weapons.

"As we get to the higher levels," the guard said, "security ramps up. It's like at the zoo — the porcupine might have an enclosure that's just a bit of waist-high glass, but you better believe the tiger has a lot more in place to keep him put."

And in that analogy, *I* was the tiger? Hell, I wouldn't have even considered myself the porcupine before. I was, at best, a meercat.

Not that I could explain that to him, or that he'd listen even if I could.

We went to another gate at the far end, and large signs hung on it.

Danger. Authorized Individuals Only. Level 1 Area Ahead.

I gulped at the way my body said *fuck this* to the idea of going past that door. I did not belong through there.

The lock clicked after the guard waved his wrist in front of it, and despite how much I didn't want to follow, I did. Perhaps it was a 'devil I know' situation.

There was no courtyard when we passed, not like the other places. I saw no rec area, no place to run laps. An even taller concrete wall surrounded us, preventing me from seeing past it, but it seemed the outside wasn't used. Three tall towers sat inside the level 1 area, each the same height, around ten stories. They reached up, imposing, like guards standing watch.

Guard Dwayne gestured at the empty outdoor space. "We don't allow level 1 shades outside time the way the others get. Level 3 can go as they please, level 2 gets scheduled time, but level 1 needs more supervision. Each shade is given short times outside, one at a time, and only in the back where it's better secured. There was a time we allowed them outside like the level 2s, but we lost too many guards and too many other shades."

Lost? Well, I was quite certain he didn't mean misplaced.

It made the reality of this place sink in. This wasn't summer camp. People died here — shades and humans alike.

A shaking started in my hand, that buzzing in my head as my anxiety grew. Maybe it hadn't before because I hadn't accepted this place, accepted what they'd said. Now that it was turning real, now that I couldn't pretend it was a mistake, my nerves struggled to make sense of it.

Not that the guard noticed — or maybe he just didn't care.

He unlocked the front door of the large building, and the inside was the oddest thing of all.

I had figured places like this, in my nightmares at least, would be like old castles. They'd be made of stone and crumbling walls. Instead, everything appeared modern. All neutral colors, but it struck me more like a public high school than a maximum-security prison.

At least, that was what I thought until another guard walked out, a gun in his grasp at the ready, body armor strapped to his chest. That dispelled any thoughts that this was anything other than what it was.

A prison.

Guard Dwayne nodded at the other guard before walking forward again. "Bottom floor is off limits. It is intake, registration and visitors."

That perked me up. Visitors? If I could just get a hold of my parents, they'd come get me—I knew they would. They both had enough pull to manage it, to get me out of this place and back where I belonged—home.

I nearly missed the rest of what Guard Dwayne said but tuned back in as we got into an elevator. "Your wristband will unlock the levels you have access for. This is the main building and houses administration, security, staff offices, classrooms and Medical. On the top floor is the bridge to the Residential Tower, which is where all living quarters for level 1 shades are located."

I frowned, thinking of the other building I had seen outside. I gestured that direction.

"North Tower is off limits." He said no more, making it clear that was the end of the conversation.

We took the elevator up, and he pointed at a map on the wall. "If you get lost, if you forget which room something is in, there are maps like this all around." He tapped and it shifted. It wasn't a paper map, as I'd first assumed, but a touch screen. He scrolled through the names, showing me how each instructor was listed, each subject, and how to locate the floor and number. "If you scan your wristband, it will also bring up your schedule for the day and the areas you're approved for. Lateness isn't tolerated, so make sure you give yourself plenty of time."

We reached the tenth floor, and past the elevator doors was an open space. It had seating and large windows that covered the walls, bathing the entire area in light.

"Top floor of both towers are set up as another rec area. Doctors told us a while back that our level 1s weren't getting enough sunlight, so we made this to give you that while still managing control. This glass is the best science can make. I've seen a gollum strike it full force and not so much as chip it."

The sun streamed in through the windows, through the huge skylights above. The entire room felt a few degrees warmer than the other areas, telling me that even with air conditioning, the glass increased the temperature.

We went to the south side, to a large door that opened with the guard's wristband, just like the others had. A bridge with glass walls, just like the top floor, spanned across the forty feet or so that separated the buildings.

"Residential here has everything you might need. A pantry, laundry, library, gym and general requisitions area."

I frowned.

He nodded, as if I'd asked the question out loud. "There's a cafeteria for those who want to use it, but it's easier to let people feed themselves at least some of the time. We don't allow anything sharp or dangerous for cooking, but we have basics available. Don't get any ideas, though, because we're quick to deal with infractions."

I hadn't even considered what an 'idea' would be in this case.

We got into another elevator, and he hit the button for floor one. "Floors are separated by source ranking. Higher the floor, the less source a shade's got. This keeps the more dangerous ones farther from the exit, since there is no way out of Residential other than the bridge. Your numbers are off the charts, so you're our only A. It means you get the bottom floor all to yourself."

I was the only A there? Out of how many level 1s? I gestured toward myself, then used my fingers to count.

"We've got about forty level 1s at this facility. Most academies have a few level 1s, but we get the worst of the worst. They send most of the rank B and Cs here, along with all the red and oranges." He paused, then let out a soft laugh. "Right, you got no clue what that means. Those colors we talked about? Red is the most dangerous. Usually means they're prone to violence and that they've killed. Orange means prone to violence but able to follow rules. Goes from there to yellow, blue, green and white is for probation— basically the time before we can assign a color. Different colors also restrict what a shade's allowed to do. Basically, Larkwood takes in the shades others aren't equipped to deal with. It's why you ended up here. Been here twenty years and only seen a handful of sirens coming through. Almost a shame they had to mute you—like taking a tiger's claws. I mean, I get it, can't ever be too careful. I've seen what a siren can do, but still, a shame."

The elevator came to a stop, and he held the door for me as I walked out. The hallway was long and reminded me of a cheap apartment complex. Ugly wallpaper with a faded floral design told me I wasn't in my old life anymore.

We went down to the end. Only six doors were there that I could see, and we went to the door with a one on it. "You're here—room 01."

He opened the door to the room, walking in before me. It chafed, since this was supposed to be *my* room, yet he strolled into it as if he had every right. Then again, he did, right? That was the reality of being a prisoner somewhere.

The room was functional. It was more spacious than I would have expected, with a living room, a small kitchenette, two bedrooms and a bathroom. The second bedroom made me pause.

I didn't need to gesture before the guard answered. "Sometimes we get families, parents with kids. Sometimes we even get kids young enough that their mom or dad stays with them at first. Besides, a second room can be used for an office. You'll have more than your fair share of work to do."

Families? That one hit me as odd. I frowned, thinking about people settling down here, having kids. Why would Larkwood allow that?

As if he could read the question, Guard Dwayne turned toward me. "We don't like when shades get knocked up here. It's inconvenient, but despite our best efforts, living creatures do what living creatures do — reproduce. All female shades have a tubal ligation procedure done during intake to block the fallopian tubes with a small device. It can be reversed more easily than traditional methods, in case someone in Medical wants to do some sort of fertility experiment. Same deal with the males — vasectomies when they arrive. Thankfully, STIs don't seem to take effect for shades, so that isn't a problem."

During intake? My hand went to my lower stomach, as if I could feel what they'd done, as I told myself he was wrong.

At least he had the decency to almost look regretful. "Yeah, you too. Think of it as a bonus. You don't have to worry about that now."

His words didn't soothe me at all, especially as I thought about the violation that had happened, about yet another thing taken from me without my knowledge or consent.

That was a worry for another day, though, since I could only freak out about so much at once. I blew out a slow breath, taking in the small space that was suddenly my entire world…

"Let's get your wristband on." The guard picked up the black band and hooked it to my wrist. It had my designation etched into a square on it and beneath that — *siren.*

I stared at the metal band, at the way it locked onto my wrist, at how trapped I felt by it. I wanted to tear it off, to throw it across the room.

A trembling started up again, and this time, Guard Dwayne noticed it. Then again, he had my hand in his, so it would be hard to miss.

"Take a breath, kid. I know this isn't how you expected your week to go, but trust me, I've seen about everything come through these doors. Do what you need to do, keep your head down and nose clean and you'll be fine."

Static came through his radio before a voice. *Issue in intake. You headed back, Dwayne?*

He sighed before grabbing the radio. "On my way."

The thought of him leaving, of me being alone in the silence of the room hit me as unacceptable. I tried to speak, to ask what I was supposed to do, but nothing came out.

"Your schedule is on the table for tomorrow. Like I said, don't be late." He paused by the door, lines etched between his eyes. "I only handle intakes, and we don't get a lot of new 1s here, so I probably won't see you again. Good luck, siren — this place has chewed up and spit out more shades than you can possibly imagine. I hope you don't end up one of them."

He shut the door behind him, leaving me alone, stuck in the silence, in the questions, in all the things I wanted to say but couldn't.

I'd never felt so powerless, so invisible.

I was trapped, and there wasn't a damn thing I could do about it.

They'd taken everything from me, even my voice.

I was alone and terrified and silenced.

Chapter Four

I stared down at the clothing set out on my bed. It seemed for the level 1s, we didn't get to pick our own. Instead, I had black and gray sweatpants, a selection of basic white T-shirts and black and gray sweaters. A pair of sneakers were on the floor of the closet, and underwear and bras had been placed in the dresser.

It all fit, something that unnerved me. Had they measured while I'd still been unconscious? Were they just that good at guessing?

It didn't really matter.

The clock on the wall taunted me. Six-forty-five in the morning, and the first thing on my list was an intro class set to start at eight a.m. I had no idea how long it would take to cross that distance on my own, and Guard Dwayne's words had kept me up most of the night. *They don't tolerate lateness.*

I'd showered already, avoiding the mirror in the bathroom so I didn't have to see my face or the scars on my throat. I was terrified I'd glance in the mirror and not recognize myself.

I *felt* like me, but I recalled seeing the eyes of shades in the past, seeing the emptiness of them. Would mine look like that, too?

I had no idea how to deal with that, so I'd avoided it.

Finally, I forced myself to pull on the clothing, since I didn't want to test the entire lateness threat. I didn't eat, since I hadn't braved the pantry and there wasn't much in my room yet.

Not that I had much in the way of an appetite anyway. Even the thought of food took me back to throwing up in that cell, to the blood I'd drank.

And there goes the gagging again.

I shook my head. If I'd managed to keep down sushi, I could keep down this. Another few deep breaths and I forced myself from the relative safety of my room. It was a straight shot to the elevator—I was suddenly thankful for being the only person on my floor, since it meant I didn't have to worry about running into anyone.

I repeated the steps in my head. *Elevator up to tenth floor, then across the bridge, then floor eight, room 806 for the intro class.*

That wasn't so hard, right?

I left the question unanswered as I crossed the long bridge that had the same windows as the top floors, still having run into no other person. Not a guard, not another resident—I'd spent all night trying to come up with a term to use that wasn't shade, as I hadn't stomached that yet.

After another uneventful elevator ride, I finally spotted someone else and immediately wished I hadn't. Two men stood outside the room and the moment the doors slid open, they turned their gazes toward me.

The two looked nearly identical. They had the same dirty-blond hair, both buzzed short, the same impressive physique, and given we all seemed stuck in the same clothing, that matched as well. The only difference?

Their eyes.

The one the left had blue eyes while the one on the right had green.

Well, there was one other thing they had in common.

The hatred in their faces as they stared at me.

I took a deep breath and tried to replace this academy with the university I'd prepared myself to go. I'd been ready to deal with cliques, hadn't I? I'd been ready to suffer through hazing and sororities and other students who didn't like me. It was basically the same situation, right?

Other than the fact that these students can and probably will kill me…

I would have preferred to slink back into the elevator, but a glance at the clock on the wall said that wasn't possible. Ten minutes until the class started meant I'd have to brave the gauntlet.

I tucked my hands into my pockets and walked forward, my gaze down, trying to mind my own business.

A snort as I approached left one of the men—I had no idea which—but I ignored it.

Somehow, I got past the two, shifting so I didn't so much as brush against either—they sure didn't help and give me any space.

I took an open seat near the front, trying to disappear into the floor.

The room was silent, making me shift and want to glance around. I'd *never* been this close to so many shades.

My best bet was to keep my head low until I could reach my parents, until I could talk to them and get them to bring me home.

I kept up that game until the back door of the room opened and a man walked in. He wore his own clothing, no band on his wrist. Was he human?

A part of me wanted to stand up and tell him I didn't belong here, that it had all been some big mistake. Sure, the guards had been humans, but *this* man wore a suit, and looked like the sort of person I'd grown up around.

I opened my mouth, but nothing came out. The good thing was it gave me time to realize what a poor idea that was. *Don't be a problem. Don't cause trouble.*

The man—teacher?—set his briefcase on the large desk at the front of the room. He reached into it and pulled out a file, then took it to the lectern and spread out the papers inside. His eyebrow rose before he lifted his gaze to land directly on me.

So much for keeping my head down.

"Our new 1A." He held two fingers out and lifted them, the universal sign for stand up.

As much as I didn't want to, I followed the request.

A few murmurs in the room hit my ears, and amazingly, I could pick them all out. It was as if I could filter through all the other noise and catch multiple conversations at once. It disoriented me as I struggled to isolate and ignore them.

"She's on floor one?"

"Have we had a floor one shade before?"

"She looks familiar."

"Did you get a look at her band? What is she?"

I closed my eyes for a second and tried to block it all out so I could focus on the teacher instead. The others didn't matter—they couldn't get me the one thing I wanted.

Out of here.

"You've done orientation, right?"

I nodded.

"Good. This class is just a basic intro to Larkwood Academy. I'm Professor Kemmel, and I usually run the multi-species courses. You'll meet the other instructors throughout the weeks."

I glanced around at the others in the room, then furrowed my eyebrows.

Professor Kemmel let out a sigh. "You're the only one required to come to this class, but whenever we set it up, the whole damn building usually shows. They like to size up the new guy—or, girl in this case. You want to introduce yourself?"

I pressed my lips together, hating that I couldn't speak. I couldn't say anything, even to express that I couldn't tell him. The idea of pointing at the scar turned my stomach, so I just stared.

He dropped his gaze for a moment to the paperwork, then cursed softly. "A mute, just wonderful. Okay, I guess I'll do the honors. This is…" He scanned the paperwork. "Hera Weston. Wait, Weston?" He did a double-take of the words, as if he might have misread them, then lifted his gaze to mine and let out an ugly laugh. "Well, well, well. Looks like we've got a celebrity here. None other than the only Weston heir. Aren't we lucky?"

It was almost terrifying the way the temperature in the room dropped at the use of my name, as if each person reacted to it on some instinctual level. The waves of aggression were thick enough to drown me, and it was all directed my way.

Which was the exact reason I didn't turn around or take my gaze anywhere except the teacher. I didn't need to see the fury — it was palpable.

The professor kept talking as if the entire class didn't seem ready to murder me on the spot. "Looks like Hera is nineteen — a late bloomer — and a…siren? We haven't had one of those in a long time. Classification 1AW."

Another wave of noise behind me made my head hurt from the noise of it all.

I'd wanted to fly under the radar, to be quiet, to be ignored, but that was seeming all but impossible. Between my last name and my designation, I had become public enemy number one in just a matter of a few minutes.

I tucked my hands deeper into my pockets and tried to hunch forward. It wasn't even like I could defend myself.

"I'd have you say a few words, but since that isn't happening, go ahead and take your seat, songbird."

The nickname made me frown. I got the joke, of course, the idea of a siren being a songbird, but given the fact I'd had my voice stolen, the name had a cruel edge to it.

Still, nothing felt better than putting my ass in that chair and slumping down, trying to disappear right into it so I could wake up from this nightmare.

I wanted to go back home to my real life. I wanted to apologize to Moa for not listening to her and cling to Aaron and forget all about my desire for something exciting. I wanted to crawl into the rut my parents had dug for me and never come out again.

Except, when I opened my eyes, the nightmare remained. It didn't change at all, didn't go away.

Kemmel started to speak, his voice dropping into a practiced cadence that told me he'd given the same spiel countless times before. Worse, he looked at me, telling me the entire thing was for my benefit.

Well, my benefit while all the other people stared holes into my back.

"Larkwood Academy was the first such place opened in this country back in 1842. Since then, another twenty have opened across the US, but we've remained at the forefront of discovery. We take in the level 1s other academies are ill-equipped to handle. We've dealt with everything here. Murderous harpies, feral amatoks…we even had a kitsune once who managed to steal every single key in the entire school, forcing a two-week lockdown. My point? Before you even think about doing anything, acting out, trying anything, know that we've dealt with it in the past, and this academy is the thing that is still standing at the end of it."

I nodded even though I didn't get the sense he needed me to agree.

"Rules are simple. Be where you need to be when you need to be there, follow the orders of all staff and security and don't murder one another. That last one is the least important of them, but still worth noting. Basically? Just follow the rules and you'll be fine. We like to hit history and legality first, then focus in on talents. You'll have evaluations with staff to work on control of your skills and to gauge your color level. Do well, and you've got hopes of making life easier on you, maybe even of release. Or don't do well, and you can be like some of the people here who have spent most of their life inside these walls with no hope of that changing."

I risked a glance around, taking note of the wide age range. There were kids, who couldn't have been older than eleven, all the way up to an elderly man in the corner. It reminded me what Moa had said, that this wasn't a school, not like people tried to sell to the public.

It was a prison.

And I was locked up inside it.

* * * *

Kemmel eventually stopped talking. A glance at the clock told me he'd prattled on for over two hours.

He'd gone over the history of the academy, some of the noteworthy residents — they'd been almost all serial killers, with the exception of a few the military used for dangerous missions. The other residents didn't appear to pay any attention to him or his stories, however.

They never took their gazes off me, as if waiting for some show.

Too bad for them — I had no intention of rocking the boat. I'd bide my time until I got a chance to call my father.

When Kemmel excused us, I lingered in my seat for longer than needed in hopes everyone else would leave and I wouldn't need to risk a confrontation.

I didn't need to cause *more* problems — my name and designation had done enough damage already. If I burned any more bridges, I'd have to swim through the ashes for safety.

When the others had cleared out, I rose and left the room, keeping my eyes down.

At least, I did until I ran directly into a large body just around the corner outside the room.

I went to say sorry, an immediate reaction I couldn't help. Nothing came out, causing me to lift my gaze.

Blue eyes stood there, his arms crossed over his chest. He hadn't tried to steady me after I'd run into him, hadn't grabbed for my arm to make sure I didn't bounce off him and fall.

It was clear he didn't give a fuck if I fell.

His gaze dropped to my throat, and I lifted a hand to hide the scar.

Why? Why do I care if he sees it?

I couldn't quite unravel that, but it felt far too personal.

"You want me to feel sorry for you?" he asked. "You expecting to walk in here and have us all take pity on you because you got bit by the dogs your family made?"

His words didn't make a bit of sense to me. Was he seriously trying to blame *me* for the fact some crazy man in a garage slit my throat?

I went to respond, but when I was, again, reminded that I had no voice, I fished the small writing pad from my pocket.

"I was attacked by a stranger." I held the pad out to him.

He narrowed his eye as he read it. "You were attacked by someone who thought shades didn't deserve to live. *Your* family has been selling that idea for generations. About time it knocked you down."

"I didn't do anything."

"You've benefited your whole spoiled life by what they've done, and the only good thing about you being here is that it's one less Weston who can fuck up our lives anymore." He dropped his gaze to my throat again. "A silenced muse is a travesty, but a silenced

Weston? A fucking miracle." He came closer, inhaling slowly through his nose as if catching something he wasn't sure he liked.

What was he? I was tempted to try to see his wristband, but fear kept my eyes on his, kept me from being willing to look elsewhere for even a moment.

His voice did what all voices did to me, now. A strange feeling washed over me, as if their words meant more than they ever had before. It was like I'd played a 2D game for years, then having it shift so I could see it in 3D, all the extra details and depth that had been missing before.

I heard the anger, the hatred, felt a rage beneath it that was deep enough to pull me under. A flash of a boy with blue eyes, just like his, being thrown into the back of a van, adults being held back and screaming, reaching for him.

Pain ran through my back, and I blinked to realize the man had moved, and by moved, I meant that he slammed me against the wall, a hand to my sternum so hard that my chest ached.

Just how strong was he?

"That's enough, Brax."

Blue eyes — *Brax?* — turned his gaze from me toward the new voice. "Didn't think you cared what we did to each other, lapdog."

"I don't, usually, but murdering our first 1A in a decade on her first day would look bad."

Brax looked back toward me, his eyes seeming to glow, his body seeming bigger somehow, angles sharper. "Stay out of my head, siren."

I collapsed when he released me. His little move had knocked all the air from me, and a crack in the drywall said I was lucky someone had come by.

That someone knelt beside me, his shiny black loafers in my line of sight. "Are you all right?"

No. The answer was so obvious. No, I wasn't even close to all right. I wasn't what I thought I was, my entire future had just been ripped away, and now, in the place where I was forced to stay, I had people wanting to kill me.

None of this was okay.

My writing pad was held out to me by whoever had helped me. I hadn't even noticed I'd dropped it when Brax had shoved me.

I took it as I looked up.

And immediately wished I hadn't.

The man was older, probably in his forties, and his eyes were entirely black. No pupil, no iris, no white, nothing. Other than that, he almost looked normal.

Almost.

It wasn't in how he looked, exactly, and it took me a moment to sort through what it was. It had been his voice.

Whereas Brax had a level of rage inside him, this man seemed solid, almost like bone, with this deep void beneath it, a gnawing, ravenous emptiness held back by that bone.

A flash of a creature hit me, something out of a nightmare, made of elongated limbs. It had a deer skull for a face, with large antlers and hands tipped with sharp claws.

I yanked backward, dropping the pad to scoot away.

The man didn't move, only tilting his head in response. "You *are* a siren, aren't you? I've always wondered what you could see, what you could learn from voices alone. My name is Kit Porter. You're Hera, aren't you?"

I didn't try to answer, especially since I'd dropped my pad again.

"I guess that's a silly question. We have so few new people here, it's always big news when there is someone. You should be careful around Brax and his brother, Knox. Those two are dangerous and clearly not fans of yours." He rose to his feet, then stuck his hand out as if to help me up.

I refused to take it, though. All I could think about were the images still in my head, that creature. Was that what he really was? If we peeled away whatever camouflage he had, if I saw what was beneath it all, was it that monster?

The memory of those claws haunted me, and I couldn't bring myself to reach out, to touch him.

He shook his head before folding his hands behind him. Not that it helped, given how he towered over me. If anything, it reminded me far too much of how I'd felt in that garage, with that man on top of me.

Panic danced at the edges of my mind, but it didn't come closer. Was it because there were just too many things to panic about? Like a whole handful of marbles trying to go through a funnel at once, but getting stuck so none could pass?

"Be careful, Hera," Kit told me, repeating his words from before. "Sirens go mad quiet often. They delve too deep into the sounds, follow voices they shouldn't and end up drowning in the darkness they never should have ventured into."

With those cryptic words, he nodded and turned on his heels, leaving me on the ground with even more questions than I'd had before.

Chapter Five

A loud bang on my door made me jump to my feet and freeze. I felt like one of those goats who fell over at the slightest startle.

Then again, not many had access to my floor from my understanding. I hadn't expected visitors, let alone someone who hit the door like *that*.

I couldn't call to tell them to come in, so instead, I went to the door, took one big breath, then unlocked and opened it.

Purple eyes, ones I'd almost thought I'd dreamed up, met mine. I recalled being on the ground, my throat slit, and staring up at those impossible eyes.

Of course, now they were housed in an entire face, one that was scowling at me.

I took two big steps backward, giving the man space. He was in his late thirties if I had to guess, but he didn't wear a guard suit or a yellow band. Instead, he wore a pair of black slacks and a white collared shirt. His hair was a dark brown and cut in the way that made me think he just buzzed it himself at home. A mustache and beard were cut the same—simple, as if he just wanted to appear clean but not stylish.

Those eyes, however, told me he was more. It was an entirely unnatural color, something that I'd never seen before beyond sci-fi shows that thought unique eyes made an alien.

He gazed around my room, a cursory look as if checking for threats, before he leveled his gaze on me. "You haven't gone to the pantry."

A frown touched my features at that, as my brain tried to make sense of the observation.

He turned around and grabbed a box from outside the door, one he must have set down before knocking. Without asking for permission, he walked in and set the box on the dining room table, then started to remove the items inside. He lined them up in two groupings—one for things that needed refrigeration and one for things that didn't.

I kept my distance, eyeing him, trying to figure him out. His voice hadn't told me anything, and while a part of me enjoyed that—it made me feel like the old me—another part wondered why. What was different about him?

He didn't speak as he emptied the box, then tossed it out of the door and into the hallway. He went about putting the cold items in the fridge, as if this were entirely normal, as if I had any idea who he was.

Which woke me up. I'd seen him *outside* of the academy. That meant he couldn't have been a resident, right?

I went for my writing pad, scribbling down words. He turned just as I held it up.

"Who are you?"

He picked up the last item for the fridge — creamer for coffee — and turned to put it in the fridge. "Deacon Laferton." He said the name as if that should be enough, as if it answered everything.

It didn't.

When he turned my way, I pointed at my eyes, then to his.

The sigh he let out was full of annoyance. He crossed his arms over his wide chest. "I'm human."

I again gestured at his eyes, as if calling him a liar.

He pointed at his own eyes. "These are a present from exposure to source."

Exposure? Shouldn't that have made him infected, thus not human?

I hit the clear button on the pad. *"Doesn't that make you a shade?"*

"No. Shades are infected. I'm *not*. All my results show I'm not a shade, just a human with these eyes due to the exposure."

It didn't make any real sense to me, but had anything else thus far?

"What are you doing here?" I asked next.

"Like I said, you hadn't gone to get any food. You have to be hungry, and I figured you were just too scared to go to the pantry yourself."

That was oddly nice. I went to write *thank you*, but his gruff voice stopped me.

"Don't get any ideas, *siren*. I'm not doing this out of the goodness of my heart. I just don't want to deal with the headache of you dying over something so stupid. Folks are pretty excited about having you here, and I don't need them breathing down my neck because you starve to death, or we have to run a feeding tube down your throat."

I pulled back at the sharpness of his tone.

He didn't apologize — I got the sense he was the sort of man who had no idea how. Instead, he shook his head. "This'll get you through a few more days, but I'm not about to turn into your own personal snack-bitch. You better grow yourself a backbone because this place'll eat you alive if you don't."

He went to leave, but something inside me snapped. He was the only connection I had to the real world, to *my* real life, to the person I'd been before I'd been thrown in here and reduced to *this*. He'd seen me out there, in some weird twist of fate, which meant he was the only one to see me before I'd come here.

I grabbed his arm, wanting more answers, needing something from him.

He glanced down at where I held him, his lips tight together. It forced him to look at the pad of paper I held.

"You were there."

"Let go of me." The words came out full of threat.

I didn't. I needed to understand. He'd saved me, right? Those men had been there, then they'd been gone — it meant he'd done that, hadn't he? Why? I needed him to make sense of it.

Deacon shifted, using a hand to shove me, sending me tumbling backward. The purple of his eyes was impossibly brighter, casting a glow on the entire room. When I came to a stop, it was across the room and yet again on my ass.

He stared at me, his chest heaving as if he struggled to control himself. "You need to understand exactly where you are. This isn't some vacation — you're at *Larkwood*. Shades come here and they don't leave, at least not alive. So grow up, get yourself a backbone and learn an important damn lesson. Trust no one and keep your hands to yourself — especially when your only real weapon has already been taken away."

I brought my legs up toward my chest, then wrapped my arms around them. The only person I thought I'd had, even for a moment, had just thrown me across a room and threatened me.

He blinked, the purple glow lessening. His gaze darted away for another moment, then came back, almost softened. He still looked terrifying, but at least some of that anger had seemed to drain out of him.

When he spoke, it came out like some sort of consolation prize, as if he said it because he felt bad about what had happened. "Yeah, I was there. You damn near blew out my ear drums even from a floor down."

"Why?" I mouthed the word, my pad having gone somewhere I couldn't see.

He knew the question, I was sure. Why had he helped me? He had to be the one to have got me medical treatment, to save me. Why?

He didn't answer right away, but at least he looked at me, as if deciding what his answer was. It took so long, I started to think he wouldn't answer, that he'd turn and leave.

Finally, he did, though. "I should have left you. A fucking muted siren, the rich daughter of a legacy? You would have probably been better off if I'd let you bleed out right there, just left you for dead."

"So why?" I mouthed at him.

He shook his head. "I don't fucking know. Call it a moment of stupidity. I knew what you were, knew that even if we saved your life, you didn't exactly have much of one to come back to. I was going to let you die, but then I stared down at you and I just…couldn't."

He sounded just as confused by his actions as I felt, as if he couldn't make sense of them any more than I could. He'd saved me and he both didn't understand why and was pissed about it.

He pointed his finger at me while he backed toward the door. "How you got here, what happened, none of that matters. You'll get plenty of lessons from everyone else here, but you want one from me? Let go of the past. Let go of whatever you thought you were gonna be. Let go of who you were. Let go of all of that, because it'll tear you apart in here. Living life in a hole sucks, but you know what makes it damn near impossible? Remembering the sky. So forget the sky. Forget whoever you had waiting for you outside of these walls. This place? It's your home, now, and the faster you accept that, the better."

He didn't wait for me a response—not that I had one—before he walked out, slamming my door behind him.

It seemed even my mystery savior wasn't all that happy I was there.

* * * *

You can do this. One foot in front of the other.

I repeated the mantra to myself like some New Age affirmation even when my feet didn't move. The elevator sat open on the rec room floor, and each time the doors went to close, I hit the button to keep them open.

I'd attended two more classes, one the day before and one this morning. Sleep had been about as elusive as the night before, but I'd started to settle into a routine.

No one spoke to me, no one did anything but glare at me. That was fine — I wasn't looking to make friends.

I wouldn't be here long, anyways.

Still, I couldn't just live in my room. I'd learned through the laptop in my room that many of the things to do existed in the large areas meant for recreation. I could get books, puzzles, games, paper and anything else to pass the time there.

However, getting those things required me going there and braving a confrontation.

The elevator dinged, and I hit the button again, keeping the doors open.

I was probably pissing off someone who was trying to use the elevator, someone hitting that call button to no avail, but I just couldn't make my legs move.

"One foot in front of the other."

The voice I'd never heard before was damn near enough to make me cry. I had no idea who they were, but just having someone speak to me as if I were a person for the first time since I'd shown up here nearly started the waterworks.

I lifted my gaze to find a man there, only in his early twenties at best, wearing sweats, a T-shirt and gloves that covered from fingertip to beyond the edge of his shirt. On his wrist was a band just like mine, but I couldn't make out the writing on it.

His dark hair was messy, with curls on the top, dark brown eyes and a surprisingly nice smile. Nice wasn't exactly something I'd seen around this place.

His words hit me, then. Had he read my mind? Was he a telepath?

His grin widened and he shook his head. "I can't read your mind. It just wasn't all that long ago I started here and had that exact look on my face, too. Come on, nothing here bites." He paused. "Well, we both know *that* isn't true. Lots of stuff here bites, but not normally on the first day." Again, he paused. "*Well,* that isn't quite right either, since I remember that time when we got this horrible new banshee and she kept screaming and it gave Brax a headache and…" He pressed his lips together, then shook his head. "Never mind that. Come on, out of the elevator before a guard comes up to see the problem."

I pointed at him, refusing to move until I had at least his name.

"My name? Wade Chris."

I stared at him, at the one person who felt like a *person* here. I had no idea what he was and for the first time in my life, I didn't care. Sure, he was a shade, but compared to the rest of the reception I'd gotten, it felt like he welcomed me with open arms. It seemed I was just pathetic enough to latch on to that, so I followed him out of the elevator, jumping when the doors slid closed behind me.

The rec floor was large, with an open space in the center and other rooms to the sides. Those never-stopping cameras hung in each corner, some moving on a clear path while others followed Wade and I as we walked.

"So, songbird, what do you think of Larkwood so far?" Wade gave me a side-eye as he walked.

I didn't bother trying to write anything in response, giving him a glare at the name.

"Not a fan of that nickname?" He dropped his gaze to my throat, a tightness by his eyes almost impossible to read. He kept going with a shrug. "You want some advice? Don't let things get to you—someone will be only too happy to use it against you. The more that name flusters you, the more people will use it to hurt you. You'd be a lot better off to claim it, to relish in it, then it'll lose all that edge."

The advice made sense, though I struggled to do it. The name felt like a reminder of everything I'd lost — my voice, my freedom, all of it. The idea that I could make it hurt less by accepting it didn't seem possible right then.

Wade shrugged, then changed the subject. "Let me guess? A few days alone and you're bored out of your mind, right?" I didn't need to nod, since it seemed as if Wade didn't mind holding up the conversation all on his own. "I remember my first week, how I would have sworn there was no way to be bored in a place like this. I mean, imprisonment, torture, shades — how could anyone get *bored*. Turns out academy life is lot less interesting than the brochure promised."

I couldn't get a feel for the odd man. Everyone else I'd met acted like this place was exactly what it was…a prison. They behaved like inmates or guards.

Wade, on the other hand, reminded me of a frat boy already halfway to drunk showing someone new around campus. How exactly did a person keep up that sort of cheeriness in this place, especially when others seemed to harden from it, to suffer from it?

"So, are you a reading sort of girl, puzzles, games? What's your poison?" He paused at the center of the room and turned toward me.

I pulled the pad from my pocket and wrote.

He read the word, not seeming to be taken back by my not speaking. "Reading, huh? Yeah, you look like you're a bit of a brainiac. Lucky for you, this place has a great library. Plus, due to 'generous donations from people like you' as the public access fundraisers go,

Larkwood gets a grant that lets them order new books and even trade with a few of the public library systems. Basically? If you want it, they can probably get it. Well, except porn. Trust me, I tried, and they told me it wasn't considered 'conducive to a calm and orderly environment.' I *tried* to explain to them that blue balls do not make for calm nor orderly, but no one listens to me."

I stared at Wade, entirely dumbfounded by his commentary. In fact, he'd so thrown me off that it took far too long before I realized he'd kept walking. It took a few quick steps to catch back up and find he hadn't even stopped talking.

"You probably have Hemet for law, right? Scheduling likes to toss the newbies in with him to scare them. The trick is to not look him directly in the eyes. I guess he spent a week or two as a statue after a run-in with a gorgon his first year here, and now he assumes eye contact is always a trick."

I filed away his advice. It might have been foolish to trust him, but he'd been the only one to offer me any sort of hope, to make me feel as if this place could be survived.

Plus, he hadn't threatened me or knocked me over at all, and that was wholly unique thus far.

We headed through a doorway, and he scanned the band on his wrist so it would open. Through it was the sort of library a true bookworm would have envied. The shelving was high enough to need step stools to reach the tops, and lined the entire large space so close that two people would struggle to pass each other in the narrow aisles.

"Wade," a woman behind a desk said, her tone suspicious but not fearful. "What are you doing here?"

"Learning." Wade gave the woman a wide smile full of mischief.

"You're enough of a problem without any additional knowledge. Besides, you never come here unless you have some grand idea that usually lands you in solitary."

He gasped as if offended, even setting his hand on his chest. "Ms. Clemmings, that is horribly unfair. I just found this poor lost new girl wandering about and thought I'd give her a tour."

"You're the welcoming committee now? I have a feeling our enrollment might suffer." The woman's words held some affection, something that unnerved me. Thus far, the humans I'd seen had treated the residents as if we were little more than cattle or product. They seemed to want us not to be harmed, but otherwise didn't give a damn.

Then again, Wade was different. He didn't strike me as someone dangerous enough to need to be *here*.

Wade kept talking as if the insults rolled off him. "Hera was bored and wanted to read. I figured I'd walk her here, show her where it was, keep the big bad shades at bay for a while."

"Well, don't cause any problems. Another fight, and you're going to end up in more trouble than you want." This time, Ms. Clemmings gave him a serious look, the sort someone gave to a kid who had pushed their luck one too many times.

"Me? Problems?" Funny enough, Wade didn't deny that he had caused trouble, or promise he wouldn't get into fights. He only repeated the statements as if they were ridiculous accusations before we passed her desk. Once out of earshot, he spoke to me. "If you want anything ordered, ask Ms. Clemmings. She isn't too bad. Well, most of the time. One time, a couple students knocked over all these shelves, and she was *not* happy about that."

"By a couple residents, you mean *you*," Ms. Clemmings shouted even though I couldn't see her anymore. It seemed she had stellar hearing.

Wade glanced my way and shook his head, as if no, that couldn't possibly be what happened.

But the look in his eyes told me it was *exactly* what had happened.

He walked me through the aisles, showing me how they were set up. The selection impressed me. Everything from self-help to history to fiction to how-tos. They had fifteen books on beading.

Finally, he stopped and turned fully toward me. "So, what do you like?"

I opened my mouth to answer, so distracted by him and the exchange that I'd forgotten, yet again. The same pain tightened in my chest as the unpleasant reminder.

Wade's smile dimmed the barest amount, telling me he understood exactly what it meant. The look held no pity, nothing so soft. Instead, he had a flash of something else, something far less friendly — anger, maybe? — but it disappeared as soon as it appeared.

He turned around and followed the shelving, squinting as he read the titles on the spines, clearly looking for something.

"Ah," he said, then reached up and pulled a book from the shelf.

Sign Language. He frowned, shook his head, then grabbed a different one instead. *Sign Language for Idiots.*

He handed it over to me. "This should get you going. It also means you won't have to carry that writing pad around like a five-year-old."

I offered him a slight glare, but it held no real heat behind it. It was odd, but the jokes felt almost kind. Wade struck me as the sort who only made fun of a person if they were worth it. In other words, the fonder he was of a person, the more he mocked them. The true sign of dislike from him would be him ignoring them.

He smiled at my glare, as if it pleased him. "So, let's see, I'm going to guess you're a sci-fi girl. If not, too bad, I'm not going to take you to the romance area because Ms. Clemmings told me I'm not allowed to go there anymore after I circled all the times the word cock appeared in it to prove my point about porn."

He didn't wait to see if that was fine, and I found myself right on his heels even though I'd never read sci-fi in my entire life.

He just felt like the only lifeline I had, and I didn't want to lose that feeling.

Chapter Six

Wade's advice about Hemet had been spot on. I'd taken a seat near the back and kept my gaze down the entire time, writing notes in the notebook supplied with a pen.

Hemet had finished his lecture — the subject being on registration laws for shades. I'd known a lot of that before, had heard my mother talk about it since she headed so many of the committees that determined those laws. Still, I'd never dug in, hadn't had a reason to learn the nitty-gritty details involved in it.

Things like the need to re-register every six months and having a home visit to ensure a shade was where they claimed to be, or the fact that random checks were allowed whenever they were deemed necessary, and that no shade could refuse them.

The list of requirements reminded me of parole, the things that the news seemed to leave out whenever discussing such legislation.

Those stories would only talk about the basics, that society needed to track shades due to the fact they were statistically more likely to commit crimes, that everyone was safer when shades were properly documented.

It had all sounded so good, even from my mother, but took on a different tone when I was the one they were talking about. The worst part was that those laws applied to lower-level shades, to the ones who had a shot at being released because they were deemed to be without risk.

That didn't include me...

I slid my notebook into my backpack, then put the book in there as well. I hadn't expected to have actual work to do, but I'd bet they figured keeping people busy reduced the risk of trouble. Busy people didn't have time to cause problems. It meant while I didn't have many classes, each one had a lot of work and study to pass.

I didn't recognize most of the others in the room. A few faces I thought I'd seen at orientation, but none well enough to be sure.

Except Knox—I would recognize him anywhere, and despite his glare not being as pronounced as his brother's had been, I struggled to ignore him.

I left my seat when Hemet released us, both glad and disappointed to be done for the day. I'd attended a morning work session where I'd helped to clean classrooms—it seemed they didn't feel I had any other use just yet—then the one class.

My course load was light, with weekends having nothing and most days of the week only one or two in addition to the work sessions.

While I was glad to be able to run back to my room, to get away from the noise and looks of the others, I didn't relish having nothing to fill the time with.

The books were nice, and I'd ventured out again later to grab a deck of cards and a puzzle, but none of that quite kept my full attention. Instead, my brain circled all the what-ifs, all the questions, all the unknowns.

Such as the fact I *still* hadn't been given the chance to contact anyone. My parents hadn't shown up, hadn't come for me, and I had no way to reach them.

Or Aaron. Or Moa.

I was entirely cut off from everything I'd once known.

Somehow, puzzles couldn't distract me from that.

Outside the classroom, a few of the residents gathered. They often did that, having their own little groups, their cliques.

And a week into being at Larkwood, I'd started to recognize some of them.

There were the overachievers—the shades who thought if they were the best resident possible, they could buy their way out of this place eventually. There were the teachers' pets, the ones who answered questions first, who cowered and called all the guards and teachers sir.

There were the old guard, the shades over the age of forty who probably had been here since they'd been teenagers, since first going through the change. They ignored most of the classes, probably because by their point, they'd already learned it all. There was a flatness in their gazes that said they were done fighting, done hoping for a way out, that they'd accepted their place and were waiting for the only out they expected — death.

Other, smaller groups existed as well. I found they often sectioned off based on what they were, as well. Demons stayed together, shifters ended up together, those who could manipulate thoughts or emotions.

A few stayed out of that, though. The twins, for one...

Brax and Knox were usually together, their identical faces almost eerie. Others, I'd found, gave them a hell of a lot of room. No one sat directly beside them, people moved out of their way when they walked anywhere. There was this undercurrent of fear, and I had no idea why.

Wade, on the other hand, blended into any group he wanted. Or, perhaps the better way to put that was that he inserted himself into any group and didn't notice or care whether or not he was welcomed there.

I hadn't seen Kit again, and I wasn't sorry about it. I still couldn't shake the images when he'd spoken. I'd woken from a nightmare a few days before with that creature in my head, the flat black eyes like a dark emptiness that threatened to pull me in.

However, seeing things when people spoke had gotten better, as well. I'd started to learn to filter out those flashes, to turn that ability into a faucet I would slow down or turn off rather than a waterfall that crushed me.

Down the hallway, toward the elevator, someone spoke to Knox. It was a man, or rather a demon, I'd guess from the horns. He leaned into Knox's space, closer than most people dared, speaking low.

Something drew me closer, a curiosity I couldn't ignore.

The demon's voice held an odd mixture of aggression and pleading. "I know you can."

Knox shook his head. "No."

"You'll enjoy it. You *have* to be hungry."

Knox repeated his simple answer, no hesitation or question there.

Hungry? The words made no sense to me. If Knox was hungry, he could easily go to the pantry like the rest of us.

The demon reached out and set a hand on Knox's chest, the action impossible to read as anything other than sexual. "What? Are you going to just wait until *they* offer you another meal?"

"I don't like men," Knox said.

"You like everything—it's what you are. Stop fighting it."

Knox's gaze turned hard, matching how his brother usually looked. He didn't remove the demon's hand, instead meeting the other man's gaze head-on. "*I* don't like men. Whatever my appetite wants doesn't matter—I choose, and I sure as shit don't choose you. I'm going to recommend you remove your hand, because it's a thin damned line between pleasure and pain, and I can walk either side of that line."

The demon's confidence fled, and despite being larger than Knox, he tore his hand away. He rushed away so fast it was nearly a dead run.

Knox followed him with his gaze, an almost predatory gleam in it before he closed his eyes and inhaled deeply. He released it in a slow breath then turned to find me still standing there, gawking and with no way to pretend I hadn't been.

And that sure put him in an even worse mood. "Eavesdropping isn't only rude, but in a place like this, it'll get you killed. There are things you don't want to hear."

I tilted my head to read his wristband. *Incubus.*

The word took a moment to work through. I knew about little about succubi and even less about their male counterpart, incubi.

Both used sex as a weapon and a food source, able to feed off their partners and draw power from either the person or the act. Worse, they were essentially walking bait, with pheromones that could make anyone want them.

Which had me taking one big step backward.

Knox's anger slid away, a moment of confusion on his features.

What, was he so used to people wanting him that it surprised him when one didn't? Was he that egotistical?

When I looked at him again, I had to admit, he had a reason for an ego... Only an idiot would try to say he wasn't drop-dead gorgeous. He and his brother could have walked off the cover of any magazine and into real life.

Beyond that, though, Knox had a sensuality to his movements, as if each were designed to draw in a person and promise them every sinful thing they had ever dreamed of.

Still, I had no desire to be fed from, so I took yet another step back just to be safe.

Knox opened his mouth to say something, but the voice of his brother broke the moment. "Is the siren causing more problems?"

Brax didn't bother to hide his distaste for me.

Knox blinked slowly, as if having to pull himself from whatever was going on in his head. Finally, he spoke, though he still stared at me. "No. Pele was bothering me, and I think she was just watching."

"Pele?" Brax's eyes flashed that unnatural blue again as he peered down the hallway toward where the demon had gone. "I thought he understood me the last time I had to talk to him."

"It's fine," Knox assured him. "I made my own point perfectly clear. He's just…overly optimistic."

"Well, maybe the siren here should teach him sign language, because if he talks to you again, I'll knock his fucking teeth out."

The threat had me moving back again, until I touched the wall, running out of space. It wasn't just the threat but the fact that, bleeding through those abilities I tried to keep turned to low, I knew Brax wasn't lying. He wasn't kidding.

If that demon spoke to Knox again, Brax planned to do exactly what he claimed.

He twisted, his gaze landing on mine. "I thought I told you to stay out of my head."

I shook my head, trying to say I couldn't help it.

Knox hit his brother in the arm. "Leave her alone— you know how long it took us to get any sort of control."

"Yeah, well, I don't like her crawling around in my brain. If she can't control it, she should put on some fucking headphones."

I frowned. I hadn't even considered that option…

Though, the idea of losing anything else made me queasy. I'd already lost my voice, so giving up my hearing was too far.

"Come on," Knox said to his brother after another heavy moment of silence, one in which he continued to study me. "No reason to just stand here."

Brax huffed, but still turned and followed him.

The twins walked away, giving me a chance to watch them leave, to wonder why the hell I cared about the two of them at all.

Because it's good to know the dangers around.

And there was no doubt they were damned dangerous.

* * * *

Deacon sat across from me in the small room, the first time I'd seen him since he'd come to my place with the food.

I should have been nervous, but I couldn't quite get there. The reason?

It was Friday.

In the past, Friday had meant a day to go out, to have fun, to enjoy the end of the week and start of the weekend.

Still, none of those had ever excited me as much as *this* Friday did.

Friday at Larkwood meant one thing — Contact Day. It was the one day a week when residents could call, video chat or even have visitors.

Which meant I sat in that small room, a video chat screen on the wall and Deacon beside me as I waited.

Finally, I'd get to talk to my parents, I'd get to explain it all, I'd find out when they were going to come and get me. As soon as I'd seen the full schedule and realized that I could make this call, I'd wanted nothing more than to reach Sunday.

"Regina and Zachary Weston, right?"

I nodded as Deacon verified the number with me. I'd already given another guard the information days before, since they scheduled the calls ahead of time with the person to be contacted.

Deacon lifted his gaze from his paperwork to me, his lips set in a line. He inhaled slowly, as if to say something, but stopped himself.

I wondered for a moment what he'd planned to say but put that aside almost immediately. I didn't care. I was too excited, too ready for this nightmare to be over.

Deacon shifted his seat so he was right beside me, and the closeness made me uneasy, especially after the last time, when he'd flung me across the room for daring to touch him. I leaned away just to be safe.

He noted it, furrowing his brows before turning his attention to the screen on the wall. He picked up a keyboard on a shelf just below the television and handed it to me. "You can use the chat with this, so you can respond. All calls and visitations are recorded, so don't think there's any privacy. Don't say or type anything you don't want seen and saved."

Fine. Whatever. If felt like someone trying to tell me the fine print as I waited to drive off the lot with my new car. I didn't care about any of that, and soon none of it would matter to me at all.

I'd be home, with my family, and this place would be a distant memory that would take years of expensive therapy to work through.

"They already have the link, so they'll join in just a minute."

I turned my head, the question clear. Would he be staying?

"Even though we record them, we prefer an eyes-on approach, especially with shades still on probation."

I gave him a deadpan look. We were talking about a video call here. What sort of shenanigans could I get into?

He snorted softly. "Clearly, you have no idea about just how dangerous some of the shades here are. There are ones who can influence humans even through technology, and ones who can control different kinds of tech."

I frowned, once again forced to acknowledge just how little I knew about shades.

I didn't have a chance to wallow long before a loud beep alerted me to someone joining the call. It took a second for a picture to fill the screen, and when it did, I lost it.

I'd wanted to be cool, controlled, to prove to my parents I could handle anything—even this. Instead, just the sight of my mother's face was enough to break me down. Tears ran down my face and my lips moved as if I were telling her the entire story.

I ran the back of my arm across my eyes, trying to clear them, as something was set in my lap.

The keyboard.

My fingers flew across the keys, typing as fast as I could. The schedule said I had thirty minutes and that didn't feel like nearly long enough.

"*I want to come home.*" That was the first thing I typed, the most important.

My mother's eyes dropped to the bottom of the screen, probably reading what I'd put. Her expression didn't change though.

"It can't be true," she said, pain on her face but no joy, nothing at seeing me. "We received word, but I just can't believe it."

"Are you absolutely certain?" my father asked. "There can't be any mistakes about this."

I went to answer, ready to tell him of course I was sure I wanted to come home, when Deacon answered.

79

"There's no question, Mr. Weston. Her tests were run four times in case there was a mistake."

"What if they're wrong?"

"They're not. I was there when she was attacked. I *heard* her. She's a siren."

My mother wrapped her arms around herself and shook her head, as if the idea was too terrible to even consider. "How could this have happened?"

Deacon shrugged. "It just happens sometimes."

"But she's nineteen. That's too late for the infection to take hold. They always turn between eleven and fifteen."

"It's unusual, but so are her numbers. I'm not a scientist. I can't tell you how it happened or why it happened when it did. I can only tell you it happened, that she's a siren, a 1A."

My father leaned forward. "A 1A? You're certain?"

Deacon nodded. "No doubt about it. The levels of source in her blood are off the charts—higher than any shade we've had at Larkwood since we started being able to test specific amounts."

I typed into the keyboard, feeling like an observer rather than a participant. "*Mom, Dad, please come get me. I don't want to be here anymore.*"

My father read the words, but when he spoke again, it was to Deacon. "I heard she was injured. Is that why she isn't speaking?"

"Yeah. The men who attacked her, one slit her throat to keep her from singing."

"And that won't heal?"

"Saving her life was the best we could do. It's possible in the future her voice could come back— sirens are powerful, and their voice is their best weapon. It could heal eventually, but the odds aren't good."

"Please, let me come home." I typed the words even through the tears, even as a sinking feeling in my stomach grew, threatening to pull me under when my parents didn't speak to me.

They hadn't really looked at me, either. They stared at me as if I were something else, like a monster who had taken over their daughter.

My father's gaze dropped, then he shook his head. "You aren't coming home."

The words hit me like bullets. All the hope I'd had, the certainty I'd held on to that my parents would get me out of this, that they'd bring me home, it all crumbled away.

My hands felt frozen, unable to move, to ask what he meant.

I didn't need to ask, did I? It was pretty clear.

"My daughter is gone," my father said. "You are not her. You are an infection, a thing that stole her from us."

I typed, forcing my cold hands to move. *"I'm still me, still the same person."*

"You're not. Why would I bring the thing that killed my daughter into our home?"

But it was my home, too...

I kept typing, pleading for them to listen, to come see me, to visit, to see the truth that I was exactly who I'd always been. I wasn't sure they even read any of the messages, though. Instead, my father spoke to Deacon.

"What are the odds that she'll ever qualify for release?"

"At her numbers? Almost none."

"Make sure it's none. I do not need the complication of a monster wearing my name out on the streets."

Deacon nodded, though his jaw was held tight.

The screen went blank, my parents hanging up without even a goodbye, without any reassurance.

They weren't coming to get me...

They'd abandoned me, left me to rot here.

Something touched my hand, and I glanced down to find a tissue held out by Deacon.

But I didn't give a damn about the tears on my face, the snot that was no doubt leaking from my nose, not when everything I knew, everything I had, everything important to me had just been torn away and destroyed.

I had no home, no family, no future.

The guard's words struck me again, and for the first time, I accepted they were true.

Welcome to Larkwood Academy. You're never getting out of here.

Chapter Seven

I couldn't get myself to move. My hips ached from lying in bed for two days, but what did it matter?

Each time I thought about getting up, about forcing myself to eat, about doing anything, it felt too far, too much.

I'd managed to make my way to the bathroom only because wetting the bed would only make my situation even worse.

The only positive was the fact that the whole 'visit' had happened on a Friday, which meant I could wallow through Saturday and Sunday all on my own.

It was Monday, now, and even the idea of pulling myself together to get to my first class around noon seemed impossible.

A noise in the direction of the door caught my attention, but I couldn't bring myself to move, to even look in that direction.

It was probably Deacon again, since he'd checked on me Saturday and Sunday, despite me not having a clue why he'd give a damn about whether or not I got out of bed or ate. He'd come in but said nothing, as if just making sure I was still alive.

Today it was probably just to warn me that I still needed to get my butt to class whether I wanted to or not.

The lock clicked open, then the hinges groaned as someone entered.

I curled into the blanket more, as if I could hide and pretend none of the last weeks had happened.

"Nope, I'm not leaving."

The voice made me frown, and I peeked out of my little den. *Wade?*

He flashed a smile my way as he walked past me and into the bathroom. "The one and only. Count yourself lucky — it normally takes a lot more to get me to go home with a girl."

The sound of water striking the tile told me he'd started the shower, and that was nearly enough to get me to sit up. Was he planning on bathing while here?

What was he even doing here?

He came back — fully dressed — and crouched in front of the bed. "You have class in two hours, and it's going to take at least one to scrub the smell of despair and BO off you. Come on."

I shook my head.

"You think I can't make you? I'm stronger than I look, and I have zero problem dropping your stubborn ass in the shower, then dragging you to class." He tossed my writing pad on the bed beside me.

I picked up the pen for it, then wrote, "*Why do you even care?*"

"Because I've seen this before. First calls home go this way a lot more than people want to admit.

However, I *don't* want to see you suffer because you start breaking rules your first month here. You don't want that either. There are some roads you start down and it's damn near impossible to get back from."

"Can't I call in sick?"

"Not unless you want to end up in Medical, and trust me, you do *not* want that."

I pressed my lips together, realizing exactly how bad my mouth tasted at that moment. I didn't think I'd drunk water, certainly hadn't brushed my teeth. I'd just lain there for two days and tried to sink into the mattress so I didn't have to think anymore.

And here Wade was, trying to drag me out of it.

"My parents aren't coming for me," I wrote.

Wade's expression said he got it, that he knew what I meant, and he was the first person I'd met who seemed to give a damn about how I felt. "Yeah, I know that moment, when things click together, when it becomes real. I remember my first night here, when I'd crawled under my bed and cried because I was so sure someone had made a mistake. I kept waiting for someone to realize it, to tell me it was a big mix-up and that I was going home."

He sighed, then shook his head as if embarrassed. "Clearly, that didn't happen, and I figured out the truth — we're stuck here. Whatever lives any of us had outside of these walls, those lives are over. There isn't anything for us out there, not anymore, and the sooner a person figures that out, the better off they are. You may not feel very lucky right now, Hera, but you are. Some of us spent months, even years pretending things were different. You, though? You know it right away, and that means you can start living *this* life now instead of holding on to the past."

"*I have nowhere to go,*" I repeated on the writing pad, trying to make him understand that life without direction was pointless. How did someone exist when they had no freedom, no hope for something better, something different? My entire life had been focused on moving in a certain direction, with achieving something. I had none of that, now.

"Sure you do. You have a shower to take, then a class to attend."

I gave him a hell of a *so what?* expression.

"One day at a time, that's all you've got to focus on. Whatever happens tomorrow, you can deal with tomorrow. For today, though?" He paused, then stared at me, expectantly.

"*Class.*"

"Close," he countered, his smile returning. "Shower first, or they won't even let you into class, not smelling like that."

And somehow, Wade's humor helped bridge the gap between what I needed to do and the place I was at, the one where I felt like that was impossible. If he could survive this place, humor intact, maybe he wasn't as dumb as he seemed.

* * * *

I arrived at the classroom moments before the soft beep from the clock would have marked me late. It let me release a long breath, thankful to at least have made it on time.

The shower had taken a while, but each moment I'd stood beneath the nearly scalding water, the more my head had cleared.

I hadn't come up with any great epiphanies, but maybe that had been Wade's point. I didn't need to.

I didn't have to know what I was going to do for the rest of my life, or in two years, or even tomorrow. Those things felt too large, too far away. They made me consider which was worse — that things could change for the worse or that they could remain exactly as they were.

Could I live my life —

I shook my head as I took my seat. I couldn't think like that. Instead, I focused on today, on this week at most.

I had two things on my schedule today — this one, which only had a room number listed along with 'evaluation' written — and a work session afterward. It seemed I'd be pulling weeds in the yard.

At least a bit of sun would do me good.

No one else came into the room, something that threw me. Thus far, all my classes had had at least another five or six residents in them.

Had I gone to the wrong room?

Fear crept into me, a worry that I'd misread my schedule, that after Wade's work to get me here, I'd messed up anyway.

The panic didn't have enough time to take hold for long before the heavy sound of footsteps drew my attention to the back door, the one I'd entered through.

Kit walked in, dressed in fancy slacks and a white button- up shirt with a tie, just as last time. The band on his wrist remained, but he still wasn't dressed in the uniforms I'd seen from the rest of the residents.

He set his briefcase on the large desk in front, then flipped it open without speaking to me, without acknowledging me.

It was also the moment I took a better look around the room. There were only a couple seats circled around an open space.

Somehow, that didn't bode well for whatever 'evaluations' meant.

Finally, Kit organized all his papers and lifted his gaze to mine. He didn't appear surprised to see me or that I was the only one there.

However, none of that quite fit. He behaved as if he were staff, but the wristband said he wasn't.

"Glad to see you made it," he said, then came around and leaned against the front of his desk, so he faced me.

The words seemed to hold some second meaning, making me frown. Had he known I wasn't planning on coming?

How? Why would he give a damn even if he did know?

It didn't seem worth it to write down the question, so I let it go, but pointed at him instead.

He nodded, then set a hand against his chest. "I already told you my name was Kit Porter. I'm what they call adjunct staff. Basically, I proved myself useful enough that they have me teaching certain courses."

This time I did scribble down my question. *"Aren't you a shade?"*

"Yes, I am. I can't leave, I still have rules, but they trust me enough for some extra privileges others lack. It is the benefit, I suppose, of being here as long as I have."

"How long?"

"Longer than I want to admit to." His tone said that was the end of the conversation, even though the answer was entirely unsatisfactory.

I nodded, knowing better than to argue. A quick glance around the room, probably clued him into my next question without me having to ask.

"Evaluations are done privately for the most part. Sometimes we have either a guard with tranqs or a void, if one is available, but I told the director I didn't feel that was needed for you." At my look, he continued, his voice lowered as if he didn't care for having to say the next part out loud. "Given what happened to your voice, you don't pose as big a threat as you would have otherwise. The rest of your abilities would be more defensive and less destructive."

Ouch. I understood why he hadn't wanted to voice that. It was true, but that only made the reminder more painful.

I dropped my gaze, not wanting to see pity in his eyes, wanting him not to see how deeply that hurt.

"Evaluations occur fairly regularly. See, Larkwood is unique in a lot of ways compared to other academies. Many are just for housing shades, for keeping them away from the public, for identifying those who could be released. The part that isn't on the orientation here is that Larkwood prefers to make use of us. That means honing talents in a way other places don't allow."

"What does honing mean?"

"It means we figure out where your skills are and track their growth. You learn to control them, to use them to their best ability, and Larkwood sees if that would be useful to them. If it is, if you make yourself useful to them, it buys you a nicer life. More freedom, access to items normally banned, even outings."

It sounded a lot like selling my soul to the devil, like playing nice with the enemy for just a few scraps from their table. Still, the opposite wasn't any better. Being difficult would only hurt me.

"So what now?"

He glanced at the pad of paper, then gestured at the large whiteboard that was at the open space. "Why don't you use that to write? It'll be easier for me to read, and some space is always a good thing. Since your voice isn't something we can test, we'll look at your other skills. How much do you know about sirens?"

I shook my head, because I knew nothing about them. Shades came in so many types, and only a few were normally discussed. The more common varieties, the vampires, the werewolves, the telepaths, they were at the forefront of pop culture. Once a person got deeper than that, though, it was hard to find reliable information.

It meant despite apparently being a siren, I had no idea what it meant.

Kit leaned against his desk. "Don't worry, that's pretty common. Not many people come in here knowing much of anything about what they are. The registry likes to keep most specifics quiet, so they don't panic people. You already know sirens are classified as level 1, and from what I heard, you got a taste of exactly why."

The memory of how I'd sang, of the blood streaming from those men's ears, hit me. Yeah, I had seen what I could do, even if it was hard to accept it had been me.

"The thing is, that was pure panic. Think of it like the difference between someone in fight or flight who attacks another person compared to someone who has spent years studying martial arts. If properly trained, one siren can take down anything in hearing range. They can even use their voice to coax and coerce others, to get people to do whatever they want. Those things all take years of training, though, of harnessing those abilities, of learning how to use them."

He spoke matter-of-factly, but that didn't erase the burn inside me. Part of it was the idea that I was what he spoke of, and the other? That something that was so vital a part of me was gone. Hearing about what I could have done if some asshole hadn't maimed me was surprisingly unpleasant. It was like losing a game but getting a front row seat into what the prize would have been.

Kit paused, then sighed. "I'm not trying to upset you—just to educate you. The reality is that there is still a chance you could heal someday, and you should know and understand what you are. See, people think sirens are just singers, but that couldn't be further from the truth. Sirens are keepers of sound, manipulators of sound. That doesn't just mean what they speak, but what they hear."

I recalled how, when people spoke, I could see images, could feel things. I went up to the whiteboard, grabbing a marker to write. *"Why do I see things when people speak sometimes?"*

"Because sound carries more than most people can identify. Think about it...if you know someone well, you can tell how they feel from their voice alone. If you don't know them, however, you can't. Sirens can hear impossibly more, the complexities others miss, and all that translates in different ways. Sometimes it means seeing images, things from the past, feelings, even thoughts. The amount a siren gets from that depends on how strong they are and how much they work at learning."

"I don't want to hear all that."

"And most vampires don't want to drink blood and werewolves don't like to change and most people don't want to ever get sick. What we want has little to do with reality. Besides, learning to control and use that power will also allow you to better dim it when needed. Werewolves learn to embrace their other form because by doing that, they also learn to control it."

I blew out a slow breath, unable to argue with him but also not caring for what he had to say.

I just wanted to deal with the evaluation to get it over with, so I could stop thinking about what I was, about what it all meant.

Though, that brought up another point, one I hesitated to ask. Still, I forced my hand to move, to write it out.

Kit stared at the question, not responding at first, his lips pressed into a hard line. After a moment, he spoke softly. "Asking shades what they are isn't considered a polite question. Most of us wear it on our wrist, but still…" He shrugged, then stood. "I suppose, however, since I know what you are, it's only fair. You'll find that for level 1 shades, there are a lot of unique creatures. The fewer there are of something, the more powerful they tend to be. I'm a wendigo."

I frowned, the word meaning nothing to me.

"I won't waste time explaining that—you don't need to know. You know what I am, who I am, but now it's time to get to work. The goal for today is to test a few of your skills and mark down the results. You'll have time to practice daily, and in a week, we'll test again." He didn't ask if I understood—I didn't think my opinion mattered.

Instead, he stared directly at me, the black of his eyes unnerving, almost feeling as if they shifted, as if they were different than they were before. "I want you to listen, to *really* listen to my voice. Not just with your ears, but with something deeper, with that part of you you don't like, the one you try to shut out, the one that tells you more. Stop ignoring it and tell me what you hear."

I closed my eyes, not wanting to do what he said but knowing I didn't have a choice. I focused not on his words, but on the sound, on how the I could feel the vibrations in my skin, the way I could feel so much more than just his voice.

When I focused, when I opened myself to it all, it wasn't just his voice that hit me. I caught the voice of a professor two doors down as he berated a resident for not completing assigned work. Deeper than the harsh words, however, was sorrow, was a hatred of what he had to do, and his desire to be tough on the kid because he didn't want anything worse to happen to him. Farther away, I caught someone moan a name — *Knox*. A feral sound responded, full of anger, of hatred, of pain, yet mixed with pleasure. Even more distant, a scream full of terror, of intense pain.

It all collided together, each one so loud and fighting for my attention. In fact, I couldn't even hear Kit's voice anymore, not over everything else.

My lips moved, forming words that couldn't escape as I put my hands over my ears. It was all too much, too loud, too massive, too painful.

Something warm pressed against my cheeks, and I opened my eyes.

When had I fallen to the floor?

The black eyes staring at me told me Kit had come closer, that he'd grabbed my face to try to wake me.

Even still, those sounds, they overwhelmed me, they threatened to tear me apart from the inside.

He came closer, so near I almost thought he'd kiss me. Instead, he curled his fingers in so the points of nails that hadn't been there before dug into my skin, and his face shifted.

Bone remained rather than flesh, the face of the creature I'd seen when he'd spoken before. Except, this wasn't some picture in my head, not a memory or a dream. This was *him*, physically, right in front of me.

His eyes were still that white, but brighter, and they drew me in. Something in them drew me back, silenced all that noise, helped me rebuild the wall that had dimmed them before.

A coldness inside me grew, as if he'd poured dry ice inside me, as if it froze me and helped me regain control.

Finally, I gasped in a breath and pulled backward, the world quiet and that feeling inside me terrifying in its depth. As soon as we broke contact, it receded, as if drawn back to him, but the quiet remained. When I looked at him again, whatever he had been, that bone creature, it was gone and the man I was used to seeing was back.

"What did you see?" He pushed my notepad my way.

"Everything. The next room, Knox somewhere, someone screaming in pain."

He didn't appear pleased. I'd done what he'd asked, given it my all, and yet he didn't look happy at all about the results. "Knox is in the Residential wing, Hera. That is so much farther than you should have been able to hear."

"And the screaming?"

He dropped his gaze, still seated on the floor in front of me. "I'd guess that's from the other tower."

"What is in the other tower?"

He shook his head. "I don't know. I don't think the staff or guards here know. What I do know is that the residents who go there do not come back."

Which sounded pretty much like Larkwood itself...

"So what does this all mean?"

Kit stared at me like he hadn't before, as if he saw something now he'd missed before. It unnerved me, made me want to draw back farther, especially after getting a good look at whatever he really was. When he spoke, he didn't reassure me at all, didn't make me feel any better about him or what had happened. "You need to be very careful, Hera, about who knows what exactly you're capable of. Useful is one thing. Larkwood loves useful. Dangerous is another. Be sure you don't draw too much attention, because standing out here is one of the biggest mistakes a person can make."

Chapter Eight

The blisters on my hands hurt, and even with the bandages I'd wrapped my palms with, I couldn't ignore the pain each time I tried to pick something up.

As it turned out, yard work outside wasn't that great of a job. I'd thought some sun, a chance to breathe in fresh air would be worth any amount of manual labor.

Boy, had I been wrong. Four hours of pulling weeds and hula hoeing had left my hands a bloody mess.

Worse, the guard assigned to watch me had spent the entire time sitting on a bench and staring at my ass. He'd made a couple comments, low enough I just barely heard them, but each made me want to gag.

Whether it was the cameras or some level of decency inside him, he hadn't acted on any of the little fantasies he'd felt the need to share that all included me naked and him taking advantage.

The longer I was at Larkwood, the more I needed to spend time outside of my own room. The walls had started to close in, started to feel more like a tomb than a sanctuary. That had left me spending more time in the general areas.

For the most part, people left me alone. It seemed no one wanted me in their little clique. Whether that was due to me being new, my name or what I was, I had no idea. All I knew for sure was that anytime I headed anywhere, others seemed to scatter.

Well, except for a few. Wade never ran the other way. Knox and Brax glared at me, but they seemed the type who wouldn't let me think I had the upper hand, that I'd frightened them away.

And the memory of the sound Knox had made, the one I'd caught, it had stuck with me. The moan from his partner—deep and masculine—had been full of pleasure. It was a sound I'd never made during sex, one I didn't know people made. It wasn't a lie, either. Then there had been Knox, that angry almost growl he'd let out, and the fact he'd told the demon he wasn't into men when clearly he'd been having sex with a man when I'd overheard him.

It was a mystery I couldn't shake.

"Yard duty?" Wade asked, gesturing at my hand and he took a seat beside me at the large table in the main rec area.

I nodded, holding them out to show the red patches on the bandages.

"Expect a delivery soon. You need a good pair of gloves, and I've got connections. It'll save your hands."

I offered him a smile, the closest to a thank you I could give.

"Well, well," came a new voice, one that put me on edge. While I'd gotten better at silencing what I heard from voices, at dimming how they affected me, some of it still slipped through.

In this case, it was violence. That had this sticky, thick quality to the words, as if it dripped off them as the new man spoke.

When I glanced in his direction, he looked exactly as I would have expected. He was in his forties and massive, with the sort of body that came from exercising when a person had nothing else to do in a day. A glance at his wrist revealed more — *ifrit*.

I didn't know much about that — like everything else — but the smoke that seemed to drift from him said it had to do with fire.

Wade turned slightly to peer over at the other man, and the difference between them was obvious. The ifrit had height and weight over Wade — along with almost twenty years and a lot of aggression.

"What can I do for you?" Wade asked the question as if he were running into an acquaintance somewhere, as if the other man didn't seem ready to kill Wade.

"What are you doing here, befriending *her*?"

"I like new people. New blood makes the world less boring."

"Her daddy and mommy are the reason we're all here, or have you forgotten that?"

"Last I checked, she's barely older than a kid. Are you blaming her for what other people have done? I know she didn't haul me in here and turn the lock. Did she manage that for you?"

The ifrit glared. "This isn't a joke. People may not want to fuck with you for whatever reason, but trust me, they want a piece of her. Be a nice message to her rich fucking friends and family if she gets sent back in pieces. You don't want to get between that."

My chest hurt, fear striking me, my hand shaking. There was no question who would win between Wade and this new man, and I didn't want Wade's blood on my hands. I didn't want to be responsible for anything that happened to him.

He'd been the only person here to treat me with any sense of kindness, so the thought of him suffering because of it made me shake my head.

"Are you sure that this is what you want to do?" Wade asked, a smile still on his face, as if we weren't moments from violence, as if none of that mattered to him.

I reached out and grabbed Wade's arm through his sweater, squeezing to get his attention.

He turned his gaze to me, his eyebrows drawn together as he looked at where I had my hand on him. I shook my head, trying to make it clear I didn't want him to get involved, that I didn't want him putting himself in danger.

Wade frowned, as if it made no sense to him, before another smile crept across his lips. "Are you worried about me?"

"You should listen to her," the ifrit said. "I don't think you want to die for her."

I again shook my head, my gaze on Wade, trying to make him understand.

He let out a soft laugh before extracting his arm. "You shouldn't worry so much." Wade rose from the seat, then turned toward the ifrit.

Never had the size difference been so obvious as it was right then, when Wade looked like a child compared to the other man.

Not that Wade noticed. In fact, he reminded me of when a tiny dog had no idea it was so small as it snarled at a dog four times its size. He tilted his head up to lock eyes with the ifrit. "Last chance. I like to give people plenty of chances, the ability to make a difference choice. This is it for you. Turn around, walk away and we're good. I don't hold grudges."

The ifrit leaned in, and the smoke increased, pouring off him as if he were on fire. "Stupid choice," he grated before reaching out and wrapping his hand around Wade's throat.

I stood, my chair knocking backward, no idea what I was going to do but unwilling to stand there and watch Wade take an attack intended for me.

Except, nothing happened. The ifrit frowned, as if he didn't understand.

"Performance problems?" Wade asked.

The ifrit tried to pull away, but Wade moved faster. He wrapped a hand around the ifrit's wrist, and for some reason, the ifrit couldn't pull free. It was then I realized Wade had removed the gloves he always wore.

Wade's eyes darkened until they turned black. Smoke started to float from Wade, just as it had from the ifrit. "You should have walked away, should have asked yourself why no one else fucks with me, then figured out that it's stupid for you to decide to be the first."

The ifrit tried to yank, the fear on his face taking over, his movements clumsier. "I'm sorry," he said, his voice weak.

"You will be. You should have looked at my band before assuming you could take me." Wade held up his band. "A void. You may not have realized what that meant before, but you get it now, don't you? Do you feel everything you are sliding away? Being swallowed up? All that strength, the power you're used to, it's leaching away, and you realize you don't have anything else."

"Let him go," came a guard's voice, who had a gun pointed at Wade.

Wade, however, ignored the guard. His black eyes remained locked on the ifrit, who had fallen to his knees. "I want you to remember this feeling each time you think about touching that girl. In fact, I want you to remember how I stole everything from you when anyone mentions doing a damn thing to her and decide whose bad side you want to be on. Spoiler alert – it isn't mine."

The ifrit collapsed to the ground the moment Wade released him, as if he had no strength to hold himself up, as if Wade had stolen all the energy from him.

"Put your fucking hands up!" the guard yelled.

Wade did as ordered, but when he did, fire coated his palms, smoke pouring off him. His eyes were still black, and he met my gaze for a moment, his smile having a dangerous edge it hadn't before.

Or maybe it had always been there, but I hadn't seen it. Wade didn't look all that scary, but then again, I'd never seen him do that, either. The ifrit had yet to move, yet to try to pick himself up. He was breathing, so he was at alive at least.

A moment later, a shot rang out and a dart struck Wade in the back of his shoulder. He didn't even wince, but the flames in his palms increased as if in response. Another shot happened, another dart. By that point, Wade stumbled, losing his footing, and one of his knees struck the ground.

A third dart hit him, and the flames died down though smoke continued to fill the rec room. He fell forward, and as soon as his chest hit the floor, three guards all but tackled him. They bound his wrists behind him and dragged him out.

I was left standing there, all the other residents in the large rec room looking my way, as if this had all been my fault.

As much as Wade had been trying to protect me, the hard looks from the others said he might have made it worse. They might be terrified of him — and now so was I — but he'd just given them yet another multitude of reasons to hate me.

As if I hadn't had it hard enough already.

* * * *

It was strange. I hadn't known Wade for long, and we hadn't spent all that much time together, yet I couldn't help but notice his absence.

Each class I'd attended, each time I'd gone to the pantry or any other community area, I'd thought about him. It was if I could feel his absence.

"Haven't you caused enough problems?" Brax's voice didn't catch me off guard, and in fact I'd gotten used to the way he spoke to me, the not even a little hidden hatred.

I turned to look his way, the items in my arms from the pantry shifting. Holding items meant I was out of luck if I wanted to talk, though I'd bet he didn't give a damn.

I didn't get the sense Brax gave a damn about whether I had anything to say back or not.

For that reason, I didn't even try to explain anything. I only moved my arms to better grip my items.

Brax glared down at the things I'd gotten, but he didn't comment on that. "You got one of us thrown into solitary."

I blew out a sharp breath, moving the strand of hair in my face away, then gave him a bored look.

He could blame me for Wade all he wanted—I blamed myself. Still, there wasn't anything I could do about it.

"Do you have any idea what solitary is like? They stick you in this dark cell—no bed, no chair, nothing to pass the time. It's just you and your thoughts there."

That sounded horrible.

It wounded even worse when I considered Wade, his incessant talking, his cheery attitude. That wouldn't have been easy for anyone, but for someone like him? Someone who seemed to thrive off connection with others, it had to be exceedingly difficult.

It made me wonder just how long that usually lasted.

I tilted to the side, trying to hold the items while I counted up with my fingers, trying to ask him about it.

Brax glanced down at my fingers before giving me an even more annoyed expression. "You care now?" When I didn't respond, he let out an unhappy breath. "They use solitary at their whim, so nothing's for sure. Usually, around a week, unless the person's got a history of causing problems."

That means Wade should be out quickly.

"Which means Wade won't get out for a while."

That made me frown.

He let out a laugh, but it lacked humor. "Don't let that kid trick you with his smile. He might look innocent as hell, but don't forget that he's here like the rest of us. He's gotten thrown in there more than a few times before."

"He somehow comes out even more cheerful than he goes in." The near identical voice to Knox's made me offer Brax a look full of disbelief. "It's true. Last time Wade got out, he wrote me a limerick."

"It was a sonnet."

"Same difference. I hate poetry."

Brax gave his brother the same sort of look he gave me—but without quite as much murderous intent. "What are you even doing here?"

"Curiosity." Knox looked my way, his gaze moving over me as if forced to pay more attention to me all of a sudden.

It had me stepping away again, just as I'd done the last time. I didn't care for the way he looked at me, especially after knowing what he was. I still had no idea what exactly that meant.

Still, I figured it had something to do with sex, with manipulating others and making them want things they wouldn't normally. I wanted no part of that nonsense, so I planned to keep my distance.

Knox lifted an eyebrow, as if that was the reaction he'd been going for.

Brax shook his head. "I don't know what you're doing but knock it off."

I let out a long sigh. Even if I could say anything, it wouldn't matter. Brax would have blamed me for global warming if he could.

I had no idea what he was talking about and honestly? I wasn't sure I cared.

It was odd how quickly I had settled into the reality of being there. Even Brax didn't strike me as quite so scary anymore.

"Leave her be," Knox said, earning him a confused look from me.

Why would he defend me at all? Especially to his brother?

Brax glared at his brother, then let out an angry, dangerous sound before he stormed off.

It left Knox and me there alone.

Knox reached out, but he didn't touch me. Instead, he stole one of the items in my arms. In this case, it was a box of crackers.

"These are Brax's favorites."

Yeah, mine too, which was why I got them.

I was pretty sure my expression didn't quite convey all that, especially when he made a soft snort in response.

"I know my brother isn't easy to deal with."

I snorted back, glad to know I could at least make that noise.

"Trust me, I know. If anyone knows how difficult it is to deal with him, it's me."

I tried to reach for the crackers, to steal them back.

Knox pulled them out of range. "He wasn't always like he is, either."

I offered a deadpan look, tilting my head and lifting an eyebrow.

"It's true. He wasn't so...hard before. This place, it changes people. Being in hell will warp people. I would bet no one here is the same person they were before they came." He looked toward me and offered a slight smile. "Well, I guess you, probably. Maybe you haven't been here long enough to be changed by it." His gaze lowered to my throat, and his smile drifted away. "Or, maybe you have."

I dropped my gaze, not caring for the pity in his tone or the way he stared at my scar.

He let out a sharp sound, one so at odds with the smooth way he spoke normally. It drew my gaze back up, startled.

He didn't speak until I looked him in the eye. "Don't hide it, songbird, not in this world. Where you came from, maybe scars are something to be ashamed of, but here?" He shook his head. "Here, people either have scars or they're dead. There's no middle ground. You should get used to them, because in your time here, you'll either earn a few more, or you won't live long enough to do so. I hope you're the sort who adds to your scar count."

He held up the box of crackers. "Thanks for this. Maybe it will keep Brax from pacing and muttering all night."

He took the crackers and walked off, following where Brax had headed for.

Those two were going to be trouble.

* * * *

"Not a chance." Deacon crossed his arms, his purple eyes hard. "And I don't like you coming to me like this. I'm not some errand boy for you."

I looked down, hit the Erase button then wrote more.

Deacon waited until I finished, until I held the pad out to him.

He snatched it from my hand, offering me one more hard glare before lifting it to read.

It gave me a moment to peer around Deacon's office. It felt strange to know that he had a space like this, something official.

I knew he was a guard, that he was one of those imprisoning me here, an enemy, but somehow Deacon didn't feel like that.

I didn't have that same fear, that same feeling that I should be wary.

So, the reminder that he was a guard was hard. The truth was in the desk with the name plaque reading Guard Deacon Harting.

He wasn't another shade. He wasn't my friend.

But that didn't stop me from needing his help.

He pressed his lips together as he stared down at the pad. "Solitary means alone. They don't get visitors."

I pointed at the words.

Deacon dropped the pad on the desk. "I don't care that he got thrown in there over you. That was his choice, and trust me, Wade's spent enough time there. He likes to press the rules, to think they don't apply to him. It isn't the first time, and it won't be the last."

I sighed and plopped down in one of the seats. He leaned against the edge of the desk, staring at me.

"Why do you even care? He'll be out in a few more days. Even if I got you in to see him, there's a good chance you can end up in trouble over it. Is that worth it?"

I nodded. Wade had been the only one to stand up for me, to make me feel like I might just not be entirely alone there.

He held out the pad to me, then shook his head. "This is a bad idea, and not just because you risk getting yourself thrown into solitary next. You need to be careful about thinking that you've made friends here. This place, it changes a person. It makes them whatever they have to be to survive, and in all my years here, I've never seen a friendship that started here last. I've seen too many die here because they got comfortable, because they thought the other folks here were their friends. I see 'em come in here, seeing the guards as the enemies and the other shades their allies, but it doesn't work like that. Lock people up and they turn into animals, and the ones here will tear down anyone else if it gets 'em a little closer to something they want."

I thought back to the werewolf I'd seen what felt like years ago, the young boy who had been digging through the trash. I'd looked at him and thought...*animal*. It had been so automatic—I hadn't been able to help it. I recalled my parents telling me that, remembered when they'd taken me to see that full-grown werewolf, to how the chains had hung off it and terrified me.

Now, however, that didn't seem to fit as it did before. I thought about Wade, about how he seemed nothing like an animal. Even after what I'd seen with the ifrit, he hadn't been what I'd expected.

Some of the others I'd met, they still did. Brax and Knox, for example. Brax was as animalistic and feral as a person could be, in fact. Knox, he didn't have the same edge, at least in his behavior. When he stared at me, that reminded me of a predator.

And Kit?

He looked so much more civilized than the others, yet I'd glimpsed something beneath, something terrifying that he managed to hide.

It meant I couldn't exactly deny what Deacon said, not to mention that he knew more than I did. He'd been here...I had no idea how long, but he had a comfort that said he wasn't close to new.

Still, I met his gaze and shrugged. What did any of that matter? I was trapped here, and I had no idea for how long. If I did as he said, if I cut myself off from anyone else, I might as well be in solitary anyway.

Deacon pressed his lips together, and for a moment, I thought he'd say no. I expected him to tell me to get out, that I was on my own. It wasn't like he owed me anything, so he wasn't entirely wrong about that.

To my surprise, his shoulders dropped and nodded. "I'll set it up. Be ready tonight around midnight. If you get enough smarts to realize this is a bad idea, then just put a *do not disturb* on your door, and I'll leave you be." He cast me one more look, something full of disapproval. "But I know you won't listen to me. No one ever does, and I have to sit around and watch the outcome. All I can do is hope you smarten up sooner rather than later."

I hope so too...

Chapter Nine

Midnight took forever to arrive. I'd gone to sleep for a few hours earlier, despite the nerves running through me. Still, I'd forced myself to close my eyes, to try to rest. I had no idea how long my visit with Wade would be or if I'd make it back to bed at all.

Eventually, however, sleep came. Maybe it was my general level of exhaustion, or maybe I was just so determined to rest that I'd managed it by sheer will.

I dreamed, but as had happened each time, they'd been odd. They hadn't been nightmares, or even dreams in the way I was used to. Instead, it had been flashes of people I didn't recognize, at least most of them.

I'd had a moment of seeing Brax, his eyes closed, his legs folded as if meditating. However, this rage had filled him, something overwhelming and deep, and he struggled to keep it under control. At the last moment, his eyes had opened, as if staring at me, and I'd woken.

Was it real? Was that like when I heard voices?

I had no idea, but figured Brax wanted to kill me enough as it was—it probably wasn't a great idea to go and ask him about if I'd accidently spied on him in my sleep.

My door opened, and Deacon's familiar scowl met me. I wondered if he ever smiled, if he ever looked happy. So far, I'd seen nothing but glares and annoyance.

And there was the time he'd tossed me across the room. Perhaps the scowling was better than that.

"So you didn't rethink the plan?" he asked.

I shook my head, then held my arms out.

He peered at my outfit and sighed. "Why do you look like a burglar? We aren't pulling a heist here. We're just going over to solitary. You didn't need to dress in all black." His cheek twitched, and for a moment, I almost thought he had to fight a smile.

Which, being at my expense, didn't feel all that great.

Still, I focused on the point and not the other stuff, not on how Deacon felt about it. Wade had spent three days in solitary, and I wanted to tell him I appreciated it. I wanted him to know he wasn't alone, since he'd made me feel that way.

In the pocket of my hoodie sat the items I'd put together for him, the ones I'd gathered as a thank you for him, to try to make up for the trouble I'd caused.

Deacon gestured for me to come closer, and I did so without hesitation.

He caught my hand and lifted it, then brought out a small tablet and held them close together, typing in information.

I snapped and when he looked at me, I lifted an eyebrow.

"I'm extending your free hours, so no alarms sound when you leave your room after lockdown. I'll open the actual doors, but without fixing your schedule, you'd be flagged the moment you passed that doorway."

I frowned at that, then reached with my other hand for my pad. I wrote down a question, using Deacon's arm as a base.

"Are we monitored when we go anywhere?"

He glanced down at the writing, then nodded. "Each doorway and elevator have a sensor in it, and it tracks each wristband that passes through. We know exactly where every single resident is and where they've gone. The bands open doorways but will also set off alarms if they happen to pass somewhere they shouldn't or at a time they shouldn't be there. By extending your schedule, you won't set off those sensors."

"Won't they still know I'd been out there?"

"Yes, but that's fine. If they look deep enough, they'll see I escorted you."

"Won't that get you into trouble?"

He frowned at the words, as if they didn't make much sense. "No. I'm given a lot of leeway to do as I wish when it comes to security here. If anyone asks, I'll simply explain I offered the visit in exchange for information."

That helped me pull in a relieved breath. The last thing I wanted was to try to make up for what happened to Wade and along the way, get Deacon in trouble for helping me.

After another moment of typing, Deacon slid the small phone-sized tablet into his pocket. "Done. Last chance to back out of this. Are you sure?"

"As sure as I ever am."

The trip through the hallways and elevators felt surreal. Something about being out at that time put me on edge.

It seemed I'd already grown used to the routine, to being back in the relative safety of my room by this time. Not to mention the empty hallways were eerie.

After we crossed the bridge, he took the elevator to the fourth floor, then went down a hallway to another elevator. Deacon waved his wrist over the sensor, and the doors slid open.

I followed him inside, taking a step closer to him when the doors closed.

He offered a side-eye, one that said he'd caught the movement and didn't appreciate it. "This elevator goes to the security floor. Residents aren't allowed there unaccompanied."

I nodded and tucked my hands into my sweater.

"Why are you so determined to visit Wade? I know he can seem charming…"

That made me twist to look at him. Was that…jealousy?

No, that made no sense. Deacon dealt with how many people coming through over the years? He didn't give a damn about some new girl who caused problems.

I took my pad out and wrote on it. *He was nice to me. That's not something that's happened much since I got here.*

He read over the words slowly, lines appearing between his eyebrows. "Is that all it takes? Someone being a little nice to you?"

"Considering everything else that's happened, yeah."

His frown deepened. "That's a pretty dangerous thing. You should keep that to yourself, or someone will take advantage of it."

I shrugged, not sure what sort of response he was expecting.

The doors slid open, but when I went to exit, Deacon put his arm out to stop me. I jerked away, recalling the last time I'd touched him, when he'd thrown me across the room. I didn't want a repeat of that.

He dropped his gaze to where I'd backed away. He didn't say anything, however, until he peered out the doors and waved me to follow. "There aren't many guards this time of night, especially because there aren't any normal patrols here since shades aren't allowed. I'd still rather not pass anyone. The fewer questions the better."

I nodded and followed him after he exited the elevator, keeping some space between us. We walked slowly, with Deacon having his head tilted slightly, as if listening for anything that was around. We managed to cross the hallways, to pass doorways, and not run into anyone. A few times, Deacon paused and would wave me to the side, either into a corner or a side room, to avoid guards.

Finally, we came to a stop after an exceptionally long hallway with only a single door at the end.

"This is it." Deacon stopped in front of the door, then turned to look at me. "Be careful. Wade is great at looking innocent and harmless, but don't forget for a second what you saw from him. Voids are at the top of the food chain—*always*." He didn't wait for a response from me before waving his wrist over the sensor, turning a red light there green at the same time as something mechanical clicked inside the door.

I took a deep breath, then slid into the darkness of the room, unwilling to accept Deacon, Knox or Brax's opinion on Wade.

I'd learned that *anyone* was dangerous when pushed far enough.

The cell was dark, and it took a moment for my eyes to adjust enough to make anything out. Just as Brax had said, there was no bed, no chair, nothing to focus on or do. It had no windows beyond the one in the door, but having been in a cell myself before, it wasn't a shock to see it was a one-way mirror, allowing guards to look in but the person in the cell to not be able to see anything.

In the corner was something dark, and it took a long moment to realize it was Wade. He lay on the ground, his back to the door, his face toward the wall. He didn't move, as if the door opening didn't matter to him at all.

I walked in, sorry again about my inability to speak. I wanted to call out, to let him know I was there. I'd witnessed firsthand what he could do, and I had no desire to startle him.

However, since that wasn't possible, I made sure to use more force than needed as I stepped, to make sure he heard it. What if he was sleeping?

I crouched beside him when I got closer, then knocked on the stone floor to get his attention.

He turned, but it happened so fast, I yanked backward in surprise. Fire covered his hand still, and that hand headed straight for me. I shut my eyes tight, prepared for pain, for whatever was coming.

It didn't make contact, though. I opened my eyes slowly, peeking through one to find Deacon with his hand around Wade's wrist.

Wade met Deacon's eyes, again reminding me how much less intimidating the younger man was. Wade, even with the smoke, the fire, with what I'd seen him do already, looked like a kid compared to Deacon.

"You really want to fry your only visitor?" Deacon asked.

Wade blinked slowly, then shook his head before looking my way. I wasn't sure at first if he even recognized me. He stared as if he was entirely confused about who I was and what I was doing there.

Except, after a long moment, he nodded.

Deacon released him, then backed away but didn't leave. It seemed he didn't quite trust Wade to be back to himself.

Wade shifted until his back was against the wall, his legs folded in front of him, the fire on his hands disappearing when he hunched forward. He stared at me, breathing slowly, seeming to calm and ground himself. "You came?"

His voice was rough, making me wonder if he'd had any water. Or was it the smoke that still filled the room?

I nodded, then reached for my pad.

Until I realized that given the darkness of the room, he'd never be able to read it. *Just great.*

"I didn't expect you to visit me." Wade lifted his gaze in Deacon's direction. "I sure didn't think you'd ask a changed for help, or that he'd agree."

Deacon shrugged, still standing against the wall beside the door, making it clear he had no plans to leave. "She was going to keep trying to find a way to see you. I figured giving her a little help would cause me the least amount of trouble."

"That's awfully nice of you. Never figured you for someone who would give a damn."

My head ached as the words carried tension and double meanings. All the history involved in them, all the things the two of them knew that I didn't, it filled the space between the syllables until it threatened to overwhelm me.

Clearly, these two had plenty of history between them.

Deacon's gaze settled on me for a moment. Could he tell my head hurt? That their conversation caused me pain? He didn't mention it but let out a soft, annoyed breath and dropped his gaze to the ground.

It was a clear sign that he would shut up and let us have our visit.

Wade brought his focus back to me, his eyes the same as they'd been when he'd touched the ifrit. It was unnerving...

"Bet you didn't expect that from me," he said, his voice soft and full of more pain than I'd noticed before. I didn't see any marks, so I had no idea why he hurt.

I pressed my lips together, unwilling to confirm or deny his guess. Of course I hadn't expected it. Who would have?

"Cat's out of the bag now, I guess. Being a void is like a counter to other shades. I can temporarily steal a shade's powers with just a touch. It's why I wear these." He lifted his hands to show his gloves.

Another puff of smoke left his hand, and I gestured at it.

"It takes a while for the effects to wear off," he admitted softly. "The more I siphon, the weaker the other shade gets and the longer it takes for me to shake it off." He let out a sigh, then rolled his shoulders as if he was tense and couldn't get rid of the feeling. "But none of that is all that important. Why'd you go through so much trouble to come visit little ol' me? I know I'm a lot of fun, but I figured you could last a week without me."

I reached into the pocket of my sweater and pulled out the items I'd put together, then pushed them across the stone floor between us.

The stone had thrown me, but after seeing the ifrit, after learning more, I understood it better.

Stone didn't burn, and when dealing with shades, fire was a real possibility.

Wade took the items, frowning as he looked through what I'd brought.

A few water bottles, a sci-fi book Mrs. Clemmings had suggested and bags of food that didn't need to be refrigerated, such as trail mix and jerky.

He got to the note I'd written, squinting in the darkness.

"Give it," Deacon said as he pushed off the wall. "My eyes are better than yours."

"It's private," Wade said.

"Well, either I read it for you, or you can wait until you're out of here to know what it says. Either way, time's running out."

Wade made an unhappy sound before handing it over.

Deacon seemed to have no issue with making out the writing in the dark. "You shouldn't have risked yourself for me, but I thank you for it. Being here, having everything change, it isn't easy. I haven't fit in anywhere, haven't had anyone look at me and see me at all. They've seen my parents or what I am now, but not me. You're the first person who seems to see me." Deacon paused at that, as if he didn't care for that part.

Then again, I hadn't written it expecting him to read it at all let alone out loud.

Still, he kept going dutifully. "So thank you for helping me, for looking out for me."

Deacon handed to letter back to Wade, who took it and stared at the paper as if still letting it all soak in.

Wade looked at me, giving me a smile that was tight at the edges, showing the pain he still seemed to be in. "You're way too sweet for this place, songbird. Thanks for the gift basket — they tend not to worry much about feeding or giving water to folks in solitary. I assume when I get out of here, I'll need to pay you back."

I shook my head. I'd done this to pay *him* back, to help ease the guilt I held about him being here all because of me. The last thing I wanted was for him to feel indebted because of it.

"Oh, I'm pretty sure I can think of a way you wouldn't mind." He winked, but even with that, I could still feel the pain below the words, as if he were burning from the inside.

Though…that didn't help stop the rush of heat through me at his words, at the not-at-all-subtle suggestion there.

I mean, who am I to tell someone not to pay back a debt they feel they owe…

Deacon cleared his throat, drawing my gaze back to him. He nodded toward the door, the meaning clear. We'd run out of time.

The window hadn't been large, which mean we needed to get going before we risked being discovered.

I offered an uncomfortable goodbye to Wade, his words still fresh in my head, before following Deacon out, the click of the door behind us as we locked Wade in unwelcome.

Still, I followed Deacon through the hallways no matter how much I wanted to go back. We took the elevator up, then got out on one of the floors with offices.

We didn't speak or interact, at least until he wrapped a hand around my mouth and yanked me into a small side room.

Being up against him made me realize exactly how much larger than me he was, and my nervous gulp had a lot less to do with fear than it should have…

Deacon

I listened, straining to hear the steps of the guard who was off his rotation. I filed that away, prepared to scold him come tomorrow about breaking routine.

As the steps drifted away, something else hit me.

The girl currently trapped between the wall and my chest, my hand over her mouth. Being this close gave me a chance to look down at her, to really see her.

She was pretty, I supposed. When I'd first seen her, covered in blood and beneath that man, I hadn't thought her pretty.

It might have been what she'd been through, that finding her attractive when she was damn close to death would have been totally inappropriate.

It's inappropriate anyway. She's a resident and a good fifteen years younger than I am.

Beyond that, however, it had been her outfit. Even with the blood, it had been easy to tell that she'd worn clothing worth a small fortune. She'd had a diamond necklace and a matching tennis bracelet. Her purse had been four figures, easy, and she'd had quite a bit of makeup on.

It had been like looking at some rich girl who wouldn't ever give me the time of day. What had drawn me to intervene, I still didn't know.

The sound of her scream had made my head throb, but being what I was, it wouldn't be fatal. It had called to me, though. Something inside it, the desperation, the fear, it had drawn me to her.

Now, with her wearing basic resident clothing, with her having her hair pulled back into a simple ponytail and no makeup, she didn't look like the same woman. It was as though the change had dulled those sharp edges, the ones I was used to people like her using against me.

It gave me the ability to admit…she was pretty. She had straight light-brown hair that fell midway down her back. Her eyes were hazel, and far too easy to read. She had a nice figure with lots of soft curves. She didn't look like the sort of woman who spent hours in the gym each day, who had clearly defined muscles. Her lean figure reminded me more of a dancer, with hips that caught my attention and a bit of stomach that showed sometimes when she reached up above her, between her shirt and her sweats.

Again, I reminded myself she was only nineteen and I was a hell of a lot older than that.

And I was in a position of power. Other guards, they crossed those lines. It wasn't like this sort of work drew the best people with the greatest moral character. It meant that if there was a resident who wanted to buy themselves something, they often didn't mind paying with their body.

And some of the guards found that acceptable.

I never had, at least not on purpose.

The idea of some woman sleeping with me just to get something didn't sit right. Sex wasn't worth it if my partner wasn't just as ravenous for it as I was. Besides, what was the point? There wasn't a future, not between a guard and a resident.

Some of the residents paired off, settled down, though that often was a disaster as well. It was hard to plan any sort of real life when at the whim of someone else.

So, even as I stared down at Hera, as I found myself drawn in, especially when her breasts brushed against me as she inhaled, when her breath warmed my hand which was still over her mouth, I told myself it wasn't okay.

Her eyes were darker in the dim room, but they were wide. It took me back to how she'd yanked away from me the last time.

Then again, I had tossed her when she'd grabbed me.

Still, I didn't like the fear. Normally I was good with fear, enjoyed it even. Right now, though? Fear was the *last* thing I wanted her feeling.

I pulled my hand away but kept it close enough to silence her again if the footsteps returned. "Stop flinching," I whispered.

She narrowed her eyes, as if that were a stupid request. It was a good thing the girl had such expressive features since she couldn't speak.

I leaned in closer to make sure I could keep my voice low, even as my attention remained focused on what was outside the door. "I'm helping you, aren't I? Is there a reason for you to act like I'm going to hurt you every time you get close to me?"

Even as I said it, I admitted, it was a dick move to hassle her over it.

She'd been fairly demure most of the time I'd seen her, but it seemed I'd pushed her buttons. She pointed at my arm, at where she'd grabbed me, then gestured her hand wildly.

"Yes, I tossed you. I get it. You needed the lesson that this place isn't safe, that you couldn't just think every person around was going to be safe. You lived a privileged, sheltered life before, and you needed to realize you couldn't keep acting like that here."

She gestured at her throat, and I could have sworn fire sparked in her eyes at that moment. And…damn, the girl had some fight in her, and I liked that. After finding her so weak at first—devastated and destroyed—it was good to see her finding her backbone.

"Yeah, I get it. You got fucked over and you've still got the marks to show it."

She threw her arms up as I stepped back, then took her writing pad. My vision was good enough to read whatever she wrote, even in the darkness.

She squinted as she jotted down words, then turned the pad around.

"You can't tell me not to trust people while also telling me to trust you."

I opened my mouth, but my brain couldn't seem to catch up. I had no idea how to argue with that point.

Probably because they were both true. Hera needed to be far more careful, to realize just how dangerous this place was, and when she didn't, when she'd grabbed me like I was her friend, all I'd been able to see were all the ways that could be used against her.

At the same time, I loathed the way she pulled away from me, as if I were her enemy. I didn't *want* to be her enemy, even if I knew that would be safer for us both.

"Yeah, well, that was before. Clearly, I'm not interested in hurting you, so your whole flinching thing is just going to waste time and risk us more."

Jayce Carter

She wrote again before turning it toward me. *"I'm not an idiot, you know? I can take care of myself."*

"Listen here, you can say that all you want, but the fact we're hiding in a closet because you just had to go see someone in solitary says differently. You want a little more advice?"

She shook her head, a defiant glint in her eyes. It was as close to *fuck you* as she could probably manage right then.

"Too fucking bad, you're going to hear what I have to say. This place is dangerous. Do you know how many residents here die happily from old age? Fuck all since I've been here. So if you're here thinking you and Wade are going to get some sort of fucking romantic happily ever after, well, get that thought out of your head. It doesn't happen anywhere, but especially not here."

The sound of her finger against the pad was loud, but I just waited as she scribbled. *"You don't know anything about me. I'm not looking for happily ever after. In fact, I have a boyfriend already."*

I let out a snort. "Trust me, you don't anymore."

"Yes, I do. You'll see."

I got closer to her, backing her up again until she pressed against the wall. Crowding her was stupid, and there wasn't a good point for me to do it other than some desire inside me I couldn't shake. "You need to start paying attention and listening. Nothing outside of these walls survives. You're not the first who showed up thinking they had someone on the outside who cared, and you won't be the last. None of them survived this place, though."

She wrote again, *"You sound jealous."*

Fuck, I did, didn't I? Still, I lifted my lip in a sneer. "Jealous? Of what? Some child who has needed everyone's help to survive just a couple weeks?"

Yeah, I really am, and that makes no damn sense...

She wrote something else, but I refused to take my eyes off her. It was like I couldn't pull away, like I couldn't break that connection.

I leaned closer, drawn by something stronger than I was. I wanted to feel how soft her lips were, wanted to feel the warmth of her breath, to hear the way she would gasp softly when I —

Knock it the fuck off, you pervert.

Hera lifted her head and leaned in as well. Was she drawn by the same thing? Did she feel it too?

The *ding* of the elevator down the hall drew my attention and seemed to wake us both up when barely a breath separated us. It snapped the dreamy moment, left us there with our eyes locked and so close I could have touched her lips with my tongue.

And, damn, that was a tempting thought.

Nope. Not going there.

Except she swallowed, her gaze dropping to my lips, and I couldn't stop myself. It was in the need in her eyes, the way let out the softest breath as if she were thinking about just this.

So I crossed the distance, consequences be damned, and I kissed her. It was everything I'd imagined and more. Her breath was sweet, her lips amazingly soft and giving, and she all but melted against me.

I didn't give her the chance to think, though. I took her over, sliding my hand to the back of her neck to pull her tighter against me. We'd both wake the fuck up soon, and I didn't want to miss out on any of this, on the way she made me burn, the way she made this moment feel different from all the other pointless ones that filled my life.

She reached for the button of my pants, her small hands eager, and that did filter past the lust inside me.

Wait a fucking minute…

I couldn't fuck the girl in a closet like this. No, wait, I couldn't have her at all.

I broke the kiss and caught her thin wrists, stopping her just as she undid the button. My chest thundered, as if I'd been running, but I tried to make my brain work.

"This is stupid," I muttered.

She peered up at me and furrowed her eyebrows as if she couldn't work out what had just happened.

I could have explained to her that it was a bad idea, that screwing in a closet like this was all sorts of wrong, but somehow none of that came to mind. Explaining things wasn't something I was good at, especially when I was uncomfortable with it.

And I was *damn* uncomfortable between the way I felt about this girl, the fact I'd bent a shit load of rules to get her here and the ache in my cock that was far too optimistic about its chances.

With all that, when I answered, it wasn't the best thing. It wasn't what I'd wanted to say.

"I don't fuck shades."

Even I cringed the moment it left my lips. It was true, but not because of the way it sounded. I didn't fuck shades who were in the academy, because of my position, not because of *what* they were.

The hurt that ran across her features said she'd taken it the other way.

I could have told her she didn't understand, could have explained myself, but I shut my mouth before I did so.

If she hated me, it made my life easier. I didn't have to worry about my feelings if she wanted fuck all to do with me.

So instead of taking it back, I doubled down and pointed my finger at her. "I don't know what you were hoping to get by screwing me in a closet, but whatever's between your thighs ain't nearly worth it."

Even saying that made me ill, but the way she pulled back said I'd done what I needed to. There was no chance that she'd want me after this, and if she didn't, I didn't have to worry about my own self-control. Waking her the fuck up was the best choice.

Hera yanked her gaze from me, and the guilt gnawed away at my stomach. She reached down and picked up her pad of paper, the one I hadn't looked at earlier, and I caught sight of the words before she tucked it into her pocket.

"I don't think you're as mean as you pretend. I think you like me…"

The words stung, reading them like some ugly reminder that I was an asshole. I could have explained it to her, could have let her down easily, but instead I'd been an absolute dick.

I could have said I wasn't *really* that person, that it was just what I had to say for both our sakes, but I knew better. I'd said what I said because I was a coward, because that was easier for me.

So even with the words she'd written in my head, accusing me, screaming at me to make it right, I shook my head and moved past her, opening the door.

It was better for us both if I was an asshole.

Chapter Ten

Hera

I frowned at the item on my bed. I'd come back from my classes for the day, exhausted after being up late the night before to see Wade, and found something placed on the bed that I sure hadn't put there.

After a long moment, I let out an annoyed breath. It wasn't like there was a wild animal in my room, so why was I acting as if it would bite me?

Because nothing else has gone right recently.

I moved forward, toward my bed, until I got close enough to make out what it was.

A book?

I picked it up, the binding a nice leather with a heft that said someone had put a lot of work into creating it. I sat on the bed, the book in my lap, before I opened it. The pages were worn, but not all that old. It wasn't put together like a regular book, with a page at the front that had all the copyright and publisher information.

Instead, I got the sense this had been created like a guidebook used across different academies? Some sort of onboarding book for new hires?

A scrap of paper stuck out of it like a makeshift bookmark. I flipped to that page, frowning as I took it in.

It had a drawing of a beautiful woman with long hair and a flowing dress, and at the top in large, bold letters?

Siren

I stared at the image for a long moment, and I wasn't sure why at first. Eventually, I figured it out.

I wanted to see myself in her. I was trying to come to terms with this new label I had, one I didn't understand, and I wanted to look at that image and have a moment of, 'oh, yeah, that's me!'

I craved a familiarity, a sense of belonging where I could identify that.

That didn't happen, though. It was just a drawing that didn't look much like me.

I sighed and used my finger to follow along the words that came after.

Siren

Level 1 Shade

Main Offensive Skills: Can sing at frequencies that range from mildly painful to lethal. Can hypnotize with their voice, but the effect is weak, more like subliminal suggestion.

Main Defensive Skills: Has exceptional hearing. Is able to determine truth and lie when others speak. Some high-level Sirens have been known to see flashes of a person's past or other telepathic abilities connected directly with another person's speech.

Weaknesses: Certain frequencies can cancel out some abilities. Not physically stronger than humans. Can be stopped by certain sounds or frequencies.

I read through the facts, over and over again, as if that would make sense of it all. Was my new reality nothing more than this? Than a page worth of information?

At the bottom was one last addition, as if they needed a too-long-didn't-read even after so little information.

Extremely dangerous. Suggest immediate euthanasia or medical silencing.

The words were written so simply, as if it was nothing, as if 'medical silencing' were the same as trimming a person's nails.

I touched the scar at my throat, the first time I'd risked doing it. The skin was rough against my fingertips, and it was the reality that the book had left out.

'Medical silencing' wasn't some easy, no-big-deal thing to do. So many of the methods used to make shades safer were temporary. Some were medicated to dull their abilities, and even those for whom they had more permanent or serious interventions, they were typically based around the extra skills.

Meaning I hadn't seen others who had lost basic human abilities.

Then again, that reminded me of what I'd heard since I'd been there. People had talked about what had happened to me, had called it 'silenced' or muted or a million other terms that didn't show how horrific it was.

I hadn't been all that loud before, all things considered. I hadn't been the sort to yell, to tell people off. I'd followed the rules as I understood them, but now?

I'd lost the ability to say anything. My voice had been stolen, and for the first time, I realized I hadn't used it much before.

Deacon and I in that closet came back to me, my cheeks flushing as if I were reliving the humiliation. I hadn't thought when I'd reached for him, had been consumed by the moment.

After so much uncertainty, after so much confusion, I'd finally found something that had made perfect sense. I'd reached for him, ready to sink into that feeling right along with him, when he'd shut me down.

No. He hadn't just shut me down—he'd done the verbal equivalent of a sucker punch.

He hadn't apologized, hadn't tried to make it better the rest of the way back to my room, and I hadn't seen him today. Was he hiding?

That was fine by me. The less I had to see him, the better. Each time I thought about it, I couldn't quite get rid of the shame that came over me at his words.

If I *had* been trying to get something from him, trying to use my womanly wiles to my advantage, I wouldn't have been so embarrassed. It would have just been a trade rejected.

But I hadn't been. I'd wanted him desperately in that moment. I'd wanted to slide my hands over his broad shoulders, to wrap my thighs around his hips, to lose myself in his scent and his strength and his certainty.

That was something I had little of, but he seemed to move through this world without fear or confusion.

I blew out a slow breath.

He didn't want me. He'd made that clear enough, hadn't he?

Beyond that, he was a horrible idea anyway. As a guard, if things went badly, he could make my life a living hell.

Well, more of one at least.

I tried to push away the thought, the memory. There wasn't any reason to let myself get caught up with that. What did any of it matter?

A piece of paper fluttered out of the book, falling to the bed. I picked it up—a sticky note, as it turned out— to find writing on it.

I won't apologize for being a dick, but you'd do well to better understand the world you're in.

Deacon.

I stared at the writing, trying to make sense of it. Deacon had left it here? Clearly, he'd avoided me when he'd left it, since he would have access to my schedule, would know where I was at all times if he wanted to.

So what did that mean?

Was this an apology? Was it his way to make up for rejecting me the way he had?

I crumpled the note and tossed it across the room.

He wasn't interested in fucking me, so he could take his vague gesture and shove it up his ass for all I cared.

Though…a glance at the book made me pick it back up. Just because Deacon was a dick didn't mean I couldn't make use of his gift. Besides, if I wanted to survive, I needed every bit of information possible.

* * * *

How did I get myself lost again?

It had been six weeks that I'd spent in this damn place, and I still had no idea how I got turned around so easily? The floor I lived on was easy — it was mostly one long hallway with my room at the end.

The rest of the complexes, though?

It felt like every other day, I found myself turned around and looking for a map.

Today was no different.

I'd finished my work and had no classes today, which had left me to go searching for the secondary pantry that I'd heard about from another resident.

Or, *over*head was the better phrasing. Not many spoke to me, which meant I'd caught the conversation from two others while I had been in the cafeteria.

They'd said the secondary pantry held specialty goods, things the normal pantry didn't carry. My ears had perked up at the mention of chocolate.

That had left me searching for the past two hours for the place, which they'd said was on the sixth floor, a place otherwise unlabeled on the maps.

I would have turned back already — or have tried to — but the lure of chocolate was too great. I *needed* something sweet, to close my eyes and think about all the things I missed. I'd stumble around all damn day if that was what it took.

The area seemed empty, though wear marks on the floor said it had been used at one time. Were there fewer residents here than before? Or just fewer of our category?

I thought about all the news stories I saw discussing the rising number of shades each year, which meant that couldn't be the case.

Door after door revealed nothing. Some were locked with old, conventional locks and no scanners and those that weren't showed only empty rooms.

The floor was set up oddly, with much smaller rooms than most of the others. It was as if it were made for something like offices rather than large classrooms or other group settings.

My feet ached, my back tired from pulling weeds earlier. At least my hands were unharmed, after using the gloves Wade had gotten for me.

A sound stopped me in my tracks. It was low, angry and in pain. It reminded me of a cat I'd found once that had been hit by a car. It had curled up and snarled at me, scratching when I'd wrapped it up to take it to a vet.

But just like I hadn't listened then, I didn't now. I crept toward the sound, drawn by a need to help whatever was suffering. As I walked farther, I realized exactly how good my hearing was. I'd assumed the sound was close, but it ended up on the other side of the floor, about as far from the elevator as a person could get.

I twisted the handle on the door, expecting to find some trapped animal there.

What I did find stopped me short, made me freeze and try to figure out what the hell to do.

On the floor of the bathroom was Knox, curled into a ball, his cheek against the tile, and that horrible sound coming from him.

I stared for what was probably too long. Or maybe it only felt that way, seemed as if the seconds crawled by.

Knox inhaled, then twisted, his eyes locking onto mine with a predatory glint that made me take a step backward and place my hand on my throat, as if protecting the already healed wound.

He blinked slowly, then swallowed hard. "What are you doing here?" His voice croaked out, so rough I almost didn't recognize it.

I opened my mouth to answer before reaching for my pad.

"Someone said there was a secondary pantry, and I was looking for it. Then I heard a sound."

He closed his eyes tightly for a moment before opening them and trying to read the pad.

And he was trying from across the room because now that I knew it was him and not some wounded animal, I was not willing to get any closer.

People should not make noises like *that*.

It took him a few tries, as if his eyes weren't working great. Finally, he let out an amused sound without sitting up, without moving from the tile. "There's no secondary pantry. It's something some of the residents like to use to fuck with new people. Also, they always say the fifth floor because they're usually waiting to jump the person."

Fifth? Damn it, I'm on the wrong floor!

I reminded myself that the wrong floor had meant I hadn't gotten jumped, so perhaps I should have thanked my poor sense of direction.

I risked writing more. *"Can I help?"*

He read that one a little better, then lifted his lips as if hissing at me. "Don't you touch me."

I lifted my hands and stepped backward. The tone he'd used said to stay away, even if I didn't hear all the violence in his voice from my skills.

His eyes tracked me carefully, but the line between suspicion and excitement made me unsure if he was the predator or prey.

Or maybe the best sort of predator was one who others thought was prey…

He shifted in a way that seemed mindless at first, until I realized he was trying to press more of his skin against the tile. It was then I noticed the sweat on his forehead, the way his shirt clung to him. Was he feverish?

I reached into my backpack and pulled out my bottle of water. It wasn't much, but it was all I had, and not only would liquids help, but I'd frozen the water and some of the ice still remained. I crouched so I could roll it across the floor to him.

It struck his arm, but he hadn't removed his gaze from me. After a moment, he sat up — slowly — and took the water between his hands. He twisted the cap off and took a few large gulps, then took the cold bottle and held it to the back of his neck. His eyes started to drift closed, but as soon as it happened, he snapped them open again.

I risked writing something else, since he seemed at least a little calmed.

"Are you sick?"

He shook his head. "Not exactly. Just…hungry."

I reached into my pack, pulled out a granola bar and held it out to him.

He stared it for a moment, then looked up at me again and let out a soft, strained laugh. "That won't help much, songbird. I don't mean that sort of hungry."

I frowned, tucking the bar back into my bag. I wasn't aware there were different sorts of hunger.

"I'm an incubus," he said, spitting the word out then waiting. When I shrugged, he tilted his head. "You really don't know shit about shades, do you?"

I shook my head.

He scooted back the short distance so he could rest his back against the wall. "We feed off sexual energy." He paused, then shook his head. "That isn't quite right. We feed off living energy, but that's created from sex."

The sudden heat in my cheeks made me wish I had the water bottle still to cool that sensation. I sure hadn't thought I'd spend part of my day on a bathroom floor with an incubus giving me the birds-and-the-bees-style talk.

Knox went on as if it weren't an uncomfortable discussion, as if I weren't squirming as I listened. "An incubus of my strength needs to feed pretty often."

I remembered the flash I'd gotten of him with some man, and I also recalled the demon who had propositioned him.

I wasn't sure what pretty often meant but it seemed to me he got plenty of action.

"When I don't, it feels like getting the flu. Fever, chills, pain, headaches." He shuddered before stretching, as if trying to center himself.

"What are you doing up here?"

"Brax likes to fix everything, to make it all better. If he saw me like this, he'd demand I feed. Hell, he'd go find someone and drag them back to my room for me."

"Isn't that a good thing?"

"He means well, but he doesn't get it. Sometimes I don't *want* to be this, you know? I don't want to be controlled by something else, by some need. So sometimes, I sit up here, where he can't see, and I just try to be *me*. I feel this gnawing pain, and I try to master it, just a little more each time."

That made me press my lips together, made me remember that desire for control. I understood it, remembered doing this for the sheer purpose of proving I could, that I was in charge of myself. It was in the way I rebelled against outfits my nannies picked out for me even when what I picked was far worse. Sometimes people needed to fell in charge of their own lives, even what it caused them pain.

I wrote another message. "*Is there anything I can do to help?*"

He inhaled deeply, the same flash of brightness in his eyes like a warning. As quickly as it happened, it disappeared, as if he'd tamed it. "You shouldn't ask an incubus that."

As soon as he answered, that burning in my cheeks intensified as his words sank in. Right, the only way to help someone who was starving and fed off sexual energy was to... —

He let out a groan that was so decedent, I could have sworn it almost brought me to orgasm on its own. "You can hear things and see things when people speak, right? Well, I can do the same with the scent of lust. Do you have *any* idea how much I like that smell from you? It's soft, sweeter than I'd have expected when I first saw you."

I couldn't breathe as I stared at him, drawn in by something I couldn't put my finger on. I'd pulled away from him before, unable to help my fear, and that hadn't gone away.

I was still terrified of him, but sitting there, I saw a different side of him. It wasn't the smoothness of his words, or even how devastatingly handsome he was. While it wasn't the outline of his erection in his gray sweatpants — and thank the lord for those — that didn't hurt, either.

Maybe it was the glimpse I'd gotten beneath the surface, a peek at the man under all that. Though, one good look in those eyes said it wasn't just a man—it was a demon, it was a hunger that couldn't be satisfied for long.

I wanted everything in that moment. I wanted to strip off my clothing, to tear off his. I wanted to kiss across every inch of his body, to taste his sweat, to dive deep into the hunger he had, to go mad with him.

Except I shook my head—hard—and found it clearing.

Even with that delicious scent in the air.

Wait, a scent? It took me a moment to realize that, yeah, there was a smell that hadn't been there before. It was something like cinnamon and brown sugar?

"You're still dressed," he said, his tone full of confusion.

That had me scooting back an inch, even though I wanted to come closer, to indulge in everything that had flashed in my mind.

"Someone this close to me, especially with me in this state, wouldn't normally be able to resist. You stepped away from me earlier, too. No one rejects me." His tone wasn't arrogant.

That was the strangest part, that despite his statement being the pinnacle of arrogance, he didn't seem proud or happy about it. Instead, resentment filled the words, and I could feel that hatred pouring through me.

I wrote something else but kept my distance when I lifted it. "*I should get back. Is there anything else I can do?*"

He shook his head but didn't drop his gaze. "No. Thank you for the water. I think I'll stay here a little longer before heading back."

I rose, letting myself have one more look at the man. He was disheveled and wild and reminded me of a sacrifice to some fertility goddess. Even pained as he was, I had no doubt that if I took him up on his offer, he'd more than live up to any fantasies I had.

The man was walking sex, as if he advertised it with each look, each step, each glance. His lips looked soft, his body solid but lean, his fingers long. Each part of him seemed made to draw a person closer, to promise them things only he could deliver.

He released another sound, deeper and hungrier than before.

Right. He can smell me…

I didn't take my eyes off him, not trusting him fully, as I backed away.

I left him there.

He was an adult, and he'd been dealing with what he was a lot longer than I had. Who was I to tell him what he should or shouldn't do?

I took myself back to the elevator, ignoring my disappointment in the lack of chocolate. The doors opened, but it wasn't empty.

Instead, Brax leaned against the inside of it, his arms crossed and his eyes on me.

It again struck me how strange it was that the twins could looks so much alike and yet so different.

Where Knox appeared calmer — even in his pained state — Brax had a wildness to his eyes, something that said he had to contain something monstrous that wanted to get out, that was always a hair from breaking free.

"You didn't take advantage of him."

I frowned as I got into the elevator. That was a hell of a thing to say to a person. I ignored the insult at the fact he thought I would.

"Do you have any idea how often I've had to deal with people who take advantage of him? Who try to push him into things he doesn't want?"

I didn't bother to write anything down. I had a feeling this was a one-way conversation Brax wanted to have.

"People like to fear incubi and succubi because they think they make them do something they didn't want to do, but that's not usually the case. They offer people something they want but something they don't like to admit they want. Knox, he struggles with what he is, with what he needs to survive. He sits up there and thinks starving himself is some penance, like it makes shit better. It doesn't."

He dropped his gaze as the doors closed, as I hit the button for my floor. "He doesn't think I know where he goes. He thinks he doesn't want to be a burden on me anymore. He's a fucking idiot, that's what he is."

I risked looking directly at Brax, especially since he seemed lost in his own head.

The angles of his face were slightly different than Knox's, but then I recalled when he'd lost his temper before, how they'd sharpened. Perhaps even now whatever change had been happening before was still there, just more subtle.

What was he?

All I heard in his voice was anger, violence, barely constrained madness. That didn't tell me all that much useful information.

Still, in this moment, I also saw something else, something deeper. I saw the pain from him wanting to take care of his brother, the helplessness a person feels when they can't, when they want to take the pain on for someone else.

"I appreciate you looking after him," Brax said, his voice low but careful. "The thing is, you need to keep your distance. You aren't good for him."

I wasn't good for *him*?

This time I did take the pad out, scribbling down a message. "*I don't need you telling me what to do.*"

He shook his head after reading it, the doors to my floor opening and Brax reaching out with his hand to stop them from closing again. "You don't understand me. I don't give a fuck what you do, so long as you do it away from my brother. Trust me, it's for your good as much as it is his, especially when he's refusing to eat. See, incubi aren't as civilized as they appear when they're well fed. When they're starving, they turn more…animalistic."

I frowned. I'd seen a glimpse of that inside Knox, the something creeping just behind his eyes. Still… I wrote another message. "*I just wanted to help.*"

"Yeah, well, don't help. If he gets too hungry, trust me, you won't be able to resist him, and if he hurts you?" Brax let out a long sigh, one full of memories too dark for me to want to see. "There are things that are impossible to get past, actions a person can't ever forget or forgive themselves for. I don't want to see Knox suffer that, don't want to see him try to carry what he could do to you if he's in that state."

I wanted to write that Knox wouldn't hurt me, that I wasn't afraid of him, but something inside the look Knox had given me made it so I couldn't say that truthfully.

Worse, there was no doubt that Brax was telling the truth, at least as he knew it. He was afraid Knox could hurt me, and he was terrified of what it would do to his brother.

He seemed monumentally less concerned about me.

Still, I tucked the pad into my pocket and nodded, then slid past him and out of the elevator.

I turned to find Brax still standing there, staring at me. "My father used to tell me, *'The most dangerous and most alluring thing is the unknown.'* Always figured he was talking about exploration—go figure that he'd actually be talking about a woman..."

With that, he stepped back, the elevator closing behind him, leaving me there alone with only his words.

I'd been called alluring before, like some trophy people wanted to have and show off, like a thing for them to own. I'd never been someone seen as dangerous before.

And I had to admit...

I liked it.

Chapter Eleven

I hit the ground hard, rolling once, groaning at the pain in my shoulder.

As it turned out, testing my skills in these damned evaluations was far harder on my body than it should have been. Then again, I'd never been the type before to take on kickboxing or rock climbing as a fun method of exercise. I was much more the 'I walked around the mall for two hours and that counts as cardio' sort of person.

So when Kit had decided to do our weekly evaluation outside, it has struck me as odd. Besides the times I'd spent weeding, I hadn't been outside much.

Now, after being tossed to the dirt for the fourth time in a row, I was over it. I'd be thrilled to get sent back to my tiny room if it meant no more of *this*.

This being another resident standing across from me and having far too much fun throwing me around.

"Again," Kit said, his hands folded behind his back, his gaze unwavering.

It was funny that I'd thought he'd almost seemed kind a few times, because he sure as hell didn't strike me as nice now. Then again, looking up at someone standing while I was in the dirt could make a person look a lot more frightening than they were.

I pushed myself upright, dust sticking to me, making my black sweats appear gray. I would have loved to tell him off, but I didn't give him the satisfaction of trying only to realize I couldn't.

The other resident, a girl around my own age, was stronger than any person that size should have been. A flash in her eyes said she enjoyed the chance to toss me around, making it clear that even with Wade's help, I wasn't well-liked.

"Again," she said, a mocking tone to her voice as she waved me forward.

I brushed my front off, wincing as I rolled my shoulder.

I had no idea what Kit was trying to prove through this little game. Most of our evaluations had been a matter of learning how to control my hearing, how to silence the noise in my head, how to home in on a single sound or piece of information in the torrent of information.

It seemed he'd bored of doing that, given today's little outing.

The girl, Gina, came forward, rolling her shoulders but I had a feeling it was for a different reason. Lord knew I hadn't hurt her at all. Watching her move was fascinating.

She had so much confidence, so much surety in her own abilities. It was something I'd discovered in the academy that I had to admit was amazing. There wasn't such a gender issue.

The reality was that a warg like her was just as powerful whether a male or female. Their danger came from the level of source in their blood and their ability to use it rather than their sex.

Gina was a great example of that. She wasn't even in her other form and yet she moved fast enough and hit hard enough to send me to the ground as if I weighed nothing. Then again, it made me glad she hadn't changed, that whatever point Kit was making at the moment was done in her human form.

She came forward, and when she slammed into me, the air rushed from my lungs. The hit was harder than the rest, sending me flying straight backward until I hit the ground.

Except, she didn't pull back, not like she had each other time. Instead, she followed me down, pinning me, staring at me. "You show up here thinking you're special. Guess what? You aren't. You're exactly like every other rich person in the world, fucking it up then acting surprised when you get taken down with it."

I shoved at her, but it didn't make a bit of difference, reminding me exactly how much stronger she was than me.

"You and your family are part of the reason I'm here, why most of us are here. You benefited your whole fucking life from the pain of shades, from places like this. You all got rich and powerful ripping families apart and torturing innocents."

I tried to push her again.

"Get off." Kit's voice was like a blast of cold air, confident and even, as if sure she'd listen.

Gina didn't tear her gaze from me. "Don't worry. I'm not going to kill her. I want her to live in the hell she helped create." The smile she gave me was not friendly. "Course, a little pain wouldn't be killing her…"

"Get off her," Kit repeated. "This is the last time I'll ask you nicely."

Gina pressed her lips together, but after a moment pushed herself off me. It seemed all her attitude and anger weren't enough to make her ignore Kit.

Kit gestured toward the fence line. "Go over there until I call you back."

She gave me a withering glare as I sat up, even though it wasn't me who sent her off. It seemed she felt safer giving me attitude than Kit.

Speaking of, he came over and crouched beside me. I let myself give him a side-eye, the bravest thing I was willing to do to show my feelings about whatever he was trying to prove.

"You're annoyed." He didn't say it like a question.

Then again, it wasn't. I wasn't hiding my frustration all that well. Still, I lifted my arms in a 'what the hell do you think, you idiot?' motion.

He shifted so he sat beside me, and I ignored how uncomfortable it made me that he was getting his slacks dirty. It just didn't seem right. Kit had appeared impeccable the entire time I'd known him, as if nothing from the real world could touch him.

"You think I'm just torturing you, right?"

I nodded.

He let out an unhappy sound. "A lot of shades think that about me. They think I get off on hurting them, on driving them to their breaking point. That isn't the case, though. Life here is dangerous, and your other skills, they're useful, but they won't keep you safe. They won't protect you if someone attacks."

I gestured at my throat.

"I know. You had your main form of safety taken, but that doesn't mean you're entirely defenseless. Believe it or not, shades are good at adjusting."

I twisted to look at him, wondering just what he was trying to tell me. I could hear really well, could understand things from other's words that weren't obvious, but none of that seemed all that useful when Gina attacked.

Kit shook his head. "You're doubting yourself. You need to trust that you have skills you haven't honed yet. If you're expecting me to give you an answer, to tell you *how* you need to do it, you're going to be disappointed. I can't tell you how to use your skills, or even what all the skills you have are."

I reached for my pad, but then recalled it had fallen the first time Gina had thrown me. The only thing worse than not being able to speak was when I didn't even have my pad.

Kit reached into his own pocket, then handed over me my writing pad.

No, wait…it wasn't mine. It was a different one, unused. Why did he have that? For me?

Instead of questioning that, I took it thankfully and wrote. *"Aren't you supposed to know that? Isn't that why you're staff?"*

"It's impossible to know exactly what any particular shade can do. It's always different. The best we can do is try to put someone in situations that might bring it out."

"So you're going to have her knock me around until I figure out a way to counter it?"

"I wouldn't have put it quite like that, but essentially, yes. Think about it, when did your abilities first show? When did you change? In a moment of extreme stress. It doesn't always happen that way, but often something stressful causes a person to change, and it can cause new abilities to show themselves. So if you get tired of Gina there throwing you around, you'll likely figure out a way to stop it from happening.

"What if she's just stronger than I am?"

Kit took the pad of paper, reading the question slowly. "You don't understand, do you? There is a reason you live on the first floor, and that reason is your test results. Trust me – if you find yourself over having Gina getting the best of you, you'll easily get the upper hand." He slid the paper into his pocket then rose and looked over at Gina. "All right, let's do it again."

Gina pushed herself off the bench where she'd sat at the far end of the courtyard, her eyes sparking with excitement. She was far too happy about the prospect of hurting me some more.

In fact, when I got to my feet, Kit barely got a foot or two away before I found myself right back on the ground, Gina hitting me even harder than the last time, as if her time waiting had wound her up even more.

I sucked dust in, coughing against the tiny particles that irritated my lungs. Everything hurt as I forced myself to my feet again, unsure what everyone was expecting from me.

I hadn't asked to be here, to turn into this, and I sure as hell hadn't asked for someone to slit my throat and steal my voice. Yet, even with that, they all thought I needed to do something.

I needed to attend stupid classes, I needed to follow a schedule I didn't pick, I needed to do these evaluations and show skills I had no idea if I even had. Each day, when I woke up, I had other people shoving me in the direction they wanted me.

That wasn't even *new*. Before this all, my parents had decided my whole life. They'd picked out my school, my future, my path, even the boy I'd need to marry. I'd never gotten to make my own choices, but never had it felt as overwhelming as now, when I choked on dust while Kit watched, while Gina wanted to take me apart.

It was once again about everyone else, about their wants, their plans for me.

The frustration ate away at me, like something alive inside me.

I shoved myself upright just as my hearing caught the vibration of Gina's shoes against the gravel, as I connected in with it. It was as if, even without looking, I could see exactly what was happening.

It gave me the chance to shift to the side and avoid the hit. She dove past me, the air whooshing by as she missed.

She let out a furious sound that was damn near a growl, sliding to a stop before turning back toward me.

I let myself sink into the feeling rushing through me, trying to let myself be what I was without questioning or doubting it. All the sounds swirled around me, but I finally was able to shut out the unimportant.

The conversation between two people in the level 2 yard? Pointless. The pacing of a guard muttering to themselves about how their boss yelled at them? Easy to ignore. I focused everything on Gina, on each detail I could absorb.

The speed of her heart, the panting breaths that showed she was more worn out than she wanted to let on. An angry sound she let out sent a flash of her in the past, fighting with boys a little older. *Brothers?* She was tackled by one, who laughed when she started to cry. "*Suck it up, buttercup,*" the boy had said.

The flash was so vivid, I almost missed when she bolted in my direction again. I shifted without thinking, as if by instinct, and she missed me by a few scant inches.

She tripped, probably expecting to strike me and off balance when she didn't. Her hitting the ground made me feel better in some weird, petty way. Still, I didn't relent as I pulled my shoulders back, staring her down.

Sure, we were both put here by Kit, but she was enjoying it. It was the hatred in her gaze, the way she looked at me, the way she seemed to revel in hurting me. She might have been told to do this, but she'd have done it herself if she thought she'd get away with it.

Gina slammed her fists against the ground before all but jumping to her feet. Her body seemed larger, telling me she'd started to lose control, that she was giving in to her other side.

She shifted her feet apart, the calculation in her gaze screaming that she was done playing. When she flexed her hand, I caught sight of long claws I was sure weren't just for looks.

"You deserve every damn thing that happens to you here," Gina shouted at me. "It's only a fraction of what you and your family have put others through. I'm going to die in these walls, like all of us, but I've never been as happy as when I saw *you* here. For once, it seems like justice got it right." She leaned forward, almost seeming as if she crouched. It took a moment to recognize the stance as aggressive, as preparing to leap at me. "And if she didn't, I don't mind making you pay myself."

She leapt at me, but I didn't run. I didn't turn or jerk away.

Instead, something inside me responded in absolute rage. It wasn't fear, not like when that man had attacked me. This was deeper, older, as if the source in my blood screamed out in anger over someone thinking they could hurt me, that they'd enjoy causing me pain.

I opened my mouth as if to scream, but nothing came out of course.

It didn't stop me. Instead, I stared directly at Gina, the world feeling as if it had slowed around me. I clapped my hands together, then pulled my hands apart and thrust them toward her.

I had *no* idea what I was doing. I didn't have a guidebook explaining the details, telling me what to do or what would happen. Instead, it was like learning to walk, something that came from inside me, something pushing me toward an instinctual action.

The vibrations in the air from my hands, the waves that created the sound of the clap, I felt them, could see them. I held on to those waves, changing them, increasing them, twisting them and sent them toward Gina.

It hit her like a wall, throwing her back harder than she'd struck me. She hit the dirt and rolled, not rising right away, as if it had shaken her.

I turned to find Kit not on the outskirts as he had been but directly behind me. When had he moved closer? Why hadn't I heard him?

Was he there because he thought Gina would reach me that time?

If he had been, he wasn't anymore. His gaze was difficult to read, but he didn't look all that happy, as if he hadn't expected *that*.

Then again, neither had I.

I swallowed hard, then turned back to find Gina still on the ground.

For the first time since I'd arrived — and maybe the first time ever — I felt in control. I felt like someone who wasn't just a pawn for other people, who didn't have to just follow the plans others had.

I was in control of my life, and it was strange that it took being locked up to feel that way.

* * * *

"Breathe." Deacon spoke without looking my way, making me want to punch him in his smug face.

He hadn't acknowledged me since he'd rejected me. He'd mostly stayed the hell away from me. He must have figured the book was all he needed to make things right, as if I'd suddenly forget how he'd treated me.

Despite it having been a week ago, it seemed I held grudges.

Or, rather, I couldn't shake the embarrassment of it, and anger was easier to deal with than shame.

Besides, it seemed rude for him to tell me to relax and breathe when he was the cause of my anxiety. He'd shown up at my room, telling me I had an appointment with Medical. It seemed those weren't put on the schedules.

Probably because people might make themself scarce if they knew when they were set to happen.

I would have done so.

Since that wasn't an option, it seemed I was getting some sort of physical.

The elevator went, just the two of us in it. Deacon turned toward me, looking directly at me for the first time. "Don't argue and don't fight anything."

I pointed at my throat. How exactly did he expect me to argue?

His expression turned serious as he leaned closer. "I'm not kidding, Hera. Medical isn't like it is here — they aren't like the guards you deal with here."

He sounded an awful lot like someone explaining to me how one man-eating tiger was not as bad as the other man-eating tigers.

It didn't change the fact they were *all* dangerous, in my opinion.

"Medical exams occur when someone is hurt, usually."

I peered down at myself, as if I'd missed an injury others could see.

He gave me the look I imagine parents give their kids when they ask stupid questions. "Of course you're not hurt. That's my point. When Medical calls for someone who isn't hurt, it's never a good thing. Push your luck out here, and you deal with angry guards. Maybe you get a few bruises and thrown in solitary. Press your luck with Medical and, well, pissing off people who know how to use scalpels and are fully allowed to use them as they please is beyond stupid."

The mere mention of scalpels made my stomach roll. I touched my throat again, a reminder of the last fight I'd had with a sharp object and just how badly I'd lost.

I had no desire to repeat that.

Deacon let out an angry sound, something close to a growl, before turning away from me. He'd been on edge since coming to get me, as if he were more freaked out about this than I was.

Then again, he had more information about it than I did. However, since I didn't have much in the way of options, I figured falling to anxiety and panic wouldn't help at all.

Plus, my little trick from the day before made me bold. Sure, I hadn't exactly managed to replicate it—it seemed it wasn't as easy as it had felt that first time—but it made me feel like I could hold my own all of a sudden, like I wasn't some fragile prey tiptoeing around things so much bigger and tougher than I was.

"Did you get the book?" Deacon didn't turn, but I knew he could spot me in his peripheral vision.

I nodded, my hands tucked into the pockets of my sweats.

"Good." He didn't say anything else for a long moment, then his shoulders dropped a bit. "I'm sorry, okay?"

Still, I didn't try to respond.

He let out an annoyed breath before turning fully toward me. "I'm serious. I don't always deal with things all that well, and I can be an asshole. That ain't likely to change anytime soon. Still, I know I went too far."

I met his gaze, listening to his words, to what was behind them. *Honesty.*

He at least thought he meant what he was saying.

Beneath that? Regret. I had a flash of him sitting in a small room alone, a beer in his hand, his gaze locked on a wall on the other side. He muttered to himself. *You are a fucking idiot, you know that? It was for her own good. She'll get over it and realize it was for the best.* He took another drink, then cursed. *Stop fucking thinking about her!*

I blinked as I brought myself back to the present, as I pulled myself from the memory of him.

Still, it gave me a new view of him. Maybe he did give a damn—maybe he did regret his harsh words.

And I certainly understood that. How many times had I wished I could take back something I said?

So I nodded at him, my way of telling him it was fine, that I forgave him. Or, at least, I'd made the choice to forgive him. It might take a while before I felt it.

He let out a long breath, as if he hadn't been sure of my reaction, then nodded. "Good. I don't want you to ignore my advice just because you're pissed at me."

I took my pad out since we'd come to some sort of truce. *"Will you go to the appointment with me?"*

"No. Guards aren't allowed during exams. Medical has their own security, so we do the hand-off and come back to get the resident when it's over." His tone told me he didn't care for that.

And I guess I didn't hate him that much, since I was disappointed by the news as well.

The elevator doors slid open, effectively ending our conversation. The floor appeared different from the ones I was used to. The lights were brighter and the doors missing the same scanners that were in other areas.

Then again, they didn't have residents wandering about like they did on other floors. It had taken Deacon's band on the scanner in the elevator to get us to the level at all, so I supposed they didn't need much security.

I followed Deacon, remaining at his heels as I tried to take in the details of the floor. It all mixed together, though. The long hallways, the twists and turns. A few people lifted their gazes my way, but they dismissed me as quickly as they spotted me.

It seemed no one here found me all that interesting.

That was rather nice. I was so used to being at the center, to being so seen and hated that people brushing me off was a nice change of pace.

Finally, we passed a doorway to find a small open room with two men standing in it. They glanced at me and didn't react, but when they spotted Deacon, they stood straighter, on alert.

It seemed he wasn't well thought of here...

"1AW Hera Weston here for a three o'clock appointment," Deacon said.

The guard on the left pulled his gaze from Deacon to me, looking me up and down slowly. "This is the siren?"

Deacon nodded. "She's been muted, so no risk there. No need for a gag."

One of the guards came closer, something in his hand. He frowned, then caught my chin and tipped my head back.

The touch was impersonal and dehumanizing. I felt like a thing, an object he was checking. He leaned in closer, peering at my neck. "This isn't an even cut. What butcher did this?"

"Not a doctor. Happened by some muggers." Deacon's tone was flat, but I could feel the anger beneath it. A glance his way showed nothing on his face.

The guard who held my chin made a low sound. "Guess that showed her she wasn't as tough as she thought, huh?" He let out a laugh before releasing me. "You're sure she's totally mute?"

"Six weeks here and not a peep. Doctor Zenwell confirmed complete destruction of the vocal cords."

The guard nodded. "All right. No gag, then."

"What're they planning with her?"

The guard stopped, turning to look at Deacon directly. "Last I checked, that wasn't your business. Medical calls and you bring up the bodies. You don't ask questions."

Deacon didn't show any sign of annoyance at the rebuke. "I have to come back and get her still, and believe it or not, I've got a lot of shit on my plate. If I know what you're doing, I know how long I've got."

The guard tried to stare Deacon down, the two of them in some macho contest I knew nothing about.

Still, it was the guard who caved first, though the way he spoke said he wouldn't ever admit it. "Do what you want for the rest of today. She won't be ready to go back until morning."

That struck a nerve with Deacon since he went unnaturally still. "What?"

"Tomorrow. Probably by nine or so? We'll make sure to clear her schedule—she'll need a few days to recover."

Recover?

The words hit me, burrowing in, carrying so many terrifying options with them. I'd expected from Deacon that the whole thing would take a couple hours. Judging by his reactions and his words, he'd assumed the same.

Yet now it seemed they'd keep me all night?

What exactly did they have planned that would take all damned night?

None of the things that came to mind were good...

Deacon didn't move for a long moment, as if trying to think up a plan.

There wasn't a plan, was there? Each time I thought for a minute that he was better than the others, that he was different, I was reminded that he was a cog in the same system that was crushing me.

He might be a nicer cog, but that didn't change that he'd help grind me down like the others.

Finally, he nodded. "Send a message as soon as she's done. Even if it's at night, I'll retrieve her."

The guard tilted his head. "You're awfully concerned about her. I'd hate to think there was something inappropriate going on, something the warden might need to know about..."

Deacon shook his head. "I've been here a long fucking time, and you should know better than that. She's our only level 1 here, and there are extra precautions with her. Everyone is safer when she's in her room where she should be."

The guard peered between Deacon and me, but in the end, shrugged. Whether it was because he believed Deacon or he just didn't care, I wasn't sure.

From what I'd seen, it wasn't like relationships between guards and residents were all that uncommon.

Though, calling them relationships felt like a far cry from the truth. Often it was a matter of residents trying to curry favor or guards who saw an easy target.

Which is why it was good Deacon stopped your insanity before you did something you'd regret.

"We'll contact you as soon as she's done."

Deacon stood there a heartbeat longer than needed, his gaze coming to rest on me, as if he didn't want to leave but wasn't sure what else to do. After another moment, he turned on his heels and stormed out, steps loud and full of impotent anger.

It left me with the two guards, one who still had a hold of my chin.

This did not seem like a step in the right direction...

Chapter Twelve

The worst part of the whole thing so far was how little the Medical staff spoke to me. It reminded me more of a vet than a doctor, and not even a good vet at that.

I recalled when I'd had my appendix out, how the nurses had been quick to ask how I felt, if anything hurt, if anything was too tight. That was a far cry from this place.

The nurse jammed a needle into my vein without so much as asking if I was ready, without a word to me at all. Instead, she tapped the inner crook of my elbow — the arm strapped down already — then placed the needle without a single glance my way.

I was nothing but a thing for them.

I couldn't ask questions — I doubted they'd answer even if I could. Still, not being able to even speak, to ask anything, it chafed. It made me feel vulnerable and cut off from everyone.

The nurse drew vial after vial of blood, placing the filled containers in a rolling cart beside the chair I sat in.

When she pulled the needle — a rough jerk that made me flinch — she held the last vial up to the light, squinting.

"How does it look?" I hadn't noticed the other person enter, but when I twisted my head to spot him in a white coat, I had to figure it was the doctor.

The nurse peered closely at the blood, shaking it slightly, and the way her lips curled into a grin made me shudder. "The test won't have a quantitative amount for another few hours, but yeah...I don't think the others were a fluke."

The doctor came up and took the vial, then repeated the procedure of looking into it. He donned a nearly identical smile as the nurse. "This can't be a natural occurrence, can it?"

"What else would it be? She isn't a Jane Doe — she couldn't have escaped from a lab anywhere. Her history is easy to follow. We've seen others with high numbers. We can't pretend this is unique. It's clearly an ongoing problem."

A lab? I had no idea what that meant, but it didn't sound good.

"This isn't a good thing, then," the doctor said. "Naturally occurring levels like this show there might be larger leaks, now. It's a worrying trend."

The nurse gathered all the blood to take it out of the room, both of them pausing to look at me for a long moment.

As it turned out, it was worse when they stared at me rather than just ignoring me. It was something in their gaze, an excitement that didn't bode well for me at all.

"Well, this might just be more enlightening than I expected," the doctor said before nodding at me. "Grab the sedative and we'll get started."

* * * *

The world had turned into soup, something that sloshed around with every movement I made. Nothing made sense, my brain feeling fuzzy, as if moss had grown over it all.

Whatever had been in the syringe they'd injected me with was not playing around. Within fifteen minutes of the first shot, I'd stopped caring what they wanted or what they'd do or what their plans were.

Nothing mattered. Nothing was scary. Nothing hurt. It was an amazing break from my own head, from my own worries, from everything that was going wrong in my life.

Hell, everything my life had become. That was the hardest part to accept, that this wasn't some temporary event. This wasn't the case of me crashing a car or losing a job. My entire future had gotten torn away and I had no idea what I was supposed to do.

At least, that was the case before whatever they'd given me, and had given me more than once. Each shot had felt like them shoving my head beneath the water again, clouding my thoughts until I couldn't hold onto anything.

Deacon walked into the room where he'd handed me off, and just seeing him got me to my feet with what was no doubt a stupid smile on my face. Then again, he looked *at* me. He was a sense of safety, no matter how unwise that was.

The world spun when I stood, shifting like those rings a person walked through in a carnival funhouse, and I ended up flat on my face.

Which should have hurt more than it did. I hit the ground hard, knew damn well I hadn't braced myself, yet nothing so much as tingled with the start of an ache.

"For fuck's sake," Deacon muttered as he crossed the room. "Did you need to give her this much?"

"They're easier to handle when they're high," the guard said without an ounce of pity. "Besides, if we did what we did without meds, the bleeding hearts would complain about cruelty or something, as if these things are even alive."

Deacon crouched beside me, taking my arm in his hands to help me to my feet. With his aid, I managed to get up, though I suspected I leaned mostly on him.

He didn't tear his gaze from me, as if dismissing the others in the room, as if they didn't matter at all. For once, that intensity in his look didn't bother me. It made me feel like I was really there, that I was alive, that I fucking mattered even if only for that moment.

"She'll be back here soon," one of the guards said.

That got Deacon's attention. He turned his head in that direction, his purple eyes hard. "What? You only do this shit once a year, if that."

"That girl has higher levels of source infection than any of our records show with any other shade since we started. Trust me, the eggheads in Medical aren't going to just shrug that off as a funny coincidence. Hell, we might be looking at another North Tower there."

Pain bled through the haze of the drugs, and I peered down to find Deacon gripping my arm exceedingly tight. I flinched, and he immediately loosened. Had he not realized he'd done it?

"Yeah, well, we'll see," Deacon spat back.

"You're way too partial to this one," the guard said with a laugh. "You better get used to the fact that she's going to garner a lot of attention. If you've just got some infatuation, bang her and get it out of your system before it causes you problems."

Deacon froze, and the look he leveled at the guard made my heart speed in fear as well. It was like a bull picking a target to charge. I might not be in his path at the moment, but I didn't care for even being red-flag adjacent. "It's not like that," Deacon said.

"No? Come on, we spend so much of our fucking lives here—it isn't like we've got time to go trolling for tail elsewhere. Might as well enjoy one of the benefits of being here. In fact, her being basically de-fanged means she wouldn't even put up much of a fight." The guard peered at me with far too much interest, and I suddenly missed how I'd been ignored before.

Deacon moved fast—or maybe it was the drugs that made it seem that way? One moment he was beside me and the next he'd twisted, one hand still around my arm to steady me and the other around the guard's throat, holding him in the air with just that one hand.

The guard kicked his feet, but there was nothing he could do against Deacon's grasp or his strength.

Which was beyond terrifying. The guard couldn't have been under two hundred pounds, yet Deacon held him by the throat with a single hand, as if he were made of nothing more than paper.

"You won't touch her. You won't look her way. If you so much as picture her when you jerk off at night, I will make you sorry you ever applied to work here."

A shiver ran through me at Deacon's voice, at the mindless anger inside it, at the way it made me want to draw closer and not farther away from the terrifying man.

He dropped the guard, who collapsed on the floor.

The other guard stood there, mouth open, as if he had no idea how to react. It seemed if nothing else, he knew better than to try fighting with Deacon, especially in defense of the idiot on the floor. That man wasn't worth dying for.

Still, the guard on the floor didn't appear quite finished making stupid choices. He coughed but tried to speak between the attacks. "You can't do that to me."

"File a complaint if you want, but first, ask yourself why I'm still here. I've been here for years, and you all know better than to fuck with me, so ask yourself why that is and if it's worth the risk."

The guard on the floor didn't bother to try to get up — maybe he was too shaken up to do so. Instead, he gave a half-hearted glare in Deacon's direction. "You're here because you're too dangerous to be allowed out. You think you're different, but you're just like *them*. Worse, actually. They're at least natural, created by a process that's gone on forever. You? You're just an experiment, and Larkwood only keeps you around so they can see what you do. You're a guinea pig, a failed experiment and a freak. You can pretend you're special, but you're just another prisoner here."

I stumbled over nothing, falling against Deacon's side. He leaned down and lifted me against his chest, giving the guard one more unflinching look. "Say what you want about me — I don't fucking care. I've heard it all before and it means jack shit to me. Just take my advice and stay away from her or you'll see exactly what this guinea pig is capable of."

* * * *

The trip back to my room took way too long. Worse, I had to close my eyes so I didn't end up getting car sick.

Or Deacon-sick?

I wasn't riding Deacon though.

God, I'd love to ride Deacon…

The thought hit me fast enough, I broke into giggles as Deacon lowered me into my bed. It was closer to noon when Medical had finished, when they'd let me go.

"Glad you found something funny," Deacon muttered as he turned away from me.

Was he going to just leave? To dump me there and walk out?

The fear that ran through me took me by surprise. I didn't have anything to be afraid of, at least no more than usual, but the idea of him going, of me being alone, struck me as unacceptable.

Thankfully, that didn't seem to be his plan. Instead, he opened my fridge and scoffed softly at the offerings. After a moment, he gathered a few things and brought them into the bedroom.

Water and a granola bar seemed to be the Larkwood bandage to every problem.

"The sedatives will make you sick," he explained as he opened the foil packaging on the granola bar, then handed it to me. "This should help keep your stomach settled. I doubt they gave you anything to eat."

I shook my head as I took a bite of what he offered, surprised to find it suddenly tasted so much better than they had before. Then again, hunger did that to a person. Hell, the absence of anything made options — even bad ones — amazing.

I glanced at Deacon and wondered if that was what was happening between us. I didn't have a lot of support, a lot of options, so maybe that made him look like prince charming to me.

He'd thrown me across a room, threatened me, was one of the people keeping me trapped, and yet I couldn't stop thinking of him as important, as a friend if nothing else.

It was stupid and dangerous, but maybe I needed that. Maybe that tiny bit of hope was exactly what I had to have to make it through.

Or…maybe I was just horny and currently high.

Probably a little of all that.

Deacon sat on the edge of the bed beside me, his feet on the floor, his side to me and his gaze locked on the far wall. It gave me a moment to look at him again, to try to come to terms with what he was.

Lab rat. Experiment. None of it made sense to me, and the drugs Medical gave to me made me bold.

I reached for one of my writing pads, the words messy. *"What are you?"*

Deacon glanced at the words then sighed. "Not like you wouldn't have heard from someone else eventually. I'm sure you know people have been trying to use source to help humans for about ever. Well, there have been a lot more experiments than people realize. Not many take, not many have the subject survive, but I was one of the successes." He let out a slow, frustrated breath. "Success being a relative term."

That made me frown. "*So you're a shade?*"

Anger flashed across his features for a second before it was gone. "I told you before, no. Shades are infected with source naturally. It changes their DNA slowly, over time, and eventually transforms them into a shade. They will show source in every cell of theirs. Me? My body never changed, never took the source and altered itself. It's the difference between having a prosthetic arm and having an entire consciousness transferred into a synthetic body. I'm considered human, but the common term is a meta—short for metamorphism. I don't show the changes that a shade would, but the source gives me a few advantages."

"*Like holding men up by their throats?*"

He nodded. "Yeah, like that. Strength, speed, senses, those are all increased beyond human levels."

"*Why are you here? Do they force you to stay here?*"

He pressed his lips together, as if he'd rather lie but didn't want to. "Not exactly. I had a lot of options after I survived, but they'd be watching me closely no matter where I went. I couldn't go live a normal life, not with them wanting to keep an eye on me. It made sense to work at an academy where they could keep tabs on me all they wanted, and I didn't have to worry about explaining to anyone what I was. I was turned into what I am in the North Tower, so it seemed oddly fitting to stay close."

I reached for the book Deacon had given me, the one with all the information. I flipped to the place where a page had been torn out and tapped on it.

"Yeah, that's what was there." Deacon took the book from me, then turned the page back to one before, to a disfigured infant that had twisted, shortened arms and the same purple eyes. "This page shows examples of failures. See, a lot of those experiments create things that aren't viable. They've been trying for centuries to use source to increase the abilities of humans, but since we can't harvest the source directly, the only other choice is to take the source from shades." He tapped the drawing of the infant. "This is what happens most of the time. The successes are few and far between, and it's even harder to figure out why those who survive do."

I gestured at the torn page again, then held my hands up to ask why.

"I tore it out because I didn't want you seeing it. I didn't want you knowing what I was and deciding you needed to be afraid of me. I don't exist in either world, Hera. I'm not a shade but I'm not a human either, and both sides know it. It's not like I didn't know you'd figure it out eventually—it's not a well-kept secret or anything—but I didn't want you to look at me differently." He let out a huff, the sort of sound a person made when something wasn't funny, but they couldn't help a small laugh at the absurdity of it. "Not that it matters now. After what you saw me do to that guard, it isn't like you could see me as normal anymore. Funky eyes are one thing—that's another."

I shifted and flinched, the action making me look down at myself. A bandage covered a spot on my hip, and I frowned before I pulled the corner of it. A bloody spot lay beneath, the reason for the pain when I moved.

Did that mean the meds were wearing off?

Deacon peered down and let out a low, angry sound. "For fuck's sake, they did a punch biopsy?"

I had no idea what that was, but the evidence was there. It made me wonder exactly what else they'd done to me during those hazy hours, during the time when the drugs had made the world hard to follow. I recalled pain, I recalled when I'd screamed out, when I'd begged for them to stop.

It was all like a dream though, and the more I reached for specifics, the further away it all drifted.

"Stop trying to remember," Deacon said.

I glared at him. What did he know about it?

He met my gaze, and shadows haunted his eyes, old things from his past so deep, I wasn't sure he saw me at all. "Trust me, Hera, our brains like to shut things down when they're too much. Going back, trying to remember it all, it doesn't help. If you don't remember, you're left wasting your time and energy on what-ifs, and if you do? You have to live with it, and I've been there. Nothing I remembered was worth knowing, and I'd sleep a lot fucking better if I didn't have the memories of my own screaming in my head."

I let my gaze fell to the book that was still open, to the twisted figure of the infant, to the reality of what he must have endured.

Maybe, just this once, I'd listen.

I finished the granola bar, and Deacon rose to dispose of the trash and get a second water bottle. He set it on the table by my bed, as if he expected me to rest. The thought of getting beneath my covers in the same filthy clothing I'd worn in Medical turned my stomach.

When I couldn't get the sweats down, however, Deacon let out an annoyed sound and helped. His hands were impossibly large and warm, and they skirted over my hips and the outsides of my thighs as he worked the sweats over my ankles. He didn't turn his back, didn't pretend not to look, even when he helped get my shirt off as well.

Instead, he swallowed hard, his gaze locked on my chest, on the simple bralette I had. It wasn't lacy, wasn't pretty, yet his gulp said he was far from unaffected by it.

Was this it?

He leaned in, pulling the cover up and over my chest. "You should sleep." His voice was rough enough to sand a table. "You've got today off, and because they did punch biopsies and fuck knows what else, I'll get you off work detail for the rest of the week. Rest."

He went to pull back, but the meds still swirling through my head made me wrap my fingers in his shirt and tug him closer.

He exhaled, his lips so close to mine that his breath was like fire against my skin. "This is a bad idea," he whispered.

Yeah, it probably was.

I didn't care, though.

I moved my lips, asking *please* even if no sound came out. I wasn't sure if he understood me or if he just couldn't not kiss me anymore, but he finally pressed his lips to mine.

It wasn't the angry kiss from before, from the closet. Instead, this was sweet. It was soft, as if he knew I wasn't up for anything rough. Funny that a man who could hold someone up by their throat could still be so damned gentle when he wanted to be.

It didn't last long before he broke it, before he rested his forehead against mine. "You're going to be the death of me," he whispered. "But fuck, maybe I've lived long enough." He nipped softly at my bottom lip, the touch not hard enough to even sting, before he pulled away. "Sleep, Hera. I'm not kidding."

With that, he left, and all I could do was stare down at the picture in the book and wonder about the page that was missing.

Chapter Thirteen

Another Friday, another day for me to sit in the contact room alone.

I'd tried to call my parents the first few weeks but had no luck after the first time. Aaron hadn't answered, either. That one I'd chalked up to his new school, to being busy, to possibly not even knowing what had happened.

My parents had all but disowned me. Maybe no one had told him. Maybe he wondered why I hadn't shown up at the school when I'd said I would, and he was worried sick. Maybe no one had told him anything?

Then why hasn't he accepted any of my calls?

Today was a last-ditch effort. It was funny how quickly being on my own made me realize I didn't have nearly as many people in my life as I'd thought. Before, when I'd been out in the real world, I'd constantly had others around me.

They'd wanted to talk to me, wanted to spend time with me, wanted to help me. I guess when shit hit the

Jayce Carter

fan was when a person found out who was there for them.

And in my life, that seemed to be all of no one.

The ringing from the large screen went on, and my shoulders dropped in surrender. There was something soul crushing about sitting there, about hearing that ringing and having no one pick up.

At least I got to experience the moment on my own, without Deacon or another guard watching over me. It seemed after the first contact—especially given who it had been with—they didn't feel the need to monitor each one.

They were recorded, if they needed anything, but it was nice not to feel the mockery or pity of spectators as every person in my life abandoned me.

"Hello?" Moa's voice almost brought me to tears, and I lost the fight against them when her image popped up on the screen.

It felt like an eternity since I'd seen her, as if we had both changed so much.

Well, she hadn't...she looked exactly as she had before. I supposed only I had changed.

Her eyes widened as they locked on me, the background behind her going still as if she'd stopped walking when she'd realized who had video called her.

"Hera?"

I nodded, then snatched the keyboard so I could type messages. "*I miss you so much.*" I typed the words without thinking about them, without thinking about anything.

"I heard what happened. I tried to call, but they won't let any communication through, said I had to wait, that you were still in your probation period. God, I was so worried."

I moved my fingers across the keys. *"My parents said they aren't going to come get me, that I should never get out. They said I'm a level 1, and those aren't ever allowed to leave. I just want to come home."*

Moa wiped a finger below her eyes, and I suddenly wanted to take back every time I'd called her a bleeding heart, each time I'd said she had no idea what the real world was like. She was the only person from my old life who seemed to give a damn about me. "I know. I talked to your dad, and he had me kicked off his property because I wouldn't stop bothering him. I'm writing letters, I'm doing everything I can, I promise."

I nodded, not believing anything she could do would make a difference but still needing to know someone gave a damn enough to try.

"What about Aaron? I can't get hold of him. Does he even know where I am?"

She opened her mouth then snapped it shut. It reminded me of what I'd done so many times, except her reasoning was pretty clear. Aaron already knew.

When she tried a second time, something finally came out. "Sometimes people need a chance to get used to a change."

Which said it all, didn't it?

Aaron didn't care that I was here. He didn't give a damn that I was locked up, that I was trapped and frightened and in danger.

It felt as if the floor crumbled from beneath me, sending me freefalling into darkness. I'd never let myself think Aaron would give up on me. Somewhere, in my head, I'd believed that I could find a way out, that Aaron and I would still have the future we'd planned. It was infuriating that the future I'd been so unsure I wanted before was suddenly the only thing that mattered.

"He's not coming, is he?"

She shifted, then a door opened behind her. She turned her head, then froze.

I would have never heard the next part if not for my skills, for my exceptional hearing. *"Who is it?"*

It wasn't the words, but the voice. *Aaron.* What was he doing there? He should have been across the country at school.

Moa shook her head, one quick jerk as if to tell him to quiet down. She must not have realized I could hear him already, that the secret was out.

"He's there."

She glanced at the chat, then more of the color on her cheeks bled away. Her expression held shame, which told me everything I needed to know, didn't it?

She'd wanted Aaron since we'd been kids, and it seemed even if she cared about me, she wasn't above trying to move into my place with me gone.

"It's not like that," she said softly. "We're both worried, so he came home, decided to take the first semester off."

"He's upset enough to take time off school but not upset enough to talk to me?"

Then the camera shifted, and I was face-to-face with Aaron.

And *fuck* it hurt. It made what Medical did seem like a joyride, made everything else I'd suffered seem like nothing. Aaron was the face of my entire life, my future, my past, all of it.

And yet he looked at me as if I were a stranger.

No, worse. As if I were someone he knew and wanted nothing to do with.

"Sorry," he said, his voice soft. "I know I haven't answered your calls."

"Why haven't you?"

"I didn't know what to say. This is hard on me, too. I mean, we had plans, things we were going to do. You're not the only one who is suffering, who's hurting here."

His words felt like a slap in the fact. He wanted me to pity *him*? He wanted me to take a moment and feel sorry for how his life was going?

Anger surged through me at that, at how unfair it was, and it made my fingers fly across the keyboard. *"Oh, I'm so sorry that you're having a hard time. How selfish could I be, not thinking about you, when I'm trapped here, under 24-hour guard, with shades who want to kill me, and guards who have threatened to rape me and a medical section that cut into me just because they want to experiment."*

He read through my statement slowly, and his pained expression hurt. Aaron wasn't a bad man, which made this all the worse. The reality was, however, that I could see it in him just as I had in my parents.

The belief that I wasn't *really* me. It was easy to write me off, to not worry when they believed that the real Hera was dead, that whatever I was wasn't the person they'd all known. It let them wash their hands clean of the problem.

"I'm just saying that you have to be reasonable. Even if I thought you were still you, what sort of future can we have? You said it yourself—you're never getting out of there. You can't have a real life anymore, can't do the things we planned. What, did you expect I'd be happy with a call once a week? That we'd have conjugal visits when they allowed them? You're a logical person, Hera. You know none of that is possible now."

And I did know it.

Even if I ever got out, it wasn't like I could just return to my old life. I couldn't go and pick up the pieces as if I'd never left. Even if legislation were changed, even if I were released on good behavior, the world would never accept me.

And neither would Aaron.

A beep from the screen said my time was almost up, that the connection to the outside world would be cut for me soon.

Aaron shook his head, as if sorry for this whole thing. It would have been so much easier to deal with if he were an asshole, if he told me he'd hated me, that he hoped I never left this place. I could have hated him in return.

Instead, he seemed as broken up over it as I was.

The difference?

He was broken up over what he thought he lost, over his dreams of a perfect future with a perfect little wife. He was upset that I'd failed that, that he had to change his plans.

I felt as if I were back in Medical, just another time when people looked at me but didn't see me.

"I don't want to end this badly," Aaron said, his voice soft. "We had a lot of good years together. Let's just…take a breather. Let's take a break so we can get our thoughts in order."

By *we* he meant him, of course. He wanted me to stop bothering him, to stop reminding him I existed. His life would be so much easier if I drifted into the shadows, never to be seen again. I'd turn into an old, sad story for him, the girl he'd loved who had slipped away.

Instead of responding—what was there to say?—I hit the End button on the keyboard.

Maybe it wasn't much, but ending the conversation myself gave me a rush of pleasure. I was trapped, forgotten, ignored, but damn it... I'd been the one to hang up. I made that choice for myself.

It was a reminder that the world outside of these walls had forgotten me, forsaken me, and I needed to stop trying to hold onto it.

I needed to accept where I was, what was real to me now.

I had more than enough problems in Larkwood Academy without wasting my time on problems from my past that had no resolution that I could see.

* * * *

Wade

Despite being a fairly sociable person, the sanctity of my room was one of the few things I protected.

This was especially true after solitary, after sitting in another room alone for over a week. Now, I wanted nothing more than to sink into the quiet of relative safety of my room.

So imagine my surprise when the door to my room opened and none other than the little songbird strolled in.

She walked as she always did, with quick steps as if afraid to draw attention. It made me wonder for a moment who she'd been in her old life.

We *all* had old lives, the people we were before we were thrown in here forever. I knew enough — that she'd been rich as fuck, that she'd been the pampered daughter of a business mogul and an anti-shade representative.

Still, had she been this timid? When I thought of rich, entitled people, I imagined women who walked into a store and berated the manager.

That sure didn't fit with the girl who seemed afraid of her own shadow. Then again, maybe having her throat slit and her entire life stolen would change a person.

"Well, look what the cat dragged in." I leaned my shoulder against the doorway to my bedroom.

Hera paused, lifting her gaze, uncertainty there. Did she think I'd throw her out?

She was an idiot, then. I'd taken a week in solitary for her — I'd have done damn near anything to get her into my room like this.

I studied her face for a moment, and realized, maybe not quite like this…

The girl wasn't in the best of spirits.

I frowned as I glanced at the calendar, the reason becoming clear.

Friday. Contact Day.

Right. Sometimes I forgot how volatile that day was for so many of the residents. Some of them, like me, had no one to contact. I never had had, so the day meant nothing to me.

Most residents settled into the routine after a few months. Even those with loving families rarely made that connection last long-term. The reality was that the world outside kept moving while we all were stuck inside, stagnating and rotting.

It was a hard lesson to learn, but those who learned it faster tended to adjust better.

"Going to guess your call didn't go well? No one answer?"

She went over and plopped herself down on my couch. I grabbed one of the writing pads off my counter—and ignored why I'd gotten it and kept it around, because admitting that I'd hoped she'd back would have been far too pathetic—and handed it to her.

She stared at the pad, a level of frustration there. Then again, having to deal with writing each time I wanted to share a thought would drive me mad.

After a moment, she ran her finger across the front. *"I talked to my boyfriend."*

The moment I read that, I wished I hadn't. She had someone back home? Of course she did. It shouldn't have surprised me, given she was pretty, rich and powerful.

Still, since relationships didn't last long, and judging by the unhappiness in her expression, I'd guess things weren't going swimmingly.

She kept writing.

"He's been ignoring me since I got sent here, but I called my friend, and he was there."

Ouch. It didn't take hearing her tone to get the point there. Her golden boy had dropped her and moved on with her friend so quickly?

"Sorry," I said, not sure what else to offer.

The scratch of the pen against the pad was loud in the silent room. *"He said he needed a break, that I'd never fit into his life anymore."*

I nodded, because, yeah, that's exactly what I'd been thinking. It was a horrible realization, but a needed one for anyone who would make it long-term in a place like this. Holding on to the past, to the things that were gone, would just tear a person in two.

Better to make a clean cut, to accept where their life was now instead of looking back and wishing it had gone differently.

"At least that means your Fridays are now open."

She gave me look that said she didn't appreciate my humor.

Too bad. I'd learned humor would fix damn near everything, and the things it couldn't fix, it would at least make easier to bear.

"I'm serious. We can make Fridays our 'fuck the past' day. We'll stay up late doing all the things we couldn't in our old lives. Boyfriend hated when you cut your hair short? We'll grab some scissors and shear off. Parents didn't like cursing? Oh, songbird, I have a whole list of new words to teach you." I lifted my eyebrow her way, willing to try anything it if helped get her out of the mood she was in. "Boyfriend disliked when you fucked other guys? Well, I'll volunteer to help you get that off your bucket list."

The red that sprang up on her cheeks was a thing of beauty, especially when she dropped her gaze as if shy.

I laughed, letting the words play off as a joke even though that was *exactly* what I wanted. Even knowing it was a bad idea, even realizing that it was probably going to end up causing me more pain than it was worth, I couldn't help it.

I'd been in this damn place so long, and Hera was the only light I'd found, the only person to make me think something could change, that things could be different. I recalled how she'd set her hand on mine when I'd stood up to that idiot ifrit, how she'd not wanted me to risk myself for her, how she'd visited me in solitary, and that had all won me over.

This wasn't the sort of place where people did anything for others, yet she had, when she'd had no damn reason to.

It seemed I was easy, that it didn't take a whole lot to get into my pants.

Or maybe there just hadn't ever been anyone else who had made it seem worthwhile.

I leaned back and put my arm out, over the back of the couch. "I'm sorry your boyfriend was a dick. You can do much better."

She moved into the space I'd created, leaning against my side. She wrote more, and the back and forth became easier, more normal. It was a different kind of conversation, but as I eased into it, as I got used to it, it didn't feel so odd anymore.

"He isn't a bad guy. At least, he didn't used to be. And I can't expect him to wait forever when there isn't a real shot at me getting out of here. That isn't fair."

"You're worth waiting for, and if he doesn't think so, then he can't see the real you, and he doesn't deserve you anyway."

She shifted so she could look up at me, her eyebrows furrowed. Another few words jotted down explained her thoughts. *"It's easy to say that when we're stuck here. Out there, though, that's different. That's the real world."*

"Is it? What makes that the real world?" I reached over and pinched her, rewarded with a sharp inhalation and glare from her. "Feels pretty real, doesn't it? The fact is that out there, people are just as trapped, just as fake. They're stuck in their little roles, in what they think they should do, in who they should be. They're not any more real than what's in here."

Her exhalation warmed my chest as she settled back in, closer than she'd been before.

And...damn, it was a nice feeling.

Even with my sweater, with my gloves, it was damn nice to have some human contact. It wasn't something I got often...

Was it because she wasn't afraid of me or that she didn't know she should be?

I risked it and ran my fingers through her hair, enjoyed the way the strands move, how soft they were. Even through the thin gloves I wore, I savored the feeling.

And Hera didn't shove me away. She didn't tell me to stop it. If anything, she snuggled in closer to my side.

"You know," I said, my voice soft. "I may seem pretty smart, like I have it all figured out, but it took me a long-damned time to get here. I've seen people arrive and leave, seen folks born here and I've seen them die here. There isn't much I haven't witnessed, and that's given me some insight into what tends to work. I know, the world outside these walls can call to us, can make us want it like nothing else, but I've seen too many shades lose themselves to that desire. I've seen them spend years trying to find a way out, wasting their time, only to end up getting taken to the North Tower when they caused too much trouble. I don't want to see you end up that way, too."

She lifted her hand, an odd motion. It took me a minute to realize she was using sign language. "*I don't know where I fit anymore.*"

My own lessons — the hours I'd spent poring over books to learn sign language — let me understand her.

That seemed an easy answer, at least to me. I caught her chin with my gloved hand so she looked into my eyes. "You want to know the secret? No one fits in, ever. Everyone tries so hard, but it never happens because there is no fitting in. There is no one group who can make a person matter, and trying to twist yourself until you manage it, until you mold yourself into something you think they can accept, it'll just leave you in knots. The real secret is being yourself and realizing that you'll find your own people once you do. Anyone who doesn't like it can fuck off."

She stared back at me, as if weighing the truth of what I'd said. Whether she believed me or just didn't want to argue, I wasn't sure, but she eventually offered a quick nod before leaning toward me.

Which woke me up. As much as I'd have loved to kiss her right there, to take it just as far as she'd let me, I couldn't.

I didn't release her chin, didn't let her come closer, and a moment of hurt skirted across her eyes.

Right, women didn't much care for rejection...

"You've seen what happens when I touch someone."

She frowned, and even I spotted the moment she remembered, the slight tremble to her lip at the way I'd nearly killed the shade.

I nodded. "I can control it to an extent. I can choose if I weaken a person, or if I'll kill them, at least usually. That doesn't change that any skin-on-skin contact will cause a shade to lose their powers while I'm touching them. If I don't want to cause harm, the effects won't linger as long, and they won't hurt them like it did with the ifrit."

She took the pad again, sitting up straight, moving away from my grasp. "*So you can't touch people at all?*"

I tried to make a joke of it, but nothing came to mind. Perhaps it was too fucking painful to make jokes about, like laughing would only cause the wound to open up, for others to see the bleeding mess.

I fucking hated how separate I was from others, how they watched me carefully. Sure, lots of shades were dangerous, were watched warily, but I was different. They stared at me as if I were something unnatural, something that could steal a part of them, of who they were.

I expected Hera to yank back, to leave, to realize exactly how bad an idea this was.

Instead, she leaned in again and brushed her soft, warm lips against mine.

A spark of sensation ran through me, a taste of her power, of the source that ran through her. It was beyond intoxicating, nothing like I'd ever felt before.

The temptation to steal it was strong, like having my favorite meal held out before me.

The trust she'd offered, though, kept my control solid. I returned the kiss, hesitant and awkward.

It probably wasn't a good time to admit… I'd never done this. I had a lot of ideas, had spent plenty of time imagining such things, but having spent so much of my life inside these walls, the opportunity hadn't presented itself.

It meant the softness of her lips, the taste of her breath, the way her hand grabbed my arm and held on was beyond anything I'd thought.

When she pulled back finally, that flush on her cheeks again, I was so tempted to push my luck. Maybe it was from having gone without for so long, but I wanted to grab her waist and pull her into my lap, to explore each inch of her body, to have what I'd never had before.

I held that back, though, and instead savored the way she curled against my side, as if she didn't have a care in the world, as if she were afraid of me at all.

In fact, she let out a slow breath, then moved her hands in another sign.

Clearly, I needed to brush up on my sign language. This one took a moment for me to figure out, but eventually, I did and smiled, wrapping my arm around her.

"*Silence.*"

It seemed she didn't mind me taking her skills, at least for a short amount of time, and if I could give her a little bit of peace...

Well, maybe what I was wasn't quite so bad.

Chapter Fourteen

Hera

The top floor was oddly soothing for me. It wasn't an official recreational area, but there were seating arrangements, and shades liked to sit up there in the sunlight. I liked to bring a book and watch people come and go, see them cross from the Residential Tower then go about their business.

It made me feel like I was part of those groups, like I had a place in them.

I didn't, and I was lucky to be ignored rather than glared at, but it turned out I was exceptional at pretending anything I needed to, and for today, it was that I had a community.

I'd read a few pages in my book, then the second the chime alerted me to the elevator, I'd try to subtly lift my gaze to get a look at who was getting off one elevator and onto the other.

I'd had an early class rather than later ones and thanks to Deacon, I was still off any work details. It left me with most of my day open.

"Good book?"

I lifted my gaze to find Kit there, seeming as out of place as he ever did. It was something about his dress, that he always seemed as if he should be a lawyer in a courtroom rather than walking around Larkwood.

Then again, he was also very good at hiding what he was, at least if no one looked too closely.

I turned the book, having nearly forgotten what I had been reading. I guess that was what happened when someone wasn't paying any real attention. I'd reread the same page over and over again, never having the content sink in.

So I shook my head, because it was true.

It wasn't that great.

Kit undid the button of his suit jacket as he sat down beside me on the large bench. "I understand you went with Wade to the library, so I'm not surprised it isn't that good. He is the reason they keep stocking romance with titles like *The Millionaire's Secret Love Child*. If you're interested in good books, I can suggest a few. I even have a private library with many options I would be more than willing to lend to you."

I closed the book, the scrap of paper I was using as a bookmark inside it. I hadn't been reading it anyway, so I welcomed the distraction. While I didn't understand Kit, knew little about him, he had a calming presence.

"How are you feeling?" he asked slowly, and it was easy to read beneath them.

He'd heard about Medical. It was funny that for a place as tightly regulated at Larkwood, rumors spread so quickly. It seemed everyone knew.

I shrugged. I wasn't all better — it had turned out they'd taken a total of six punch biopsies from my body in different areas — but I wasn't that bad, either.

The time off had been appreciated, though. While I could attend classes, the idea of pulling weeds or raking when such motions aggravated the wounds sounded dreadful.

Kit nodded, then stared across the room with me. "Well, you're scheduled for an evaluation this week, but we'll stick to simple things that won't further harm you."

I recalled the last lesson, the one where I'd gotten my ass handed to me before managing to put Gina on *her* ass. Yeah, that did not sound like something I wanted to repeat in my current state.

Or, well, ever really.

Sure, that rush of power had been intoxicating. It had felt like someone else, like the sort of person I'd always wanted to be. It was the lead-up to that I hated, and the fact I wasn't sure if I could do it again.

"I didn't report what happened with Gina."

At that, I looked his way, trying to understand his meaning.

He went on. "When I filed my report, I left out what you did. I also *suggested* to Gina that she shouldn't mention it either."

"*Why?*" I signed.

"Because the warden has already taken too much of an interest in you here. Between your political usefulness and your source levels, you're already a target. The only reason you've been left alone to some extent has been because you can't use your voice. If they realized what you're capable of..." He let out a long sigh. "I don't want to see you suffer that way.

Larkwood uses everything it can, every skill, and it'll use them until nothing is left of the shade but a husk. There isn't a shade here who isn't used for their abilities, forced to comply. It's a part of life here, but I don't want to see you having to deal with that."

I thought about that, tried to think if I'd seen any other shade forced to do anything other than work details.

Then again, I hadn't seen what work some of the others did. I had assumed it was similar to mine — manual labor of some sort, probably as a means to keep us worn out.

"Like what?"

"Well, think about it. If there is a dangerous mission where a water approach is needed, what better time to use a mermaid for it? If a building needs breaking into, a shapeshifter with a small animal form would be ideal. If a suspect won't speak, it's the perfect use for a telepath to dig through their brain. The more useful a shade's skill, the more in demand they become. If they need to force someone to help them, why not use a succubus to twist the person?"

I grabbed my writing pad, knowing my knowledge of signs wasn't good enough for a full conversation yet. *"Why stop that? It sounds better than pulling weeds."*

He peered at the words, then shook his head. "It isn't. It seems like it, at first, especially because the warden likes to promise a lot of things in order to get shades to agree. The thing is, doing someone else's dirty work is dangerous. There comes a line for each person, something they won't cross, but I've found Larkwood doesn't have those same sensibilities."

I frowned, unsure what he meant.

Kit leaned forward so he rested his elbows on his knees. "I remember a phantom who was here, a long time ago. He was only too happy to help the warden, to gain access to buildings, to kill enemies. I think he enjoyed it, felt as if he were a part of something larger, of something good. He was young, naïve and felt as if he were being patriotic. The thing was, Larkwood doesn't like to let anything go to waste. They sent him on a mission, and when he came back, he was different. Darker, quiet, angry in a way I'd never seen from him. He didn't tell me what had happened, didn't tell anyone. The guards found him dead in his room a few months later, after he managed to steal pills from Medical."

"What happened?"

"I was able to get access to his records in order to seal them, and I took a look at that mission, the one that changed him. The warden had sent him to a place in Florida, where a local judge wasn't ruling the way they wanted him to. He'd gone, expecting to need to frighten the judge, to make him see reason. Unfortunately, they knew that wouldn't work. For those few real good people, it won't work to just try to scare them. Their ideals mean more to them than their lives. The warden knew that, so he'd already created a better plan — target one of the judge's children."

A sickness rushed through me at that, at the immediate reaction my entire body felt to such an evil idea.

Worse, I knew how the story would go. There was only one way, only one thing that would make sense since I already knew how it ended.

Still, I let Kit tell it all.

"The report shows he said no, that he refused. He came back walking slow, but I didn't know until I saw the report why. They'd damn near killed him for refusing, using drugs, torture, whatever they needed to get him to agree. Eventually, he did."

I reached out and set my hand on Kit's arm, unable to help it. There was so much pain in his voice, so much regret, as if he held himself just as responsible as the shade or the warden.

Kit reached with his other hand and set it on top of mine but didn't look at me. "My job here is to help teach, to serve as a liaison between the staff and residents. I might be hated by the shades, by the guards, but I do my best to protect the shades I can, to try to keep them off the bad side of the warden or the guards. I failed him, though. When he started, I should have made him understand it wasn't a game, that it wasn't something he could ever win. Surviving this place, it has to do with walking a line. You need to be useful enough to keep around but not so useful as to draw attention. I changed the report I turned in on you because I don't want to see you go down that same path, and I can only imagine what they'd use you for."

I stared at where his hand was over mine, at the scaring on his knuckles, the only real sign that he wasn't quite as fancy as he let on. It made me wonder...what were his skills?

I hadn't risked looking for him in the book yet, maybe too afraid of what I might find. The scars said he hadn't had the quiet life his dress and behavior would have implied.

The elevator made a sound again, and we both jerked our hands back as if caught by parents.

Then again, Kit probably didn't want the complications of anyone thinking he was involved with another shade.

The doors to the elevator opened, but it wasn't just a resident who walked out. Instead, there were four guards all wearing black — that wasn't something I saw often. The guards for Larkwood wore gray and Medical had light blue. These men, however, wore black uniforms.

Between them was a shade I'd seen around, a young boy who couldn't have been here that long.

He had his hands bound in front of him in thick metal cuffs and the guards to each side had a hold of his arms.

He yanked, struggling against their grip. "I don't want to go there."

"Too bad," one of the guards snapped and yanked him harder, trying to get him to move.

The boy dug his heels in, and amazingly, he seemed to be giving the four guards quite the challenge. I had no idea what the boy was, but whatever it was, clearly he had strength to spare. The more he pulled, the harder it was for the guards to keep their grip on him, to keep him moving.

"Fuck you," the boy snarled, his voice far less human now. Worse, I felt his fear beneath it, my head throbbing from the impact, as if he'd struck me with it. "I'm not going. No one comes back from the North Tower."

"You don't have a choice," the guard said. "Your name's on the list, so you're going."

The boy shook his head, anger and fear swirling together for a dangerous combination. He pulled again, managing to toss off all the guards with a fling of his arms. His body shifted, his back arching before he leaned forward, the popping of bones sickening. The cuffs snapped as he moved, freeing him.

I was confused at first, figuring he was a werewolf and wondering why he'd be in level 1.

Except, the reason became clear as scales appeared on his skin, as his body shifted more, became even larger. The change was fast—not instantaneous, but the whole thing only took a few seconds. The next thing I knew, a dragon stood in the center of the large room, smoke trailing from his nostrils, his eyes darting around and furious.

The guards dragged themselves backward on the floor to avoid when he stomped his foot and swiped his tail around like a whip. He caught a small table and flung it.

Kit grabbed the back of my shirt and yanked me down, so I barely missed the piece of furniture that had soared my way.

Not that I thought the boy had targeted me on purpose. I could hear the terror in the sounds he made, even in this form when he couldn't speak. I could feel it crawling around inside me.

"Stay here," Kit snapped before rising.

The thought of him going to face off against *that* seemed impossible. There was something more to Kit— I knew that—but the boy in the center of the room was a real-life *dragon.*

That seemed like a top-of-the-food-chain sort of creature.

Still, Kit walked forward as if unfazed by the beast before of him. "Gerald," he said, his voice loud in a way that made me cover my ears.

The boy—Gerald—turned his head toward Kit. He didn't attack, but he didn't stand down either.

"There isn't a way out. There aren't any exits where you can escape from. You are trapped."

My stomach sank at the fact Kit wasn't helping him. Was he playing a game? Trying to trick the guards?

"You'll only make this worse if you fight it here, and we both know you won't succeed."

Gerald made a soft, low sound, one that broke my heart. It was full of fear, of pain, of the unknown and a desire to escape it. I knew those feelings, had lived with them since coming here. Every shade here, whether they admitted it or not, had the same fear of the North Tower.

"I know," Kit said as if he understood Gerald. "But some things can't be helped. If you go, there is still a chance that they'll bring you back, that there could be another way out of this. There will be no other way if you don't, however. If you continue to fight, they'll kill you here."

Gerald's gaze darted around the room, as if he were searching for an escape, for some other option.

One of the guards lifted his weapon and fired, a dart sticking out of the side of Gerald's hip. It had to be a tranquilizer, but I would bet it would require a hell of a lot more to bring down a creature that size. Even Wade had taken a few shots to bring down.

Kit's gaze moved to the dart, to the guards, then across the way the North Tower. He pressed his lips together, and I could see the conflict inside him. The last thing he wanted was for Gerald to end up over there—whatever it was that was there. Still, he wasn't wrong. There wasn't a way out, not from there, which meant Gerald would go that way alive or dead, but he *would* go that way.

"Don't make me do this," Kit pleaded softly.

Gerald let out another sound, louder this time, like a real roar. It shook the windows, so deep that I felt it. Another dart hit him, this time on his flank, and he responded by inhaling, smoke leaving his nostrils even as he did it.

He opened his mouth, red sparking deep inside his throat, the starts of a flame he seemed to plan to spew across the room.

And I was pretty sure I wasn't fireproof.

Kit let out a sound of frustration, just a split second of helplessness, before he changed before my eyes.

It was the creature I'd seen from him before, the white bone as a head, the elongated limbs, the horns, the black eyes fitting in this face as it didn't in his normal one. "Stop," he said, his voice nothing like his old one. It seemed to slip into every person in the room and demand they obey. It rooted *me* in place.

Gerald didn't close his mouth, but neither did he let loose any flames. His tail twitched, swinging back and forth like an unnerved cat's.

Kit walked forward, his steps eerie and calm and terrifying. He reminded me of something dead, something cold and evil that shouldn't exist. He made me want to pull away, to run.

He grasped Gerald's chin, Kit's hands long with huge claws at the tips. He stared deep into Gerald's eyes, as if they could have a conversation without words at all.

Kit moved, a hard jerk of his hand, and the crack of bone seemed even louder than Gerald's roar had been. The dragon collapsed, his body shifting back until it was the boy on the ground there, his head bent at an unnatural angle, his eyes still open and blank.

Kit stared down at the body, opening and closing his hands, then turned to look at me.

Whatever he saw, he must not have liked, because he twisted away to shift back. Still, when he faced me that time, I couldn't see the man I'd gotten used to. I didn't see Kit, the pseudo-professor, the classy, well-dressed gentleman.

I saw the monster he had become, felt the chill that threatened to devour me when I saw it, heard the terrifying depth of his voice, the way I couldn't make sense of it the way I did everyone else's. It was like a sound that wasn't meant to exist, one that wasn't natural.

"Well fuck," one of the guards said as he got himself to his feet. "They wanted this one alive."

Kit peered over his shoulder at the guard, as if trying hard not to look at the body anymore. "You should know better than to try to move a frightened dragon shifter."

"Maybe I'll tell them it's your fault he's dead."

Kit nodded, as if the threat meant nothing to him. "You're welcome to do so. Please, have them review the footage where you lost control and nearly allowed him to set this entire floor on fire. I'm sure they'd be interested in that."

The guard tightened his jaw, and I could feel his desire to lash out. Whether it was fear of Kit—which seemed pretty damn reasonable—or fear of his bosses, but he made an angry sound and hauled Gerald's body up and over his shoulder. He headed toward the North Tower door, the other guards at his heels.

Once he left, once Gerald was out of sight, I turned my gaze on Kit.

I'd just watched him murder a child... He'd snapped the boy's neck instead of helping him, instead of doing anything useful. I thought about all the times others had whispered about Kit, about how he wasn't one of us, that he was nothing more than a lapdog for the warden, and it suddenly made sense.

I hadn't understood it before, hadn't believed it. Kit spoke so nicely, so calmly, that it had been hard to think of him as being as bad as people said.

That was before I'd watched him kill someone in cold blood.

He stared at me, the room silent after the chaos that had consumed it moments before. He took a step toward me, and I leapt away. The thought of him being anywhere near me seemed all sorts of bad.

Kit froze, swallowed, then nodded as if letting me know he understood the boundary I'd set. "You need to be careful." His voice had returned to the way it had been before, to that controlled one. "What you just saw? That is where everyone here is headed. Some faster than others, and if you make the wrong choices, if you draw attention to yourself, you'll find yourself there a lot quicker than you want."

I kept my distance as Kit looked toward the North Tower once more, then headed back toward the elevator, leaving me there.

The North Tower might have been dangerous, but Kit had just reminded me of another truth — everything here was dangerous.

I thought backward, to how I'd suffered in Medical, to the fact they planned on bringing me back there. I remembered the way that boy's body had crumpled into an unmoving pile after Kit had broken his neck. I saw my parents' faces, the way my father had told them to make sure I never got out. I heard the way every last person had told me there was no way out.

It all washed over me, and I realized I couldn't stay. If we were all headed for the tower, if there were no other options for me, if my options were to end up there or die to avoid it, then I knew my choice.

I'd get out of Larkwood Academy, even if it killed me.

Chapter Fifteen

I pulled at the shoulder strap of my backpack as I walked down the long hallway toward my class—legal requirements for shades.

I tended to hate the legal classes the most. History, biology, even the evaluations had to do with facts. They were about who shades were, about what they could do.

The law classes instead felt like the world reminding me that I would never have a normal life, that I would always be trapped, that even if I was released, I'd always have this shadow watching over me.

Worse...my mother's name continued to get brought up. As a senator and one of the main forces behind all modern shade laws, she was spoken of often. It felt like a kick each time the instructor said her name, each time I realized she'd had a part of each of these laws that ruined my life.

And the swinging of angry glares my way from other residents said they all knew it too.

This made my steps slower than usual. I'd left early enough that I had plenty of time to make it and walking slowly made me feel as if I had some control.

"Thank you," Knox said as he fell into step beside me, his hands tucked into his pockets. He wore a pair of the gray sweatpants, a reminder to me that it was unfair how much better men looked in them than women.

I lifted my eyebrow, unsure what he was thanking me for.

"For the bathroom." He didn't go further about that, but I couldn't blame him for that. I recalled how he'd looked there, on the tile floor. It probably wasn't something he wanted to remember much.

I nodded, then pulled out the writing pad. *"You look better."*

He shrugged. "Yeah, I'm doing better."

Which meant he'd fed, right? It meant he'd found someone to be with, that he'd gotten what he'd needed. Otherwise, he'd still be starving, just as he had been there.

The shot of jealousy that hit me was beyond surprising. It was a moment when I had to admit...*I must like him.*

I wouldn't have thought so, but there was no other way to explain why I'd feel jealous over some faceless person who had given Knox what he needed. It wasn't just the sex, either.

I mean, it was partly that. The man had a way of moving that screamed sex, that said he knew his way around a person's body, could deliver on any promise he made. I sure as hell was curious about what that would be like.

However, that wasn't the only part. I remembered how fragile he had seemed, how broken. The idea of him going to someone else, of him seeking out a stranger, bothered me. I recalled the demon propositioning him the first day, remembered what Brax had said about people who took advantage.

It was strange, since I would have assumed that an incubus would be a predator, that he'd be in control when it came to sex. The thing was, after seeing him in that bathroom, after listening to Brax, I wasn't so sure anymore.

My mind seemed to do what it wanted, and at that moment, it was thinking about Knox, about what it would be like to have him feed from me. I recalled what the book had said, thought about how incubi could draw a person in, could make them want nothing more than the shade. Was that what this was? A fascination? Something he'd created in me?

Maybe.

Did it matter?

"Do you have any idea how distracting you are when you smell like that?"

Heat burned my cheeks. He wasn't supposed to just come right out and say something like that. *"You could try not sniffing me."*

"That's like telling someone not to see what's right in front of them."

"Yeah, well, your voice makes me see flashes of you screwing some man with short brown hair, but I don't bring that up."

A tic in his jaw started after he read the words. "You have now."

Guilt settled in my stomach quickly. It hadn't been fair to lash out like that. *"Sorry,"* I wrote, unable to help apologizing. Even if he was mentioning things that didn't need to be mentioned, I didn't need to be a bitch over it.

He burrowed his hands farther into his pockets. "It was a fair point. I guess we can't help what we get from our skills sometimes, right?"

We walked a little more before he spoke again. "You know, I'm not into men."

The statement sounded odd, especially since I still had the image in my head of him with that man. I went with an answer that didn't commit me to anything. *"Isn't my business."*

"No, it isn't, but you saw me at my worst. I don't sleep with men. I feed from them. That's it."

"Why men if you aren't interested in them? I bet there are women who are more than willing."

He nodded. "Yeah, there are. It's more complicated with women, though."

I waited, wondering if he'd continue, if he'd tell me more. The silence made me doubt it, at least until he let out a sigh. "Feeding is one thing. It's something I can't help, something I need. I don't like mixing that with anything real. People can get addicted to being fed from, can crave it, and I don't like doing that with anyone I might actually care about."

That made sense, even if I didn't like it. I felt like it was a line in the sand he'd drawn, one where he made it perfectly clear—he had no plans to use me.

It wasn't that I wanted to be used, yet I couldn't shake the disappointment. I wanted to help him, wanted to feel all that intensity directed at me.

Since that wasn't going to happen, I tried to bury the desire somewhere deep inside me. *"I'm glad you're*

Silenced

feeling better," I went with instead. That seemed like a nice, safe answer.

"I thought maybe you'd want to come over to my place later."

I didn't bother to write anything, giving him a 'what the hell are you talking about?' look instead.

Knox grinned, the smirk making him seem younger and somehow carefree. "What? I know you've got the law class, and that one isn't easy. I've passed it, so figured you might want to come over and study. He uses the same quizzes each time, and I still have all mine."

The offer felt entirely out of place. It was funny, because just months before, in my old life, that would have been normal. Some boy inviting me over to study was just a part of life.

Now, however?

It seemed shades, attacks and twenty-four-seven guards were normal and a boy asking me over to his place to study seemed entirely out of place.

Still, the temptation to sit down with Knox, to spend time with him, was strong.

So I nodded, agreeing to it.

Knox flashed a wider smile. "Good. I'm on floor two, room twenty-four. Come around six o'clock? I'll have food."

His words made it feel like a date, but what he'd said before stuck with me, the fact he'd made it clear he wasn't interested.

So what was the study session about?

The way Knox looked at me, an odd sweetness to him, made me push off any worries. I deserved something that was almost normal, and damn it, I'd let myself have it.

205

* * * *

Somehow, a glare had the same weight as someone continually poking me with a pointy stick.

At least, it did when Brax was doing it. He sat two tables behind me in the main eating space, staring holes in the back of my head the entire time.

His brother wasn't anywhere around, but I'd learned they were often apart. The two weren't joined at the hip, didn't need each other to function.

That was a good thing, since I had a feeling my little study session with Knox wouldn't be nearly as much fun if I had to deal with Brax there. He was someone who could ruin the mood without even trying.

For all those reasons, I ignored him. I kept my gaze instead on the people who came and went. I watched the shades who came in to eat, the guards who patrolled, the staff who worked the pantry, the interaction of them all.

I noted the shades who were closely watched, the ones who created problems and the ones no one noticed. They all made for so many data points, so many tiny details that I couldn't make sense just yet.

Still, I filed it all away, hoping any of it would be the piece of information that would allow me to figure out a plan. I never knew what would be important, so I just watched it all.

"You're awfully interested in what everyone is doing." Brax sat down across from me, his gaze hard and nothing like his brother's.

I wrote a message for him. *"What do you want?"*

"Just curious why you're watching everyone. It's smarter to keep your nose down and don't worry about others' business. It'll get you in trouble."

"I didn't ask you for your advice."

He narrowed his eyes. "You show up here, thinking you're special. Maybe you're used to being important, to being in charge, to getting to dictate how things work, but that isn't here."

"I'm just trying to live my life – alone."

If my jabs landed, he showed no sign. Then again, he was always scowling at me. It was harder to tell if he hated me more. "You buddied up with Deacon, with Kit, with Wade. Now you even have Knox's attention. Are you hoping to wrap them all around your finger? To have some harem of men who do your bidding? Who keep you safe here? Because you aren't dealing with trust fund babies here – you're dealing with shades who won't be so easy to cuckold."

His words made me roll my eyes and scratch down another response. *"Look. I'm not trying to do anything but survive here. If you have a problem with that – too bad."*

He let out an angry sound, and the lines of his face shifted again, a sign of his control slipping. I'd never seen him fully transformed, never seen the monster beneath the surface.

Part of me wanted to see it. I'd learned that while it was terrifying to see the reality of people, it was safer.

Whatever he was, it was dangerous enough people avoided him, were cautious around him.

"Watch yourself. Whatever plan you've got won't get you very far, and if it involves screwing over Knox, I'll damn well step in."

I looked away from him, having no desire to continue this little pissing contest. Instead, I spotted the way one of the guards stopped a shade across the room, patting him down. The guard pulled a blade from the man's pocket before slamming him down on a table.

Random searches weren't all that common, I'd found. It seemed there were moles, however, because each time I saw someone searched, they always had something on them.

It meant I needed to keep things close to my chest, keep from sharing them. I had no idea who could be the one snitching, but I didn't need to get caught before I could think up the best way out.

The problem was clear, however. Despite my watching, despite all my studying, I hadn't found any good path. I had no idea how to escape the building, how to escape of the property.

The yard was watched too closely. The buildings were secured well, none of the windows opening, no access to the doors on the ground floor to get out. Both the main buildings had similar features, and in the Residential Tower, there wasn't even a door to get outside from.

It left me with one choice…

The North Tower.

I had no idea what was in it, how to get there, but there weren't any ways out that I could see anywhere else.

It meant if I wanted to escape, if I ever wanted to try to get some form of a life back, I was going to need to go the one place I didn't want to.

I had to find a way to get taken to the North Tower, then hope I could survive it.

Chapter Sixteen

I'd had so many years where I had access to whatever I wanted, years when I'd taken that for granted. I recalled how I'd looked at my closet and been annoyed, as if my hundred thousand dollars' worth of clothing hanging there were an inconvenience rather than a blessing.

What I wouldn't give for just a tiny fraction of those things. Hell, I was pretty sure I'd pay about anything for just one cute little black dress. Anything that was date-ready, that would make me feel like I belonged there, beside Knox, who was unfairly handsome.

Once again, I was hit by how unfair it was for men to look so good without much work. The men walking around in their sweats looked like snacks, whereas I looked more like a co-ed senior who had given up on looking nice than a girl meeting a guy I sort of liked.

All those doubts kept me standing outside of his door, staring at the number, frozen in place and afraid to actually knock.

This was a horrible idea.

I was trapped here, looking for a way to escape. The last thing I needed was to entangle my life with others, to risk letting some crucial piece of information slip that could screw up my whole plan.

Still...my plan, which hadn't even started to come together, could end up taking me years to make happen. Was I supposed to have nothing in my life but *this*, nothing but classes and work and horrible medical visits? I was supposed to pretend no one else existed for what could be years of time?

That was beyond unreasonable.

I took a deep breath, then knocked on the door, needing to do it before I lost my nerve, before I took off and gave up on the whole idea.

As I stood there, waiting, a horrible idea struck me. After how bad things were between Brax and me, what if this whole idea had just been a way to humiliate me?

I recalled how those other shades had sent me to an isolated floor, had planned to jump me when I was alone.

What if this was just an even crueler form of that? If Knox had asked me here so he could laugh with his brother over my stupidity, over the fact I'd believed him, that I'd shown up thinking Knox wanted to see me?

I was halfway into my own self-doubt, ready to turn tail and run before I had to suffer the humiliation of Knox answering, but it seemed I was slow. The door opened, and one look at Knox helped calm my frazzled nerves.

He wore what he always did—a pair of sweatpants and a shirt. However, he had no shoes on, and that felt odd.

It made me realize, I hadn't seen anyone without shoes since I'd been here. It was a strange realization — it wasn't like I had some weird fetish with feet and wanted to see them — but what I figured out standing there was that it was a type of vulnerability and comfort.

People removed their shoes in their own private space, when they were safe, when they were home. The fact that I hadn't seen anyone like that since getting here meant I hadn't seen anyone that comfortable.

"You came," Knox said, his smile showing the signs of unease.

Which was strange.

Why would he be nervous whether or not I'd show? I recalled again how others looked at him, how almost all the shades in Larkwood wanted him. It was crazy to think he might be nervous about me.

I nodded, not sure what else to try to tell him. Of course I'd come.

Well, at least because he'd opened his door quickly. If he hadn't, I would have bailed.

I walked in when he gestured for me to do so, and his place made me stop short.

My room was basic. No real decor, nothing personalized, just what I'd found when I moved in. While Knox's room was identical to mine in terms of layout and size, it looked nothing like what I had because he'd changed a lot.

The walls were a soft green, and a large, U-shaped couch sat in the middle of the room. Instead of a dining room table, he had a bar in the kitchen with stools. Through the cracked open door, I caught sight of a messy bed with a red comforter, something that was, again, not standard that I'd seen.

His place reminded me of an actual home, of a place where someone lived, a place they'd changed for their own comfort.

"What?" Knox glanced around the space, his eyebrows drawn toward each other. "It's not much, but it's not that bad."

I shook my head and pulled out my writing pad. *"Your place looks comfy. Mine is like a cheap motel room."*

He read it, then smiled as if relieved. "Well, you just got here. You have to remember that I've lived here for over a decade. That's given me time to collect stuff, to make it the way I like it."

"How did you get the furniture?"

"Every job you do earns you some credit. The more difficult jobs get you more. You can trade that for items. Since it isn't like vacations are a possibility, most of us pick things for our rooms. Talk to Kit about it—he does the negotiations, and he's usually pretty reasonable. You've done mostly manual labor, which doesn't earn nearly as much, but given how nice Kit's been to you, I'd bet you could get quite a lot out of him."

Knox didn't say that with any amount of censure. He didn't say it the way people talked about a woman sleeping her way to the top, but more like there was nothing shameful about using someone's desire to get what a person wanted.

Then again, he was an incubus. He likely had an odd relationship to sex in general, since it was something required for his survival. That had to cross a few lines, mix up feelings.

I let myself look closer around his living room, enjoying the peek I got at the real man. See, a room would tell me a lot about a person, especially when they lived alone. Outside of it, people portrayed who they thought they should be. They weren't honest.

However, inside one's home, that was the real them. They filled the space with things they loved, that made them happy.

In Knox's case, that seemed to be magazines? I peered closer at the shelf of them to find they were all on farming? Home-steading? The one that made me smile was near the end, where he had three different magazines for making preserves.

That sure as hell wasn't something I'd expected to find in his room.

"You don't have any allergies, right? I don't think sirens do."

I turned back toward him and shook my head. I hadn't even considered whether sirens would have any issues with food, like vampires with garlic. Nothing had hurt me yet, so I had to assume it wasn't a thing.

Knox nodded, then pulled a wooden platter from the fridge and set it down on the bar. I came closer, drawn mostly by curiosity. There had been a lot of foods in the pantry but trying to make something had proven damn near impossible. I'd grown up with a private chef and more than enough staff around the house that I never learned to cook anything beyond eggs. To make it more difficult, there weren't a lot of the basics when it came to utensils.

Knives were obviously off limits, and even forks had been missing from my place.

So how had Knox managed to make a charcuterie tray? It had slices of meat, cheese, fruit and bread, all perfectly arranged.

I lifted my gaze to his, a question there.

"Like I said, I've been here a long time. Guards end up trusting people more—well, some people—and we're given extra leeway. In my case?" He reached into a drawer and withdrew a large kitchen knife, holding it up to show me. "The food they give out in the cafeteria is horrible, so one of my first focuses was to get enough of a kitchen set up to make my own. It isn't perfect—they refuse to allow an actual gas stove—but it's something." He put the knife away, then gestured toward the items behind him. "Induction range, an oven, I even have a deep freezer tucked away in the extra room. Anything that could be weaponized—like the knife—have tags inside them. Alarms will go off if I take it out of my room, so I don't go and stab people with it."

The idea that a person's life in a place like this could be good struck me as odd. Perhaps I'd been so wrapped up in my own life, in my own worries, that I hadn't tried. I hadn't realized that a person could settle in here, that they could have access to some of the comforts they missed from before.

It didn't change that I'd be getting out, but it meant I might have an easier time, might just manage access to some things that would be useful.

I took a seat at the bar then waited for him to sit beside me. The food looked amazing. It reminded me of the old parties my parents would throw, where fancy hors d'oeuvres were passed around and people gathered to talk about themselves while pretending to listen to others.

Except, I'd never been happy in those places. I'd never fit in, never felt at ease there. Somehow, sitting across from Knox, I did.

He tapped the tray and pushed it closer. "Go on, dig in."

I took one of the crackers and set a piece of cheese and a slice of meat on top. I gave myself the chance to stare at it, to savor even the look of it, the smell. I'd lived off what the cafeteria made for the most part, supplemented by boxed crackers and one night, when I was hungry, just plain slices of bread.

I couldn't believe that others had lived such different lives.

Knox leaned forward and reached over the bar for something. It made his shirt ride up, gave me a look at his lower back, at where his tan skin showed solid muscle beneath. How could an inch or two of skin excite me?

I felt like a man in the past, when seeing a woman's ankle was considered sexy and taboo. Here I was salivating over a tiny strip of skin.

Pathetic. Then again, it had been well over a month since I'd had sex. The last time had been with Aaron, a week before everything had changed. We'd been at his place, the small apartment his parents had rented for him for his senior year.

It had been about what it always was. Not unpleasant, just not all that exciting.

So maybe I was just hard up for action.

It meant I needed to take care of myself in the privacy of my own room soon, because I couldn't start ogling men each time they showed the tiniest bit of flesh.

Knox made a low sound in his throat as he settled back in, meeting my gaze for a heartbeat, the heat there saying he'd known exactly what I was thinking. Still, he didn't call me on it.

It seemed he'd learned how to pretend, and I was more than willing to do the same as I took a bite of the food.

It was even better than I'd imagined.

"So, for the law class, the trick is to read the wrap-up at the end of the chapter. He always pulls the questions from there. If you can memorize those ten questions, you'll ace all his tests."

I frowned, thinking back to the test I'd taken a few days earlier. Now that I thought about it, he was right.

The questions hadn't been in the same order or even the exact same phrasing, but they'd all been from the study quiz at the end.

Which seemed rather lazy.

Then again, it wasn't like this was an actual school. They weren't educating students so they could go out and have fulfilling lives or do complicated jobs. Instead, they were filling time to reduce riots and fighting. They offered classes so when overseers showed up, the school could say, 'look, we're educating them! We're taking good care of them!'

It was a lie, of course, but it made sense that the staff wouldn't give a damn if a person learned anything.

I picked up my pen and wrote on the pad that sat between us. *"Why did I need to come here if that was all the advice you had?"*

Once I wrote it, I realized how much of a shrew I sounded like. It wasn't that I was complaining about coming, it was that I didn't quite understand why I was there still.

He stared at it for a long moment, then lifted his gaze to mine. "I wanted to see you. Is that so hard to understand?"

I nodded. It really was. He had a lot of options, and those were probably far less complicated than I was. Not to mention, he'd made it clear he wasn't interested in anything physical, so what was the point?

Knox let out a sigh before sitting back in his stool. "I'm sure you know how many prying eyes there are in this place, least of all my own brother." He let out a soft laugh at that one, but there was a fondness in it. "I wanted a chance to sit somewhere quiet, to talk to you somewhere without everyone watching, without having to play some game or worry about what we say or what other people think about it. You know the worst thing about this place? Just how much we have to hide, have to keep close so others don't use it."

"You don't even know me."

"You're right, I don't. Don't you think that's why you're here, though? I mean, how else am I supposed to get to know you?"

Which was a fair point.

It seemed so normal, but in the context of the absurd, normal felt wrong.

"You really are suspicious, aren't you?" He asked the question with a smirk, as if it amused him.

"Can you blame me?"

That wiped his smile away. "Guess not. I think it's just easy to forget you're new, that you haven't had the same time to come to terms with this all that I've had."

"How old were you when you changed?"

"Fourteen. Brax and I changed the same night — scared the hell out of our mom."

I frowned as I thought about that. It was hard enough to deal with this as an adult, but how would I have felt so young? Forced to grow up, to leave everything I'd known?

I reached out and set a hand on his, squeezing gently to say the sorry I couldn't with words.

The shocking part was when he shifted, twisting his hand around and lacing his fingers with mine. It was intimate and personal and so beyond welcome. I'd had so little contact with anyone since being there, beyond the few stolen kisses, or getting my ass kicked a few times. The warmth and softness of his hand was beyond welcome.

"So I've had a while to get used to it all. I've seen people come, I've seen them go, and realized life is what it is. Some shades here, they're looking forward, looking for a way out. Brax is like that, always hoping for some escape, for something to change. Me, though? Why waste now because you're hoping for something else later? I've watched shades come here, watched them strive so hard for some future they thought they could get, watched them ignore and reject every good thing that's here now, and do you know where they all are?"

I shook my head.

"Most of them are dead or gone—which might as well be the same thing. They didn't get out, they didn't get the future they wanted, and the time they had, they wasted. I won't do that, won't ignore what's in front of me now because Brax thinks he can figure a way out *this* time."

Knox rubbed his thumb against my hand, his words less angry and more sad. "I think Brax is the way he is because of what he is. Berserkers are tricky, driven by anger, but it means they don't think things through that well. They're controlled by their baser instincts." He paused, then let out a soft, hollow laugh. "I guess we all are, right? Just depends on which instinct it is that rules you."

I didn't have siblings, so the closeness of the two was something I was unused to. Sure, there was annoyance, but that was true of any relationship. The surprising part was how much affection there was, how much respect.

Knox might not agree with Brax's desire for freedom — or it might be better phrased that he didn't feel it was a productive goal — but he seemed to still care deeply for his twin despite the two being nothing alike.

It made me yearn for that sort of connection. I recalled how quickly my parents had tossed me aside, how quickly Aaron had been ready to move on, even how Moa had used my absence for her own means. I had no one in my life who had my back the way Knox and Brax seemed to have each other's.

It made me feel all the more alone.

At least, it did until the gentle stroking of Knox's thumb turned into something else, something harder to ignore. A scent teased me as well, similar to what I'd found in the bathroom when he'd been starving. It was a draw, something that made me want to lean in, to feel more of him.

I shuddered, my skin feeling as if it were electrified, as if tiny shocks ran through it, just waiting for any sort of touch.

Knox made that same sound again, drawing my gaze up to meet his green eyes, to find them locked on me in that same predatory way.

Maybe this had all been a bad idea…

Knox

Hera was beyond alluring. I had no damn idea why, what it was about her, but it was if she'd woken old instincts inside me, ones I'd worked so hard to smother and eliminate.

I'd been so sure I could handle this, that we could have a nice time, that I'd walk away from it better understanding my reaction.

Why did I need to feed more since she'd arrived? Previously, I'd only needed to feed once or twice a month unless injured. Since she'd shown up? It seemed I couldn't go a week without those hunger pains growing.

Worse, though? The fact that it wasn't just hunger. The old predatory instincts it had taken me years to rein in had woken as well, and they were all directed right at *her*.

Why, though? What was it about her?

Perhaps sirens had some connection I hadn't known about? It made sense, in some twisted way, that perhaps we were bound. Both of us used skills to draw humans in, could both harm and help with the same skill depending on how we used them. Maybe that was what caused it?

Don't be an idiot. This is about her.

As much as I wanted to argue, it was true. I felt a pull stronger than any I'd felt before, as if she'd sparked back to life parts of me that had withered. She made me feel excited, eager and ravenous in a way I hadn't before.

It was the difference between having a salad in front of me when I knew I needed to eat, and being given a delicious steak. One was something I had to do for survival and the other was for pleasure.

When was the last time I'd wanted to touch someone just because I'd wanted to? When it hadn't been my nature driving me to do so, when I hadn't wanted to throw up afterward?

Years, at least.

Staring at her, I tried to make sense of it, tried to see if I could figure out why or what to do. Our time together hadn't lessened my reaction at all. I'd hoped it would have, that I'd have been able to relegate her to the place where all the other people here were.

It didn't seem likely that would happen now, though. If anything, I found myself more drawn to her, wanting to learn more. The softness of her skin called to me, the way she'd touched me.

When had been the last time someone had touched me not wanting something in return? When they hadn't stared at me with the desire that said they wanted what I could give them rather than wanting *me*?

"Maybe this was a bad idea," I said, my voice soft as if I could make the conversation less awkward.

She looked down at where we touched, then took her pen in her other hand. Getting used to reading half the conversation had already become less strange to me. *"Brax said I should stay away from you, that it could be dangerous."*

That hurt. It made me pull my hand back, the same old shame filling me. Brax had been taking care of me our whole damned lives. He was only ten minutes older than I was, yet somehow, he'd taken on the position of the much older brother, the one who had to watch out for me.

The fact that he didn't trust me, that he felt the need to warn her off, dug at old wounds that hadn't healed.

Still, she deserved the truth.

"It could be dangerous. I won't lie to you about that. Especially if I'm starving."

She tilted her head. "*I don't think you'd hurt me.*"

That felt like a cool breeze on a sweltering day, like a drink of water after a long run. It was something I'd wanted to hear but never believed before.

"Brax worries," I admitted. "He worries about damned near everything, but at the top of that list is me. He worries I'll do something that gets me into trouble, that I'll make the wrong choice, that I'll get hurt or hurt someone else. Brax doesn't have a whole lot of faith in others, and certainly not me."

She shifted in her seat, and the action drew my attention to her thighs. Her sweats were baggy, which did her no favors when it came to her form. I had a feeling she had a body that could bring me to my knees beneath all that fabric, but it was difficult to tell.

Still, the place where her thighs pressed together as she crossed her legs called to me, made me desperate to drop to my knees right then, to press kisses up her skin, to strip her out of every scrap of that clothing that kept me from my goal.

I swallowed hard, that need so strong it took everything I had to not reach for her, to not try to draw her closer. Even I could smell the pheromones I released in response to her, in response to my own hunger.

I'd fed just two days before, and yet I was suddenly ravenous. My head clouded, made it so the world shrank to that place, to between her thighs.

Had I ever wanted anything more?

Fuck, I doubted it.

The scratch of something drew my gaze up to where Hera had pushed her writing pad closer to me. "*Are you hungry?*"

I almost pretended she meant the food on the bar, but I was too raw for that. Instead, I was honest. "I shouldn't be, but yeah, I guess I am."

"What if you fed from me?"

Fuck. The words went straight to my cock, made me want to tell her yes. She was offering, and I really wanted, so why not?

A flash of memory, of some faceless person before me, me on my knees before him. I recalled the taste of him, the way his fingers had wrapped in my hair, the sickness inside me afterward.

It was like eating rotten food. It might keep me from starving, but it was slowly killing me, too.

I shook my head. "That's not smart."

"Why not?"

I didn't want pity, didn't want to look weak. I was *always* weak, always the one who needed help, who couldn't seem to make it on my own. I liked the way she had looked at me before, as if I mattered, and I wasn't willing to lose that.

So, I went with what was close enough to the truth but saved my pride. "I told you, I don't feed from females."

She let out a sigh, her shoulders dropping. *"Why not? Do you not like me? Why am I even here, then?"*

"I just wanted to spend time with you."

"But you're hungry. You're hurting."

"So?" My temper slipped. It felt as if she'd backed me into a corner. It wasn't fair, since she wasn't pushing me to do something I didn't want. She was trying to understand, but it was something I didn't want to talk about, that I didn't want to admit, something I didn't want her to know. "So what if I am? I said no."

She pulled back, sitting up straighter in her seat.

Still, I kept going, because I'd rather she be pissed than to risk opening my mouth and telling her anything more than she already knew. "I'm tired of people thinking I'm going to fuck them just because of what I am, thinking I owe them that, that I'm not supposed to be able to say no. Is that what you want from me? For me to just get on my knees?"

I got off the stool, that energy rushing through me, spurring me to keep talking even when another part of me pleaded to shut the fuck up already. "I'm not an animal, damn it, I'm more than just my cock and my tongue and my fingers."

Even as I spoke, I knew the real problem.

I didn't believe that myself.

There was only one person in my life who saw me, and even he doubted my ability to control myself — Brax.

Even I wasn't sure I was more than that, that I was worth more than that. Worse, as much as I hated how much I craved that, how I hungered for it, I still had that pull. I still gave in.

Which was why a part of me wanted Hera to push. I wanted her to ignore my words, to strip off her clothing and tease me beyond my ability to resist. If she did that, I could hate her — hate myself. I could do what I wanted and not have to make a choice, not have to argue with myself. I could blame her for it all.

If she did that, I could give in and know she was exactly like everyone else.

Hera didn't reach for me, though. She didn't try to talk me into it, didn't tell me to take my pants off, didn't ignore me. Instead, she left the writing pad on the counter, repeating the sign for *sorry* as she got off the stool.

I pressed my lips together to keep myself silent, so I didn't beg for her to stay. She kept repeating the sign as she hurried out of my place, leaving me there with the leftover food.

I stared at it, wondered how I could have been so stupid. How could I have thought this was a good idea? What had I expected to happen? She'd come over and I'd magically be different? That everything would change? That I could just be fucking *normal* for once?

I grabbed the tray and threw it across the room, needing some way to deal with the frustration inside me.

"Didn't go well?" Brax stood by the door, his arms crossed as he moved his gaze over the food all over the floor.

"Are you happy about it?"

He frowned, lines showing in his forehead. "Of course not."

"Really? Because you've been clear this is a bad idea. You're *always* clear about it being stupid for me to want anything."

Brax sighed but kept his arms crossed. "I don't want to see you getting hurt. That's it."

"Right, that's always it. I'm just a fuck-up who needs you around to fix my mistakes."

Brax came in, stepping past where the mess of food laid on the floor. We might have our own places, but we tended to consider each other's space our own. It meant he was more than comfortable to walk into my room, to treat it like his own. "This is why I said it wasn't a good idea — you're too fucking naïve and optimistic. You think things are going to work out

Jayce Carter

magically, and when they don't, when reality hits you, it crushes you. I don't like to see you crushed."

I let out an angry sound in his direction before plopping down on the couch. The hunger from earlier was still there, a whisper telling me follow Hera, to apologize, to bring her back. At least sitting kept me from giving in.

Not that Brax would have let me go. He'd have tackled me if that was what it took.

"You're hungry again?" Brax asked the question quietly, something he rarely talked about directly. He tended to prefer vague statements, to not address it head-on.

I dropped my head forward, into my hands, and nodded.

"This is getting out of hand. Your hunger hasn't been like this, not even at the start. It *has* to be her. You can't keep going like this."

"What do you expect me to do, then?"

"Deal with it."

I lifted my gaze. It wasn't fair to be angry with Brax, but fairness had nothing to do with feelings. I wanted him to understand the unended hunger inside me, the fact that even when I was well fed, I still saw almost every person and had an immediate desire inside me, wanted to do things that turned my stomach.

He dealt with anger, but that was different.

"What do you think I was trying to do tonight?"

"I think you were trying to play house, trying to have a cute little fantasy where you got some happily ever after."

"Yeah, well, it didn't work."

"Course not. There is no happily ever after, especially not here. You've got two choices. Deal with the hunger with any of the more than willing people here or fuck that siren and get it out of your system."

"This isn't some sickness that will run its course."

"Isn't it?" Brax leaned against the bar. "I don't think that girl is anything special. I think you've just got some stupid fantasy in your head. You think you're gonna get some magical moment with her, and everything will make sense, will fall into place. She isn't anything new, she just happens to be the focus of your little obsession. If you get inside her, you'll see she's like everyone else, and it'll clear your head."

The way he spoke about her chafed, made me want to lash out. I took a deep breath instead, reminding myself that while Brax and I sometimes fought, while we bickered the way all siblings did, he wanted the best for me.

"I think after snapping at her and her running off, that isn't a possibility anyway."

"She left?" Brax's lips tipped down. "You didn't kick her out?"

I shook my head. "She offered to let me feed from her, and I didn't react all that well."

"What does that mean?"

"I yelled at her and told her I didn't appreciate her treating me like a piece of meat only there to fuck her at her whim."

Brax's flinch said it all, didn't it? He wasn't warm and fuzzy, so for even him to realize just how bad that was said I'd fucked up.

I knew it already, but his face sure as hell drove home the point.

"And she left then? She was able to just leave?" He turned, finding the pad on the counter still. Hera had left it?

Guilt tugged at me, wondering if she had another. She'd lost her voice already, and I didn't want her to feel as if she'd lost her only other way to communicate.

Brax picked it up. "I didn't mean to upset you or push you. I just wanted to help. I'm sorry." He frowned at the words, as if they didn't make sense. "You're about drowning this room in pheromones, and she was able to just walk out?"

That hadn't hit me before—probably due to my own turmoil. Most people, when exposed to that much of my pheromones, would fight to stay, to get closer. Instead, Hera had left. She'd apologized and left me be out of worry for me.

"Knock it off," Brax snapped.

"Knock what off?"

"I see that look again. You're all but planning a future over *nothing*."

"If she isn't affected by my pheromones—"

"Then nothing. Even if that's true, it doesn't change a damned thing. You still need to feed—you still are in the same exact place. The last thing you need to do is complicate your life by trying to create some goddamned fantasy with that girl. You already know your two options, so grow up and pick."

With that, Brax turned and stormed out, taking a moment to kick the tray on his way out, showing that perhaps our tempers were a family problem.

The idea of feeding from anyone else turned my stomach, but the thought of feeding from her was *worse*. What if it turned out like it had every other time? What if I realized she was like everyone else, just interested in what she could get from me? Just smitten with the idea of me like some personal sex toy for her?

It left me stuck between two options that were equally impossible. It might have been easy for Brax to say whatever he wanted, but he wasn't *me*.

All roads led to Hera, and one way or another, it was clear she was important. I just had no idea if she'd change my life for better.

Or worse.

Chapter Seventeen

Hera

Secretly watching the guards turned out to be harder than I realized. Whether that was because I was just exceptionally bad at surveying others or because I was being watched myself, I wasn't sure. Either way, it seemed each time I tried to subtly keep an eye on someone, within a minute or two, I had another guard watching me without all the subterfuge.

Still, watching had given me *some* information. Having lived with occasional bodyguards, I was accustomed to the reality of guard rotation and security. That background let me identify details others might miss.

Such as the difference between a guard who had just started his shift and one who was exhausted and waiting to leave. I was also able to identify which guards were sticklers for rules and which were the type to let things slide.

I found more, too.

I spotted one guard shaking hands with a shade, but when they separated, the shade had something tucked into his palm. I filed that information away. The sort of guard who smuggled things in for shades was someone for me to take notice of.

Everything started to come together — or perhaps it was better to say that there were enough details that I started to get a feel for how things were run.

Every place had an ebb and flow, a routine of its own. If I could understand that, read that, I'd be able to use it to my advantage.

Or so I hoped.

The memory of Knox a few days prior hit me and made me cringe. Damn, it was just my place in life to get turned down by damn near everyone, wasn't it?

Was there anyone who *hadn't* rejected me at this point? Maybe I needed to set up the opposite of a kissing both, where people could come and make it clear they were not interested in kissing me.

If they pay me, at least I'll get something out of my humiliation.

I let out a long sigh, trying to push that to the back of my mind. At least Knox seemed to turn me down because of himself instead of anything I'd done. He had his own hang-ups that revolved around sex, and I was only connected in the most roundabout way.

Though, when I'd spotted him the next day coming out of a room with someone else, a flush on the man's cheeks, I had a pretty good idea that he'd fed.

Meaning he'd yet again turned me down but found someone else good enough to feed from.

Which burned.

I wasn't a great daughter, a great girlfriend, a great siren, and I wasn't even good enough for a meal.

"Stop bothering me," came a voice that made me flinch. While I was getting better at distancing myself from people's emotions, the stronger the feeling, the harder it was to block out.

The indignant anger from the shade speaking, a woman in her forties, was one such time. It battered against my skull, made me swallow down sickness to try to settle my stomach.

I turned toward the voice, finding the woman standing there with Deacon.

He leaned in, speaking quietly.

It made me watch closer. They seemed far too cozy for strangers, despite the tone that she'd used.

Deacon had made it clear he didn't sleep with residents, but I suddenly wondered if that had always been his rule, or it had been created because of a bad experience he'd had.

Jealousy gripped me, especially on the heels of what had happened with Knox.

"Why are you hassling me?" the woman asked, but she didn't pull away from where Deacon had his hand wrapped around her arm.

I focused this time, so when he spoke, even with his voice low, I could easily pick up the words. "You think I don't know you're hiding a knife?"

"You don't know shit," she answered, but the lie was loud and clear to me.

Deacon stared down at the woman without flinching. "I find it, you still get to walk away and go back to your room. Someone else pulls you to search and you'll spend a week in solitary for it."

A muscle in her jaw twitched, but a smile spread across her lips. It didn't reach her eyes, was fake enough to easily spot. In fact, it seemed practiced, as if she were used to doing it when she needed to. "Come on, Deacon…You let me go, put in that you searched me, so I don't get selected again for a random, and I'll make it worth your while."

He lifted his lip into a sneer. "You know better than to ask that."

"Why? We used to have a good time."

That got my attention. What exactly did she mean?

Well, the answer was clear. Despite Deacon's whole noble shtick now, he hadn't always been so principled. It seemed he'd been more than willing to sink that low in the past.

He didn't give an inch. "Don't play with me, Layla."

She set a hand on his chest. "Why not? You used to love my games. Come on—we can go to your place, and you'll feel much better afterward. What's one little time looking the opposite way compared to that?"

He held his hand out. "Give me the knife."

"Maybe I'll take my chances with a random search. I mean, what are the odds that I'll get picked today?"

"They're about a hundred percent."

Her smile slid away. "I'm on the list?"

He nodded.

She let out a soft curse. "Who ratted me out?"

"Does it matter?"

Her eyes flashed a bright icy blue for a moment, as if frost had covered them. When she spoke again, her breath looked like fog. "Yeah, it does. I deal with people who get into my business."

"You're welcome to do that, but it won't solve your issue right now. You're losing that blade — it goes to me or whoever searches you."

She dropped her gaze to where Deacon held his hand out, then jerked her head in a *no* motion. "I'll try my luck with whatever guard does it. Maybe he'll be more reasonable than you are."

"You mean more easily manipulated."

She tugged at where he held her, then lifted her eyebrow. "Let me go, unless this is just your attempt at a game to get me back to your place. I'm up for a bit of cavity searching if you are. No?" She jerked her arm again. "Then let me go."

Deacon lifted his gaze across the room, spotting a guard entering. He released Layla, and she backed up a few steps.

She took off, her head down as if trying not to draw any notice. However, she didn't have to do much to draw attention, given that the two new guards zeroed right in on her.

It seemed Deacon had been right — they'd been tipped off.

She lifted her hands, trying to look innocent as they closed in on her. They escorted her out, but I could hear her starting to spin her tale already, trying to play them as she'd tried with Deacon.

Speaking of, he watched her from his spot, crossing his arms and shaking his head. He looked no happier about her being caught, which made little sense to me.

He went to leave, but when he turned, he caught sight of me. A hesitation there surprised me, as he froze for a moment, as if unsure what to do.

I made it easy for him by rising from the table, pulling my backpack over my shoulder, then walking out of the room.

Heavy footsteps told me he had followed me without needing me to turn around.

"I was trying to help her," he said.

"Don't care," I signed.

He snorted. "Course you do. If you didn't, you wouldn't be running off like this."

"I have places to go."

He caught my arm to pull me to a stop, and because he was far larger than me, it worked. It forced me to stop, and I stared up at his face, trying to give him my best annoyed *what?* expression.

"I tried to get her to hand it over so she didn't get caught with it. I saw her name listed for a search today."

"She said you used to have fun together."

He pressed his lips together, no doubt cursing my good hearing. "That was a long time ago."

"So you do sleep with shades." I left out the last part of that thought—*just not me.*

He let out the long-suffering sigh of a man who knew he wasn't going to come out ahead. "You're being ridiculous. You know that, right?"

I lifted my eyebrow, unwilling to agree to that. I mean, *was* I being unreasonable? Probably. Knowing that didn't change how I felt, which was damn unwanted.

Which was the ridiculous part of it all. Here I was, trapped inside Larkwood, needing to focus on how to escape, and instead I was busy worrying about if men wanted me.

It was the most absurd thing about it all.

Still, knowing that didn't ease the sting.

What was it that Layla had that I didn't?

Especially because he hadn't seemed to mind trading sex for favors, and I wasn't even asking anything from him.

He caught my arm before waving his wrist band over the sensor to a room I hadn't been into, an unlabeled one, and pulled me into it.

I yanked away from him as the door slid shut. It wasn't with fear—I guess I'd moved beyond being afraid of him. Maybe that was because I'd gotten used to the weird, to the fact that no person was all that trustworthy. Instead, I pulled away because of how he'd rejected me, how he had apparently *not* rejected Layla, how little I felt he deserved to touch me at all.

A glance around the room clued me in on where I was. Filing cabinets that lined the walls told me this was a files room. I frowned at the names on the different cabinets—the labels showing different types of shades, different levels.

Were these our files? The records of the different shades that had been here?

The huge room had tall ceilings and the filing cabinets stretched all the way up to the top. A part of me was in awe at the sheer number of shades who had to have come through these doors.

What happened to them all?

It made me feel oddly connected. For the first time, I accepted that *my* name was in there, along with so many others.

"Okay, let's do this." Deacon drew my focus back, and for a moment, I forgot what we were arguing about.

The sight of the room had distracted me, had taken all my focus, and suddenly Deacon's issue didn't seem all that important.

He held his arms out, as if my lack of respond annoyed him.

I dug out my writing pad, not wanting to have to search for the right signs to make my point clear. Nothing was worse than having to come up with synonyms, with sounding stupid instead of making my point clear.

"Why her?" I ignored how pathetic that sounded. If he wanted to have this conversation, we're have it.

He read it, then let out a sigh. "The thing with Layla, that was a long time ago."

I crossed my arms. That was a bullshit response. It didn't address what he'd done or the past or anything else. It was like someone saying, *'sure, I murdered someone, but it was like…five years ago.'*

Five years or not, that was the sort of thing a better explanation was needed for.

He gave me a threatening glare, but it didn't do a damn thing. Once he realized a stern look wouldn't work on me, he made a rough sound that probably didn't have the effect he wished it did — that was an unbelievably hot sound…

"Layla and I were sort of together about twenty years ago."

"What does together mean?" The response wasn't the one I'd hoped for. The idea that he'd had some crazy one-night stand was one thing, but to think they'd been dating or whatever the equivalent here was made it worse.

He started to pace, moving back and forth across the room. "Life here…it's lonely. You should get that by now. Twenty years ago, I guess I hadn't quite accepted that. I was still trying to find my place, figuring out how to make a line between myself as a guard here and yet not being entirely human. Layla wasn't as hard as she is now—I guess none of us were." He paused, turning toward me as if he wanted to read my expression as he finished talking. "I didn't trade her sex for favors. I'm sure you were thinking that, given what she said, but that wasn't how it was. At least, not at the start."

That made me frown, unsure what that meant.

"It started like anything does—I liked her. I thought it was a weird thing, but figured we'd make it work somehow. I spend all my damned time here, and the regular guards don't look at me like I'm one of them, so I figured, why not? As time went on, though, it didn't stay so easy. There are certain realities in a situation like that. I still had to enforce certain rules, and there was no way to win. If I was stern, she was mad and if I gave her leeway, the guards were suspicious. There wasn't anything I could do that didn't make my life worse, and I'm sure Layla ended up taking her share of shit from it. The real problem started when Layla began pushing for favors. At first, I did some of them. I saw it like some real relationship, figured fixing a few problems here and there, turning my back on a few issues, getting her things from the outside, they were the same as flowers out there. Fuck, what did I know about dating?"

That caught me off guard, made me furrow my eyebrows.

He let out a hollow laugh. "That was my first year, when I was eighteen. Before that, let's just say I didn't live a life where dating was possible. So, Layla was my first time trying to figure out what the fuck women even want, and as it turns out, I don't fucking know. Clearly, I *still* don't know."

"What ended up happening?"

"I got her a few different things. She said they were for trading, to buy her stuff or favors from other residents. I knew that was how things worked here, and she swore up and down that she wouldn't do anything violent with them. I asked her and every fucking time she said she wouldn't break any rules, wouldn't attack anyone, wouldn't do anything to risk either of us. Well, one day, she took the shit I brought for her, managed to craft them into a blade and buried it in the stomach of another guard. I can't blame her for wanting out, but when I confronted her later, in solitary, she made it clear that she'd do it again, that she'd use anything I did, anything she could get me to do, to her advantage. I wasn't angry with her — can't say I wouldn't do the same — but it became clear that any sort of real relationship wasn't going to happen between us. This would always be between us, and it would probably get one or both of us killed. She never gave a damn about me. Or maybe she had at the start, but this place changes people. By then, she saw me as a resource — nothing else."

He sighed, and for the first time, I saw how it wore on him.

"So I learned my lesson. This place doesn't foster anything real, not between residents and guards, at least. It's too easy to become manipulative or abusive or transactional. I don't want that — I've seen where it leads."

I stared at him, an ache in my chest. It was so easy to assume that as a guard, he'd been at fault for whatever had happened. I recalled how Layla had responded to the idea of trying to get another guard to do what she wanted.

"*I'm sorry,*" I wrote, meaning it.

When had I become so damned worried about everyone else? It took me back to people thinking I was vapid and selfish. That had all changed.

Which was hilarious, in a twisted way. The people of my old life, they thought I was a monster now. They thought who I was before was gone and had been replaced with something else, something dark and dangerous. As it turned out, I'd been more monstrous before, and turning into a shade had softened me.

He looked at the note, going still. It was as if that had broken the spin-out he'd been on. "You are, aren't you? Even after all the shit that's happened, how fucking unfair this all is, you're actually sorry for me."

I nodded, because I was. I knew I shouldn't be. I had my own problems, and all things considered, a bad relationship didn't have the same level of severity, but I still was. I understood how it felt to be used, how it felt to be alone. I wouldn't wish that on anyone.

And the more I learned about Deacon, the more I realized he wasn't as bad as others thought. He *was* a guard, sure, but it didn't seem like his ideal choice. He seemed as stuck as the rest of us.

Deacon moved toward me without a word, and even me jerking backward didn't deter him. He slid a hand behind my neck and pulled me closer, crowding me for the kiss he seemed to suddenly need. The kiss was passionate but not so angry as the one we'd shared when going to see Wade. It wasn't the one from my bedroom, either, after he'd brought me back from Medical. That one had been sweet, like a test. This one?

It was like giving in to something we'd both wanted, something we'd denied for too long until we couldn't for another minute. I was tired of doing what was smart, and it seemed he felt the same.

He slid his other hand to the small of my back, tugging me closer. I felt his erection against my stomach, and he did nothing to hide it, to pretend he wasn't as lost in this feeling as I was.

Which was damn reassuring. After how many times I seemed to get tossed aside, it felt wonderful to finally feel wanted.

That emboldened me. I curled my fingers into the front of his shirt and stood as tall as I could, trying to get closer, to ensure he couldn't get away. I finally felt this rush, was able to enjoy it, to feel something other than the questions of my future.

"Fuck," he muttered, breaking the kiss for a moment and grabbing my thighs and pulling me against him. My ass pressed against something hard, but I didn't give a damn what he'd set me on, especially because he kept me on the edge of it, and it lined us up so every rock of his hips ground his cock against me.

And it was the first time I realized exactly how much I wanted this. I'd been in the middle of survival, in figuring out how to just live, so even if there were moments there where I wanted more, where I felt some rush of desire, I'd tried to ignore it.

Especially given the reactions people had given me.

Yet when Deacon ground against me, when he crowded me, when he touched me and kissed me, I fell into the moment so powerful, it kept everything else away.

I pulled him closer, tilting my head, wanting more of his kiss, more of his touch, more of everything. Even knowing that, however, I didn't allow myself to reach for his pants. That had broken the spell last time, and I couldn't risk that.

"Can I taste you?" he asked, his breath spilling over my lips.

I frowned, his words making no sense. It wasn't that I was a virgin or unaware. I just was so deep into the haze of want that my brain couldn't keep up.

He slid his hands down, over my hips, then shifted so he grasped my thighs, his thumbs on the inside, and grazed over my pussy, though my sweats.

Oh.

That made it clear what he'd meant by *taste*.

And there was no chance I was turning that down, especially when he stared at me with his purple eyes, when he waited for my answer. He didn't push me, didn't try to get me to agree.

That was what made it even easier to say yes, because right then I was desperate for that. For a moment to drift away, to have that rush of sensation through me that blocked out everything else.

So I nodded, not needing any time to think, to consider. Maybe it wasn't smart. Maybe it was a horrible idea. But right then, I just didn't care.

Deacon's lip curled, and a smile on that man's face was devastating. I hadn't seen that before, hadn't seen any real happiness or excitement from him before. He'd always been serious, suspicious.

Seeing something softer from him drew me in more, made him feel like a real person who had suffered, who had his own share of scars, and one who I wanted more than anything in that moment.

He dropped to his knees, and it made me realize he'd set me on a large metal table beside the filing cabinets. He still appeared massive, and there was no confusion over his strength as he curled his fingers into the waist of my sweats, then pulled them down as I lifted my ass. The metal was freezing against my heated skin, but that was just another rush of sensation.

Deacon grasped my knees and spread them wide, then slid his hands up the insides of my thighs. I hadn't worn underwear—the only ones I had were uncomfortable, and I hadn't seen the point.

Deacon didn't seem bothered by it. He dragged his thumb up my slit, his gaze locked between my legs as if nothing else existed in the world.

"You shave?" he asked, tilting his head.

I shook my head.

That made him frown, glancing up at me. I mouthed back at him, having no idea the sign—and even if I did, I doubted he would—and not willing to try to reach for a pad to write. *Lasers.*

He let out a soft growl, one that said he liked it, before he leaned in. That sight was nearly enough to get me off. Deacon nearing my bare cunt, him on his knees there before me, the intensity of his gaze—it was all so much more than I could have imagined. It put me on the edge, and the first swipe of his tongue made me gasp out.

Which had him lifting his eyes to me, watching me as he repeated the motion.

It was somehow even better the second time, and each touch after seemed to grow, to combine with the previous, to make me need more.

Deacon wasn't slow and careful, not methodical. Instead, he seemed as caught by it as I was, as if each taste made him only hungrier for more.

After a moment, he used his forearms to spread me wider, then used his thumb to move the hood of my clit out of the way. Even the cool air in the room teased me, made me squirm and want the warmth of his mouth again.

"I hate that I can't hear those moans I know you'd be making," he said, then blew a stream of air over me, one that made me shiver hard. "But at least it means I can lick you like this just as much as I want and I don't have to worry about you making noise, about you letting anyone know what's happening. You're all mine, Hera, and there's nothing anyone can do about that."

The statement was surprisingly possessive, but I understood that. While I wasn't a jealous woman for the most part, it was easy to feel possessive, to want all of him in that moment alone. Clearly, he felt the same.

Deacon pressed a kiss to my thigh, a sweet touch that added to everything else. "I've wanted this since I first saw you. I tried to tell myself it was stupid, that there was no chance of it happening, but I couldn't stop thinking about it. No idea what it is about you that drives me this crazy, but fuck, it's powerful. Every fucking time I see you, it's right back there with me again. It makes me crazy, makes me hungry, like this feeling of something I have to have. I kept thinking if I ignored it, it would go away. Then I thought, if I gave in, I'd be free. Now, though? After a taste? I think you're a drug, and each fucking time I taste you, I'm more addicted." His gaze locked on my pussy, again. He lowered his voice to an almost terrifying level, something deep and primal. "I don't think I'll ever not want you, but fuck it, I'm fine with that."

I didn't need to respond, because Deacon leaned in again. He delved in this time, not as careful, not as cautious. He seemed wild, like he'd been right, like my taste was enough to drive him out of his mind, as if he needed nothing more than me, than to get me off, to swallow down every drop of me he could.

And the man was talented.

I recalled Aaron doing this, and it had been nice. It had been a few licks, more of something for him to be able to say he'd done it rather than for its own enjoyment.

That was nothing like my experience with Deacon. He licked me as if the meaning of life were there, like he could get everything he wanted between my trembling thighs. He wasn't attempting to just get me excited enough to fuck me, but was driven to get me off, to please me.

I arched my back, that pleasure rushing through me, overwhelming me. The orgasm hit me so hard, I felt as if I shattered apart. It seemed as if all those parts of me, the cracks that had been put there by life, the things that had happened, the orgasm managed to break it all.

A loud sound filtered in through the crushing release, but I couldn't pay attention to it, couldn't figure out what it was. It just wasn't important when compared to the way my body reacted.

Once I was able to breathe again, when my muscles unknitted, when I all but collapsed backward and leaned against the wall, I opened my eyes and peered around.

Filing cabinets were open, and a few of the things hung on the walls were askew. It seemed like a dust devil had torn through the room. What the hell?

Deacon glanced around, as if just as confused, as if he'd been so distracted by what he'd been doing he had no idea, either. A sheen on his lips made it impossible to not be distracted by what we'd just done.

Deacon lifted his gaze back to mine, and the surprise there said that neither Kit nor Gina had spilled what I'd done before, since clearly Deacon had no idea. "So you're not entirely helpless," he said, his voice careful.

I held my breath, waiting to see if he'd turn me in, if he'd haul me back to Medical, if he'd let the warden know. Even now, even with my pants still off, with my wetness on his face, I wasn't sure I could trust him.

"Don't let anyone know," he said. "Learn to control it, to hide it, and don't let *anyone* know what you can do."

I nodded, because that was the same advice I'd gotten before, and it seemed the best path.

On the floor, I spotted files that had been blown out by whatever I'd done as I'd lost control for a moment. Just as I'd suspected, they were files on the residents. Some names I didn't recognize, and I didn't have time to study them all.

One caught my attention, though. *Gerald.* That was the boy I'd watched taken when Kit had stepped in, who he had killed.

Marked for processing into Lazarus. Killed while being taken into custody. Body given to North Tower for use.

I frowned. Processing? Lazarus? What did that mean?

While I wasn't sure, I did know one thing.

I needed to get back in this room at a time when I didn't have a guard staring at my cunt as if it were a meal and he were starving.

Though, knowing that didn't stop me from spreading my thighs again when Deacon ran his tongue along his lips.

If I can't do anything about the plan right now, I might as well enjoy…

The look on Deacon's face said he could more than deliver, so why not?

* * * *

"You know, I don't normally get called for electronics house calls." Wade spoke as he entered my room without any prompting, as if we were already halfway into a conversation.

We weren't, of course. It made me wonder if that was how his brain worked, if he was always going and just let other people jump in when they could manage it.

It sounded about right. He was random enough for that to make sense.

I knocked on the desk in my secondary room that I used for an office to let him know where I was.

He walked in, the large device in his hand as he peered around. He held it up like some conquering hero bringing home a prize.

Then again, I wasn't sure just how much he'd had to give to acquire it. It couldn't have been an easy thing to get ahold of.

Sure, I'd realized there was plenty of contraband around. It was funny, since people would have assumed a place like this would have some of the tightest control. As it turned out, when people were trapped, they made the best of it.

In this case, that meant having drugs, weapons—I'd even seen someone with a kitten. I'd decided they'd wanted it for a pet and not food, because that helped me sleep at night.

Still, finding a sensor for a door that was still in working condition was far more difficult.

At least, that was what I figured.

Wade set the piece down on the desk. "So, what is it you're doing with this?"

I had the pad of paper out already since I knew I'd need to explain. *"I want to see if I can unlock these."*

"Why do you think you could do that? These are made to resist shade powers. Even the shades who can control electricity and some technology can't do anything."

"I can hear it when people use them. There's a sound when the code is accepted."

His lips tilted down. "Well, this one isn't connected to the main system, so no alarms will go off if you get it wrong. It'll flash green and click if it unlocks and will flash red if it gets a wrong sensor reading. I had them set it to open with my band to show you." He waved his wrist over the sensor, and sure enough, the light turned green and an internal click showed it had worked.

I waved my band over it, but it turned red.

Which was perfect.

Wade left the room and came back with a chair from the kitchen table, then took a seat there as I studied the sensor. I tapped it to gesture for Wade to open it again and closed my eyes to focus only on the sound.

Just like I thought, there was this tiny wave that I could hear, before the light switched, before the click of the lock. It was quiet, but I recalled hearing it each time a sensor had successfully unlocked a door.

It was exactly what I was looking for. I let my mind pull it apart, play with the sound like a toy, to feel the depth and width of it. I recognized just how much more complicated noise was than I'd known. It felt like I'd gone through life with earplugs in, thinking that was what the world sounded like until they were removed suddenly.

I waved my band over the sensor, noting the difference in the sound, the sharper edge to it.

"I told you, I don't think this'll work." Wade leaned back in his chair. Without even opening my eyes, I knew that by the squeak of the wood and the slight exhalation he released.

When I gave myself over to the sounds, it was strange just how much I could hear, how my brain fit it all together and made sense of it.

Which meant I just needed to manipulate it.

I held one hand in front of the lock as I passed my band across the sensor. I focused on the sound, but tried to change it, to manipulate it.

Again, the red light flashed. No luck.

I let out a slow breath, then tried it again. Over and over again, I tried to alter that quiet sound, tried to twist it to what I needed.

"Don't take it personal," Wade said, his voice full of consolation. "I've seen every type of shade try to get one over on these things. I saw a storm demon pour a full lightning strike into one and, while the thing fried, it didn't open."

I tried to ignore him, each time I worked closer to that sound. It felt like a puzzle, one that I had to shift the tiniest bit each time. The continual failure got to me. It made me sigh, my head throbbing as I pulled back.

"Why do you even want to do this?"

I reached for the pen. "*Locked doors annoy me.*"

Wade laughed softly. "Yeah, I think that's the whole point of them. You wouldn't be putting in all this work if you just wanted a good breeze, though. So, songbird, what's the real reason?"

I met his gaze, trying to decide just how far I could trust him. The fact so many people told me not to tell anyone, not to trust anyone with the truth, forced me to keep it closer to the chest.

I knew some shades sold information to guards, and I didn't want to have my plan ruined before I got anywhere.

So even though I wanted to tell Wade, wanted to get his help, I just couldn't. Instead, I went with a safer reason. "*I'm going to be here a long time. If I could open doors, wouldn't that make my life easier? Wouldn't it make your life easier?*"

The unhappy expression he gave me was odd on his youthful and usually smiling face. "Open doors would be incredibly useful. What isn't useful is that sort of heat if you get caught."

"*Which is why I'm trying now instead of on a real door.*"

He shook his head. "I remember back when I first got here, a long time ago. There was a hellhound who, as it turned out, could melt his way straight through the fencing. He never used it to escape, but the second the guards realized it? When they figured out he was capable of it?" Wade let out a sigh. "They took him to the North Tower and we never saw him again. This place doesn't like when people are capable of too much, when they shine too bright."

I shrugged. *"I can't change what I am. It's better to understand and control it."*

"Uh-huh." The way he spoke made it clear he didn't come close to believing me.

Which I wasn't shocked about. I'd never been a great liar, and even now, when I didn't have to speak the lie, it seemed I hadn't gotten much better.

Still, he went on. "Well, whatever it is you're planning, be careful. Larkwood has a long memory. No one gets away with anything."

I took a deep breath, then set my hand over the sensor and ran my band over it again, using all my focus on that tiny sound, the one too soft for others to pick up, and put everything I had into it.

And a split second later, the light flashed green, and the lock clicked.

"Holy fuck," Wade muttered then let out a low whistle. "Never thought I'd see that."

I stared at the green light, at the fact I'd done it, that I could open any lock in the entire academy. My world suddenly felt larger, not so scary, not as dangerous.

I might not have an exact plan, but I had options, now.

That was far more than I had thus far.

Chapter Eighteen

Waking up to someone crawling into my bed didn't startle me. It should have, really.

I was in my bedroom, and I sure as hell hadn't invited anyone over. Still, when the heavy, warm weight settled in behind me, when an arm wrapped around me and pulled me closer, I snuggled into the heat instead of questioning it.

It reminded me of Aaron, of how he had come over in the past, snuck in my window and slid into bed with me.

It took me back to what the world had been like, when my biggest worry had been schoolwork or colleges or the color of my roots.

"*Aaron.*" I mouthed the name despite making no noise, my brain still half asleep and willing to accept the impossible because the momentary fantasy seemed worth it.

A gruff sound from behind me clued me in before the person said a word. Aaron didn't sound like *that*. "Not Aaron, whoever that is."

Brax. I'd recognize *his* voice anywhere. He must have been able to read my lips…

I went to turn, to face him, but he tightened his arm around me. "Just let me lie here." His voice was low, like a whisper.

It was tempting to tell him no, to throw him out, but I didn't. As I lay there, I realized it wasn't even for him. It was for me. His body was solid, comforting a way that made me crave more.

I didn't pretend anymore that he was Aaron, knew damn well who it was there behind me. It wasn't the sweet boy I expected to marry, the one who had been a part of my life for nearly as long as I could remember. Instead, it was a shade who was locked up like I was, who had made it clear he detested me.

It gave me the freedom to relax. We were on the same page, understood one another, had no illusions about a future or anything else.

It meant fuck it. I could rest against him, could enjoy the heat and weight of his body against mine.

"Why are you like this?"

I frowned, unable to ask what he meant. The pad was nowhere around, and he didn't know sign language as far as I knew.

Whether Brax knew that, or he just didn't care what my response might have been, I wasn't sure, but he kept talking. "You're like poison. You got here and crawled into my life, and you keep spreading. Knox keeps talking about you, thinking about you, and as if that weren't bad enough, *I'm* stuck thinking about you, too. You calm me."

He hadn't acted all that calm to me, hadn't in any of the time I'd dealt with him. If anything, his temper seemed worse each time he interacted with me.

"You do. I don't know what it is about you, but you quiet that voice in my head." He sounded angry about it, as if he were insulting me, threatening me. "You don't get it, do you? My anger is what keeps Knox and me *alive*. It's always been what's kept us safe. So here you come, and you throw him off his game, and you steal the *one* thing I have to protect us. My anger, that's my berserker and it's my power. Can you blame me for hating you?"

When he put it like that, I guess I couldn't.

Though, it still felt unfair for him to blame me, when I'd done nothing, when it was his reaction to me.

What had changed?

He let out a slow breath that teased the back of my neck. "This is a bad idea—I fucking know it, but I don't think I care anymore. You're in my fucking head all the time anyway, so how much worse could it be if I'm here?" He shifted closer, as if he couldn't get enough contact, as if he needed more. "I want that quiet, just for a minute, when I don't feel controlled by this rage. It reminds me of how I felt before I changed, before this thing took over me."

I let his voice slide through me, the pain in it, the anger. I understood that all so well, had experienced it when I'd laid in this bed alone, when the life I'd expected had been torn away.

He shifted his fingers so they dipped beneath my top and touched my skin directly. It felt like a jolt of sensation, an unexpected gentle touch that immediately sent my brain in the direction my body wanted. Which was funny, as it had only been a few days since Deacon had absolutely exhausted me, when he'd spent more time than I could have tracked on his knees, when he'd made me come over and over again.

I would have figured I'd be good for sex for the rest of my life after that, yet the tiniest touch from Brax's fingers got me right on plan for another round.

"You're so warm," he whispered before a shiver ran through him, as if he were frozen deep down. "Who's Aaron? I know everyone here and he isn't here. Old boyfriend?"

I went to nod but hesitated. He wasn't an old boyfriend, was he? He was still my boyfriend, wasn't he? Or was I just being naïve and stupid? It wasn't like I hadn't already moved on — still, calling him my ex felt too far.

Brax huffed as he traced the waistband of the underwear I'd worn to bed. "If he isn't here, he's an ex, songbird. That's how it works. Nothing from your old life survives here — not who you were, not family, not relationships. Don't waste your time wishing for something that isn't possible."

I wanted to argue with him, to tell him that wasn't true. Sure, things were weird with Aaron at the moment, but I'd escape and they'd all see. Everything would be different. I'd talk to Aaron, I'd make him understand, and he'd realize I was the same person I'd always been.

However, given conversation wasn't much of a possibility, I set my foot on Brax's leg and dragged it up, over his calf. It was one hell of an invitation.

Was it cheating? Maybe. The reality was that my life was too uncertain to worry about such things.

While I still believed with all I was that I could make Aaron understand, that I could explain it to him when

I reached him face-to-face, that was for the future. For right now, I had to take what I could get.

That meant there was no reason not to give into what I had a feeling Brax had really come for.

He groaned, and the sound simmered through me, warming me. It was deep and hungry…and I felt the same.

"Knox'll kill me if he finds out about this," Brax whispered. "I've spent my whole goddamned life doing whatever I needed to do keep him safe, no matter how hard, how dangerous. I've sacrificed so fucking much, and I don't regret it, but I don't want to sacrifice this. I want to be selfish this once, have you just because I want you, and I can hate myself for it later."

The amount of upset in his voice hurt. It held years of responsibility, of feeling like a failure because no one could protect anyone else. The real world always got a piece.

He slipped his fingers into my underwear, so close to where I wanted them. "Do you want this? I'll walk out if you don't."

Instead of nodding, I arched my back and ground against him, the point clear.

He let out a sigh, one full of frazzled nerves as if he'd been unsure if I'd agree or not.

He pressed his lips to my shoulder, a kiss that seemed too soft for the sort of man he was. He slid his hand farther into my panties, his fingers finding my clit with ease. He didn't struggle, didn't seem to have an issue with figuring out female anatomy. He was careful, not stroking hard at first, keeping the hood between him and my clit, until I grew wet. When I did, he traced his fingers over my slit, then touched my hardened nub, lubricated by my own desire.

He moved his lips over my shoulder, my neck, groaning as he touched me. "You're so soft," he said, his voice having lost some of the anger he'd had before. "Goddamn it, how can you be this soft? There's nothing this soft in this whole fucking world."

He drove me mad with his talented fingers, and before long, I was a panting, desperate mess. I was so close to getting off, to that wonderful moment of bliss, but it wasn't what I needed. My pussy felt neglected and empty, and a roll of his hips made it clear what I wanted.

I reached behind me, sliding my hand over his hip, then dropped it to cup his groin, to feel his hard cock through his sweats. It melted me more, made me all that much hungrier.

The sound he made was almost strangled, as if he hadn't expected the touch or the forwardness. "You sure?" he asked.

I nodded, beyond sure. I was downright *eager.*

He shuddered, then pulled his hand away, out of my panties, and I wanted to cry from the loss. Even knowing I'd have more soon didn't soothe the way my body rebelled having the feeling stolen.

Brax shifted behind me before he caught my thigh and lifted it back and over his hip.

I frowned, my underwear in the way, but as it turned out, he didn't care. He hooked his finger in the crotch of them, pulling them out of the way, a moment before the head of his cock pressed against the damp heat of my pussy.

And *fuck* did I want him.

He held still for a second. Was he savoring the feeling? I couldn't imagine it was that great, but he must have felt differently. He rubbed the head of his cock along my folds, grinding it against my sensitive clit, before *finally* sinking into me.

The stretch from his thick cock was beyond perfect. It stole every thought from my head, let me have a moment of perfectly quiet bliss.

He was far from silent, making enough noise for us both. The dark sounds he made said he enjoyed the snug clutch of my pussy, as did the way he grasped my hip tightly. The drag of his shaft on my sensitive body set off tiny sparks of pleasure inside me, ones that grew and combined and took over.

Brax wrapped my hair in his other hand, using it to tilt my head backward. He was larger than I was, letting him wrap around me. He didn't try to kiss my lips—I doubted we were those sorts of people—but rather pressed a kiss to my throat, to the scar there.

Which felt *far* more personal of a touch. People kissed strangers, but for him to press his lips to my throat, to the scar I carried from my attack was so much more intimate. He didn't say anything about it, didn't apologize or try to make me feel better about it. He didn't need to say anything, though.

His body said it all. He kept hold of my hair, the grip solid despite the softness of his lips and the roughness of his thrusts. He took me hard, each time bottoming out, filling me entirely.

It was passionate and intense but had far less anger than I would have expected. It seemed Brax and I had little between us beyond that anger, that simmering rage, so it was strange that in this moment, that would be missing.

Sure, he took me roughly. There was no doubt that it wasn't some sweet, gentle lovemaking, but it didn't feel like it was hatred, either. Instead, Brax held my hip tightly and plunged deep into me, holding me as if terrified of my escaping.

Not that I wanted to escape. I pressed backward, needing him deeper, needing as much of him as I could get.

He rumbled, a near-feral sound that soaked into me. It sparked visions for me, a sound he couldn't contain, one that gave me a real view of what he was beneath his control.

I closed my eyes, and the image that flashed behind my lids was beyond terrifying. It was like Kit, something deep and hungry. However, where Kit was like ice, Brax reminded me of flames, searing everything in its path, a desire to burn it all. Despite seeing Brax's eyes there, the face, the body, it was nothing like the man I knew, the one behind me, the one *inside* me.

Brax was scary in his own way, but he looked human. Whatever I saw there wasn't even close to human. His skin was reddish, and his body was larger, the angles sharper than usual. His cheekbones were obvious, the edges of his face distinct, no real softness there at all. He had sharpened teeth, like fangs, and claws on his fingers.

And yet, seeing that didn't steal the flames raging inside me at all. Knowing how terrifying he really was didn't shock me like it would have months before. I'd fallen into this world, gotten used to it, become a part of it. Everything in it was scary, everything wanted to kill me, everything was a threat. It meant being able to see just how scary Brax was felt normal, felt almost safer than humans who were monsters beneath, whose other side I couldn't see. They came out of nowhere, no way to predict it.

At least I knew exactly what sort of monster Brax was.

There was a safety in that.

Brax let out a deep growl. "I can *feel* you in my head," he told me, his voice rough. "I feel you crawling around in there. You can see me, can't you?"

I nodded.

He growled again as he paused. "Are you going to kick me out, now? Now that you're getting a good look at me, you want to turn me away like you woulda done your whole life?"

The question struck me as entirely stupid. How could he ask that? How could he think that, for even a moment?

I couldn't even imagine turning him away. What he really looked like didn't bother me, and the way he made me felt meant there wasn't a chance of that. I'd have done about anything to get him to continue.

I shook my head and pressed back against him, tugging against his grasp in my hair to make the point clear.

He paused, his breath rough and uneven, his body still.

That was damn near torture, the way my cunt pulsed, the way I needed the friction of his moving body. I shuddered in need, wishing I could beg him. A roll of my hips must have driven home my point, because Brax seemed to wake up.

He moved, and for a moment, I feared he'd leave. Thankfully, he didn't. He rolled me to my front, sliding out of me for just a moment before his weight settled back over me.

I pulled in a rough breath when he plunged back into me, then gripped the pillow since I had nothing else to hold on to. A part of me wished I could have rolled over, that I could have seen him. I wanted to wrap my arms around his shoulders, to hold him tight, to bury my face in his throat and lose myself in the beat of his heart, in the strength of his body.

That didn't seem possible, but I was glad he blanketed me with his body at least. I could feel his heart pounding as he was pressed against my back, and he thrust deep into me.

Even without touching my clit, the edge of my orgasm crept closer for me. I arched my back so he could fill me more, offering everything to him in that moment.

He groaned. "Fuck, songbird, I'm close."

Was he trying to give me another out? I didn't need that, wouldn't tell him to stop. I wanted exactly what he did — for him to come, to follow him into that same moment of bliss, to feel for a second a connection, to not feel alone and adrift.

I reached behind me and set a hand on the back of his neck, holding him closer.

Brax released a heated breath, then sank into the touch. He pressed his lips to my shoulder a moment before he came with a sound that went straight to my core.

That sound was almost better than someone touching me, than anyone teasing my clit. It was full of lust, of desire, of the pleasure that ran through him as he came. It took me over that edge, swarmed over me and dragged me under.

Brax didn't move off me right away. Once I started to come down from that high, when my overly sensitive body woke back up and shivered, he shifted. His softening cock slid from me, the drag of it making me tighten my fingers that still clutched the nape of his neck.

He groaned before settling beside me, forcing me to release him. He didn't get out of the bed, though. He didn't take off, didn't insult me and leave me there alone.

Instead, he threw his arm around me and tugged me back against him, so similar to how we'd been when he'd come in at first.

The questions threatened me, the desire to figure out what this meant, what to do now, but somehow his body kept it at bay. The way he wrapped around me, the way he kept me against his chest, it all meant I could let go of tomorrow.

For tonight, I could just enjoy the moment.

Lord knew nothing good ever lasted that long.

* * * *

As I woke, I reached for Brax. It was something I did without thinking, before I even got far enough to consider it.

What woke me was the empty bed, the lack of a body beside me.

I frowned as I pushed myself upright, as if I needed the chance to see clearly that Brax had left.

I wasn't sure why it surprised me. Brax wasn't the sort of person to stay, to wake up and having breakfast together. Expecting that sort of thing from him was foolish on my part.

It wasn't like he'd promised me anything, like he'd sworn we'd end up falling in love and having some big romance. That was my old life, the world outside of Larkwood. Here, that just wasn't possible.

Here, a quick lay was the best a person could hope for, and I needed to accept that.

I wasn't even sorry about it. Maybe I should have been. I heard my mother's voice in my head, telling me that nice girls don't give it away for free.

Nice girls are quiet. Nice girls listen. Nice girls don't make much of a fuss.

I'd tried my whole damn life to be the nice girl she said I needed to be, the one who would have some magical, perfect life.

It hadn't worked so far, so why was I still striving for that? Why was I still trying to be what my parents thought I should, despite the fact they'd turned their backs on me?

So I refused to be ashamed. I refused to feel bad about sleeping with Brax. I'd wanted to have a moment of feeling like a person and not a shade, not a resident, nothing but alive.

The fact I had something going on with a few people — so what? Men played the field all the time. I wasn't dishonest, hadn't promised or been promised anything. I wouldn't allow guilt to take hold even when I thought about Aaron.

He'd been clear that I wasn't a priority of his at the moment. When I escaped, when I was out and free, well, we could deal with that when we came to it. I still had to believe that I could make Aaron understand, that if he just spoke to me directly, he'd see I was the same.

That was a very long time in the future, however. There was no reason for me to live some weird life of mourning celibacy, because I was quite sure Aaron wasn't doing the same.

People had to find comfort where they could, and there wasn't much of it here in Larkwood.

Still, the fact I'd slept with Brax stuck with me. What did that mean? Was he right? Would Knox be angry?

The last thing I wanted was to cause problems between the brothers.

I shook my head. It wasn't *my* fault if they fought. I didn't owe either of them anything, and neither had promised me anything.

In fact, that could be said about any of the men who orbited me.

Deacon had given me mind-blowing orgasms, but he'd also made it clear that any sort of relationship wasn't in the cards for him. Wade was sweet, and we'd shared a kiss, and he was the most clearly in support of me, but he'd also made no move to imply he was interested beyond that. I had no idea what Kit thought or wanted—he'd made no attempt to get closer to me despite being a part of my life. Knox turned me down constantly, shoving me away at every turn.

In the end, *none* of them seemed to give a damn about wanting me to themselves—or wanting me in any real way.

The reality was that none of them had proven themselves enough to be any sort of partner, so taking what I wanted from each seemed fair. Maybe, together, they could form a single almost decent boyfriend.

Maybe…

I braided my hair back after a long hot shower, then paused when I returned to my bedroom. The sight of rumpled blankets kept reminding me of what had happened, of the fact that Brax could have left flaming skid marks with how quickly he left.

No, that's not fair. Skid marks implied rapid movement, and Brax had managed to sneak out without me knowing at all.

I pulled the sheets off the bed, because the last thing I needed was to crawl back in later and find myself wrapped up in Brax's scent. I stuck them all, along with the comforter, into a basket.

I didn't have a washer or dryer in my place, but there was a large communal laundry room on the fifth floor. The machines were keyed to each person's band, which meant it wasn't needed to watch them. Usually, I'd take a load there in the morning, switch it during the day, then pick it up when I headed back for the night.

It had taken a few times to figure out how to run the damned things, since I'd always had staff at the house to do such chores. The odd thing I'd learned was that I enjoyed the folding and putting away.

The clothing was warm and smelled nice, and it felt like home in a way not much did anymore.

Which meant clean sheets would be an amazing thing to crawl into and managing to do away with the evidence of the night before sounded good to me.

In the laundry room, I took up two machines. One for the sheets and pillowcases, the other with the comforter. A large lid-full of detergent was the last step before I closed both machines, happy to clear that away at least.

"Laundry?" Wade made me smile before I even turned around. Something about his voice caused that reaction in me, as if I knew it would be a good conversation just because he was there.

I hit the start button before turning, because as it turned out, washing my sex sheets while talking to a different man I was interested in felt all sorts of wrong.

Which meant my whole independent woman who didn't mind scratching an itch when and where I wanted wasn't as deeply a held feeling as I'd pretended.

I patted the machine and nodded.

Wade lifted one of his dark eyebrows. "Laundry doesn't usually call for a blush like *that*. What exactly are you washing?"

I used my signs, spelling out the words to make it easier, since Wade seemed to understand at least that much. "*Just my sheets.*"

"Sheets, huh?" Wade's voice made it clear he knew I wasn't telling him the entire truth, but he seemed more amused than annoyed by it. "Maybe I'll hang out until it's done, then, help you carry it all back. I mean, putting sheets on a bed is a two-person job—minimum." He crossed his arms and leaned his hip against one of the washers, and the arrogant man just grinned. Funny how often he almost looked like a kid, but not when he smirked like that.

I shook my head and tried to wave him off. The last thing I wanted was for him to hold those sheets, to help get them back onto my bed. It felt like if he did that, if he saw the sheets, he'd know exactly how I'd spent the night.

Which had been having sex with a man who didn't care much for me. It made me feel stupid for a second, that Wade was there and yet I'd slept with someone who couldn't stand me. It felt like one of those 'nice guys finish last' things.

At least, until I reminded myself that Wade hadn't been in my room the night before. I hadn't tossed him aside for someone else.

He chuckled. "Fine. I guess I'll let you have your secrets."

I let out a breath of relief at the fact he'd let it go. I was pretty sure if he wanted to press, I'd end up outing myself.

"Since you're still here, I'm going to assume you aren't using your new nifty key trick, huh?"

I shook my head again. "*I just wanted the skill in case I needed it.*"

"Right." That couldn't possibly have sounded any more like *bullshit.* "Still, I'm glad to see you walking around free instead of being trapped in solitary." He paused, then shrugged. "Well, free-ish. Though, if you do end up in solitary, I have to say, there is a lovely spot in the back that is worn down more than the other spots. Easier to sleep there."

And there went another one of those smiles I couldn't seem to help. Wade just took everything in stride. Whereas so many others in my life reminded me of exactly where I was, of how different life was than it had been before, Wade made me think that *this* life might not be so bad. In fact, he made me wonder if I couldn't be happy. He made me smile, made me feel like life was more than just this place, more than just a struggle to survive.

I set my hand over Wade's, which rested on the top of the washer. He looked down at the touch, his eyebrows furrowing. Even through the gloves, I could feel the heat of his skin.

"I don't think I'll ever quite understand you," he said softly as he stared. "Most people here wouldn't dare risk getting close to me. Even the brush of my skin against theirs would put them at a disadvantage, and this isn't the sort of place where people wanted that to happen. Then there's you, who doesn't seem to worry about it."

I signed back to him, going slowly to make it easier to keep up. "*I'm not afraid of you.*"

"Maybe you just haven't been here long enough to gain a good amount of fear." Even as he made his own joke, he let out a hollow laugh, as if he knew it wasn't that funny. I could hear the nerves beneath his words. "I've been here a long time, and I've never had anyone else seem comfortable around me."

"*How long?*"

"I changed younger than most. I was six when it happened, or, at least, when I used it the first time. I could have changed earlier, but I didn't have signs the way other shades do."

"*How did you find out?*"

"I was out with my mom at a bank, and this group of people came in to rob the place. They had guns, made everyone get on the floor, the whole deal. Well, it seems the government wanted to show off just how wonderful registered shades could be, because they sent in a small group of them to take out the robbers."

I frowned as I listened, trying to understand where it was headed. Usually, I could pick up the horrible way it would go wrong. This time, I couldn't seem to.

He didn't move, didn't pull his hand away as he continued his story. "It was three shifters who came in, and they made quick work of the robbers. Afterward, I think for photo ops, one of the handlers for the team asked me if I wanted to meet them. Sometimes, I wonder what might have happened if I had said no, if I'd gone home. I was a kid, though, and I'd just been saved by real-life superheroes. So I said yes, and the handler brought me there to them, ready to show off how well-trained their pets were, how safe, how taxpayers should give them a lot more money to keep their work going. One of the shifters grabbed me to pick me up for a picture, but the moment he did so, that draw started. I felt his powers, the way they slid into me. I couldn't control it, didn't mean for it happen. It was like pulling the stopper in a tub—it was sucked into me like water down a drain."

And there it was, the part of the story that gave me insight, that made me understand him better. I tried to imagine being six, having that happen, how terrifying it must have been.

"He didn't know it was me at first—no one did. Voids are extremely rare, only a few have ever been documented, so no one knew what to look for, knew to suspect that. When he started to fall, another one grabbed me so I didn't hit the ground, and the same thing happened. It was terrifying and painful to have all that power inside me, especially because I didn't understand it. It didn't take long before all three shifters were on the ground, when the handler realized it was me that had caused it. I got a tranquilizer from one of the guards there to watch over the shifters, and I woke up here, in Larkwood."

I squeezed his hand, trying to use it to say what I couldn't.

He offered me a tired smile, one that lacked the humor from before. "That day changed everything. I went from being a normal kid to being a pariah, hated by humans and shades alike. See, the other shades, they're dangerous, but not just by touch. I've lived every day since then with people keeping their distance, with them afraid to touch me."

That drew me short, thinking about my teenage years, about all the ways I'd grown during that time. How different would that be in a place like this? Or, worse, being *so* young and alone and in this place? Around so many older shades, in the vicious world that was Larkwood.

Then something else struck me...

I recalled when we'd kissed, the hesitancy there, the parts he hadn't said but I could read between it all.

I lifted my hands then froze, trying to think of a way to ask. Men didn't tend to like others knowing their shortcomings, and I had a feeling this would be a topic Wade wouldn't have been thrilled to discuss.

"Yeah," Wade said, turning his gaze across the room, as if he were answering something I hadn't actually asked. He let out a sigh, then went on. "You're smart enough to figure it out, and I can see those wheels turning as you come up with a way to ask. If people aren't that keen to touch me, that means yeah, I don't have what you might call a long romantic history."

"How long?" I signed.

"About one kiss long."

I tapped my chest, my eyebrow raised.

He nodded. "It's not like you wouldn't have figured that out, huh? Experience is something that's hard to fake. I guess I'm telling you because it's better you know now rather than have you staring at me later wondering why the fuck I'm as bad as I am." Again, he made a stupid joke, one I had a feeling he wasn't sure how to deal with.

It left me staring at him, wondering exactly how to respond...

Wade

I held my breath. If I passed out, who cared? At least then I wouldn't have to know what Hera would say back, what she thought about it.

The reality was that no man wanted to admit to being a virgin. It felt like the biggest check mark against my manhood. Sure, I could be modern, I could be one of those men who were against all the toxic masculinity bull, but that didn't change that I felt about two inches tall at the moment.

Hera was beautiful. She was smart and brave and way too damned good for me, and I was absolutely sure she had more experience. I'd seen other men sniffing around her. The rumor mill at Larkwood worked overtime, and I knew damn well that both Knox and Brax had spent time with her, knew she had some friendship with Deacon, with Kit.

Those men weren't virgins.

I wasn't a jealous man, one who tended to give a damn about what others could or couldn't do. Maybe that came from what I was, from being unique, from being nearly untouchable by other shades, but I'd never needed to feel inadequate.

At least, that had been my reality before now.

Now, I couldn't help but compare myself. I noted Knox's appeal — I'd seen people with no interest in men *beg* to sleep with him. Brax had that whole 'brooding bad boy' thing down. I knew the history of Deacon with Layla — along with Layla having no problem praising the man's skills in bed. Kit was a black hole when it came to history. He was good at keeping a low profile.

Still, it all came down to the same point.

What the hell did I expect Hera to see in me? My very presence around her threatened her ability to protect herself, could steal a part of her. So why the hell would she be interested in me?

I blew out a slow breath, then said what I knew I needed to. "It's fine. You don't have to worry about it, okay? We're good." I tried to withdraw my hand, wanting to run the hell out of that room and pretend the whole exchange had never happened.

I could avoid her for a week or two, enough time to let the whole thing fade, then walk back in with a grin and a joke and go back to just being buddies. She was sweet enough to let me off the hook, I was sure.

When I tried to pull away, however, Hera didn't let me go.

I forced my gaze to hers, since it wasn't like she'd speak and tell me what she was thinking. I braced myself for disappointment, for pity, for her to look at me like I wasn't really a man.

None of that was on her face, though. She didn't stare at me as if I were weird, as if I were any different than before.

"Come on, Hera," I said softly, all but pleading her to understand what I was trying to say. Better to end things now rather than let it drag out so I could prove how little experience I had.

She reached toward my face, and the moment she made contact, I could have moaned. It still shocked me just how much I craved the touch of another person after being denied it so long.

She didn't stop there, though. Instead, she stepped forward as her lips found mine. She kissed me softly, and it said what I didn't need to hear from her.

That she didn't give a damn about my experience, or whether I lived up to others, or anything else.

And that removed the weight, the fear, the feeling of inadequacy. If Hera didn't give a damn about it, why should I? Her kiss wiped away my worries, and let me give into instinct, into what I wanted that I hadn't been able to have before.

I set a hand on the back of her neck, but the touch felt empty. I pulled off the glove, wanting to feel her skin directly, needing to experience the softness, the warmth, to trace each freckle without nothing between us.

Her power was intoxicating, something unique and different I'd never felt before. It didn't hurt the way others did, didn't burn me, didn't scratch inside me.

Why? Was it because she wasn't fighting me? Because she chose to touch me, because she trusted me?

Whatever it was, the experience wasn't painful as usual. Hell, it was pleasant. The powers from her were warm and light, almost like a song inside of me, one I borrowed from her instead of stealing.

I kissed her the way I'd wanted, without worrying about anything else. She was so easy to lose myself in, to forget about the rest of the world. I moved my bare hand down, then slipped my fingers beneath her shirt, wanting access to as much skin as I could get. If we were in private, I'd have stripped her out of every stitch and worshiped each inch of her body. I wanted to lose myself in her, to kiss each of her curves, to trace my tongue along every part of her.

I felt like playing catch-up, like someone who hadn't been allowed sugar, then set loose in a dessert buffet.

The beep of the sensor on the door woke me up, reminded me we were in a common area that got used plenty.

Good thing I hadn't tried to strip her.

Then again, at the moment, I wasn't sure I gave a damn if I had an audience.

She must have been smarter than I was, because she yanked backward and put distance between us just before the door opened.

I turned to find a shade walking in with a basket of clothing, and my brain was so scrambled, I couldn't recall her name, or what she was, or anything.

It seemed that the whole theory that men could only operate their brain or cocks but not both at the same time checked out, since all the blood in my body was located south of my waist.

"Oh, sorry," the shade said, pausing, her gaze moving between us.

I would have sworn we had 'screwing in the laundry room' written on our foreheads with the way she stared, the way she seemed to know exactly what had been going on.

My normally fast mouth had abandoned me, because I had nothing to say back.

Instead, yet again, Hera stepped in. She nodded at the other shade in an awkward greeting before she scurried out of the room.

I was left standing there, a not-at-all-subtle erection, her taste on my lips, and I suddenly didn't feel unexperienced. I didn't feel broken or unwanted or like someone who hadn't grown up.

Hera made me feel like a man who wanted a woman, who was wanted by that woman, and that was a powerful thing.

I might not have experience, but I'm a quick learner, and there's never been anything I cared about doing right more than this.

Chapter Nineteen

Hera

I sat in Deacon's office, shifting in my chair. It was strange that I could feel so comfortable with him much of the time, that I could manage to not fear him the way I did the other guards, yet sitting here reminded me of the truth.

It made him not just Deacon, but a guard.

"Stop squirming." His gaze remained on whatever he read on his desk and not me.

I froze at the sharpness of his tone.

After a moment, he sighed and lifted his gaze to me. "You want to tell me why you're here?"

I held up the paper, the one I'd already written, had planned out each word of. "*I want to know about the North Tower.*"

And there went Deacon's disapproval. Lines appeared between his eyebrows, a sure sign that he was not a fan of what I was saying. He hadn't been happy to see me, as if he'd known me showing up at his office meant something he wouldn't like.

He didn't answer, but gave me one hell of a glare before he shook his head once, a quick and decisive no.

I hit the Erase button on the pad and started to write again, but Deacon tapped his finger on the desk, drawing my attention back to him. Another shake of his head, then he rose. "Look, I can't force the staff to learn sign language. The ADA doesn't matter here." He opened the door to his office, as if to usher me out, and I got to my feet by instinct alone, as if all those manners my mother had raised me with took over.

His words didn't make any sense, as if we were having two entirely different conversations I couldn't piece together.

When I went for the door, he held a hand out to stop me before he shut it, then opened the one behind the desk and gestured for me to follow.

I'd known he had a door, but where I'd assumed it had been to a closet of some sort, it seemed to lead to another room. I trailed behind him, frowning as I realized it led to a living space.

Was this where he lived?

Deacon shut and locked the door, then turned to face me. "You shouldn't ask things like that, not in public."

I gestured toward his office and shook my head. His office was *not* public.

"You don't think they record offices? *Especially* mine?"

I pointed at the floor of his living room.

"I sweep my living quarters to check for microphones. Leaving them in the office has meant they don't bitch at not having them in here."

I pressed my lips together, unhappy about the idea that others were watching so often. I'd known it, but the reminder chafed. Though, at least since I couldn't speak, I probably hadn't given anything away.

"Why do you even want to know?"

"I want to understand this place."

His suspicious expression called me a liar. "Nothing good comes from that question."

"I'll ask someone else, then."

A tic started in his jaw. "Well, at least you'll get your answers then, since if you're caught asking questions you shouldn't to the wrong person, they'll send you there."

"At least I'll know."

It was funny how his face shifted, how terrified I'd have been months ago when I'd met him if he had looked at me that way. Now, though? I just stared back at him.

Moa had told me before that when someone showed you who they are, believe them. Deacon had shown me already—he'd huffed and puffed and growled but hadn't hurt me. What I'd learned was that no matter what Deacon wanted me to believe, he wasn't as bad as he tried to pretend.

I mean, I wasn't planning on telling him my real goal, but I trusted he wouldn't act on whatever annoyance he had with me.

Instead, he turned away and stormed through another door.

If he thought he could walk away and end this conversation, he was wrong. I followed him, ready to continue pressing for what I needed to know.

As far as I understood, *no one* else had been to the North Tower, hadn't seen past those first doors. No one but Deacon, which meant he was the only one who could tell me anything.

I poked my finger against his back in a jab while his gaze was on a bookshelf.

He peered over his shoulder at me, and the look in his eyes made me wonder what the fuck I was doing. As it turned out, that courage I'd felt didn't last as long as I wanted it to. Still, I swallowed and didn't back down despite the way my heart pounded.

He shook his head, as if he saw my fear and was annoyed that even that wasn't enough to get me to back off. He then turned back to the books, tracing a finger across the spines. Finally, he pulled one out.

"You want to know what the North Tower is? It's hell." He held the book out to me.

It made no sense, the book a hardcover about the history of guns. When I flipped it open, the truth became clear. Inside wasn't the book it showed. Well, it was for the first few pages, but further in were other pages tucked inside it. The pages were written by hand, not mass produced, and I couldn't even start to count how many were there.

I lifted my gaze to his.

He nodded at the book. "That tells you everything about it. At least, everything known about it. The fact is that if you want to understand what exactly they do, why they do it, you'd have to talk to someone who works there."

"You don't?"

"No. I'm not given access there—none of the guards are. Just like Medical has their own security, so does the North Tower. Anyone else who goes in there doesn't get out of it, doesn't come back."

"You did."

He tapped on the book. "And that's what's in here."

That made me drop my gaze to the book, scanning over the page.

A section was scribbled in black ink, the letters formed messily as if by someone young. *It still burns when they give me shots, but not so bad. The doctor seems happy about that.*

Below that was a drawing of a syringe, detailed and shadowed well.

It hit me then…this wasn't just a book. It wasn't information Deacon had collected. Instead, they were journal pages from him, something he'd created out of what he'd written.

I flipped pages, to another with a drawing of a chair that had straps. The writing beneath it was more formed, telling me he was older when that page had been written.

I'm different, now. I tried to pretend it wasn't true, that I haven't changed, but I can feel it. I hear things no one else does — I thought I was crazy at first, that whatever they're pumping into me had turned me psychotic. I've seen it happen to other kids here, watched them lose their minds, turn feral and wild. Is that what this is? Is my mind snapping? If it does, I just hope I kill as many of them as I can before they take me down.

The words tore at me, and I looked at him then mouthed *"how old?"*

He peered at the page, as if he needed to see which part I meant. "Twelve, I think. That was when the experiments they did started to take effect. First, it was my senses that improved. I could hear, see and smell more than humans. Others like me, they changed in different ways. I think the doctors were using different substances, trying to find a way to give humans shade powers without changing them. Most of them didn't survive. Some died quickly, some died later, and some went crazy, losing their mind and attacking anyone around them."

He lifted his shirt, and a deep scar sat on his side in the shape of a bite. "One of them took a chunk out of me. He was wild, like he had no idea what he was doing."

I moved over and sat on the bed so I could rest the book open while taking out my writing pad. *"They were kids?"*

Deacon didn't sit—in fact, he didn't seem to notice I'd moved at all. "Yeah. From what I heard, they'd tried the experiments on adults, on teenagers, but found they couldn't survive it. The only successes they had were when they started dosing young kids. It seems like kids' bodies can adapt better since they're still growing."

"How old were you?"

"I don't know. I don't remember a life before this place, don't know if I had parents or a family or anything. Maybe they stole me, maybe my parents happily gave me up for a handful of cash, or maybe they found me at an orphanage."

That tore at me. Sure, my family weren't my favorite people, but I still had a whole life of memories with them, where I'd felt wanted and loved. Deacon made more sense suddenly, though, to think that he'd never had any of that, that he'd never had a safe place or felt wanted.

"That's what the North Tower is, Hera. It's a lab, a place for them to figure out how they can use shades, how to fight them, how to destroy them. Medical here tests on residents, but they do it expecting the shades to survive. The North Tower doesn't care about that. The shades they pick, the ones they want—they never return. They never come back, never are seen again."

He finally looked right at me. "I know you, Hera. I know you want out, that you're thinking you can figure out a way to use the North Tower and escape. You aren't the first to come up with that, you know, the first to think you can figure out a way to use it. There's nothing new, no idea that someone hasn't come up with before. It hasn't worked, not a single time. Any person who goes through those doors doesn't get a happy ending. Whatever you think you've figured out, let it go. There's only pain and death behind that door—trust me, I've been there."

I stared at him, at the pain in his eyes, at the sincerity there.

Deacon might be right. Maybe it was a horrible idea, maybe it would get me killed, but I didn't have a choice.

I had to try. Staying here was dying too, it was just slower. I'd rather take the risk instead of fading away like the rest of the shades here, instead of becoming just another name in that filing room, in the cabinet of dead shades.

If I had to die, I'd rather it happen because I tried something instead of just drifting away.

* * * *

One of the strangest parts of my life was how fragmented it felt, how I had two different lives that I had to fit together.

On one hand, I had my plans to escape. For this part of my life, I practiced with the sensor to ensure I could open doors quickly when I needed to. I watched the guards. I gathered all the information I could. I read the book Deacon had lent to me.

The other part of my life was playing the part of a good resident, a responsible shade who didn't need to draw any attention. That one felt like the game, like the ploy.

It was strange, because before I'd always wanted to be that person. I'd wanted to be the perfect student, the good girl, to live up to everyone's expectations. I wasn't sure if I'd grown, if I'd realized how little living that way had gotten me, or if I just knew only one of those paths would get me anywhere I wanted to be.

My current part of that pretending had me yet again at an evaluation with Kit. We'd worked on controlling my power, but always in private spaces, where others couldn't see.

Today, we were in an empty classroom — or rather, what had been a classroom, I thought. There were no chairs, no desks, but there was a white board on one side. The room was located on one of the many floors that seemed to not have much use.

Why were so many places empty? The studies seemed to say there were more and more shades, so why was so much of the building no longer used?

"You look confused," Kit said, pausing from his tirade.

Kit was a man who could talk. Not in the same way that Wade did, where the younger man liked to talk to just fill the space, full of lies and jokes. Instead of that, Kit spoke like a man mid-lecture, someone who knew a hell of a lot and had no problem showing off.

Except, even then, it didn't feel like a flex, like an ego-driven thing.

I reached for my pad, but he shook his head. "I know enough sign language. I can figure out what I don't know."

I frowned. Had he known sign language before? He hadn't mentioned it.

Still, I did as he said and signed my response. *"Why are there so many empty floors here? I thought there were more shades now than ever?"*

He didn't respond right away. "Not many people notice that, and even fewer question it."

"That's not an answer."

"No, it isn't. I can't answer you, though. I may work as adjunct staff, but the warden doesn't share such things with me. I have limited access to the outside world, and yet, I have heard that there are more shades changing every year. Still, fewer come through these doors each year."

"Why?"

"I don't know. We only have high-level shades here, so perhaps there are fewer of those while more overall?"

I pressed my lips together, feeling like that was another piece of a puzzle I didn't understand, one that I couldn't see how it fit together. *"And no one cares?"*

"The people who care either don't have access to the answers or they already know them and don't want to share."

I shook my head, then risked looking right at him. *"I heard you're just a lapdog for the warden."*

He didn't frown, didn't wince. I had a feeling he'd heard that plenty of times before, so what did it matter if I thought it, too? He let out a long sigh before taking a seat across from me. "Larkwood is more complicated that most people want to admit. Survival here isn't as easy as it is in other places, and we all do things we wished we didn't have to."

"People like to give me half answers. I'm sick of it."

He made a soft amused sound. "You aren't as timid as you were when you first arrived. I'm glad to see that—too often this place dulls people." It took another moment before he went on, before he continued with what I'd asked him. "The longer a person is here, the more they give up of themselves. Everyone likes to look at me like I'm a sellout. Maybe I am, but I'm not the only one. Do you not wonder why some of the residents have so many things in their rooms? Why they have access to free time? To the internet? Those things aren't given out of the goodness of the warden's heart. They get them because they work for them, because the rewards are payments for things they've done. Brax has gone on a few missions and returned covered in blood. Knox has gotten information out of suspects the guards have brought. We all sell what we have to get what we need—I am simply more successful at it than others."

"And what payment do you get?"

He leaned forward, the first time I'd seen him not sitting straight, not as formal-looking. "I came here like most of the others—so sure I'd find a way to survive it, to be myself, to not bend or fold to the evil warden. I had years here where I did that, where I spent more time in solitary than in my own room, where I fought with every guard and every staff member around. I spent far too much time sitting down with the warden, having her stare me down, threaten me, but I wouldn't bend."

He offered me a soft smile. "I know, that doesn't seem much like the person I am now. We all grow and change, bend to the world we live in, and I'm no different. I wanted to be that rebel hero, the one who this place couldn't change. It *did* change me, though. It changes everyone."

"Why, though? What happened?"

"This place always finds your weakness. They found mine, knew how to wield it and used it to create a muzzle and a collar. I know they call me the warden's lapdog, and I wish I could tell you they were wrong, that it wasn't true, but they're right. Twenty years ago, back when I still thought I could live however I wanted here, I was foolish enough to fall in love."

That was the last thing I'd expected him to say. Love, in a place like this, with a man like Kit?

"People find comfort where they can here, and I found it with Jasmine, a banshee. It was everything I ever wanted, more than I thought I could have. It was this break in the horror of this place, a moment when I thought I could have what every person wants — some happily ever after."

"What happened?"

The sadness in his voice told me already, but I forced myself to sign the question.

"Well, she isn't here, is she? There isn't a happily ever after here. The warden is always watching, always looking for a leash to use on us, and if you give her enough time, she *will* find one."

I thought about that, considered what could had happened. I still didn't quite understand. If the warden had Jasmine killed, why would that make Kit obey? If anything, wouldn't that have made him angrier? More difficult?

I went to ask, but Kit rose to his feet in a smooth, quick motion, cutting me off before I could continue the line of conversation.

"Today we're going to work on how to control your powers when your emotions are high. It's usually those moments of stress when a shade struggles to control themselves, when they do things they don't intend to. With the sort of power you have at your disposal, that's especially important, more so because keeping some of those quiet is best for you. Have you had an issue with that?"

I thought back to what happened when I came, to the way my powers had slipped free and knocked things in the rooms I had been in. I nodded, unable to deny it.

He tilted his head. "Interesting," he said, his voice soft. Through his tone, I could tell he knew it wasn't anger I was talking about. Instead of calling me out on it, though, he went on. "Well, losing control of your powers at those times is as dangerous to yourself as it is to others. We'll work on that, on those difficult times, because you don't want to let the warden know what you're capable of."

He faced me, locking eyes with mine, and I spotted a moment of his other side, the terrifying depths of him that he hid so well. "That's a leash you don't want her to grab on to."

Even if I didn't trust Kit, I knew he was telling the truth here.

Chapter Twenty

I hesitated at Knox's door, knowing I was early. He'd invited me to come over at eight p.m. to watch a movie.

I hadn't gotten to watch a movie in the months since I'd arrived. I didn't even have a television or access to any sort of media beyond a radio that got horrible reception, which meant I didn't care what we were going to watch. I'd happily sit my ass down.

In fact, I'd brought a bag of popcorn and LED candles, which I'd gotten from another shade by taking her weeding tasks last week.

However, my day had ended sooner than I expected, which meant I'd gotten ready almost an hour ahead of plan.

Would Knox be angry with me? Would he be upset that I showed early?

Knox didn't strike me as that sort of man, and I was just too excited to wait. Knox was a surprisingly calming presence for me. Sure, things were weird, but they were still good.

We hadn't discussed Brax, of course, and I had no idea if he knew what had happened between us. I didn't plan to bring it up — it wasn't any of his business. We weren't even romantic exactly, so I could chase whoever I wanted.

Instead of worrying about it, I knocked.

No answer.

Maybe he was out?

It gave me another idea…

I used my trick on the sensor, and the flash of green felt like a rush of pleasure through me. I was getting better at that.

I went into his space — I didn't feel bad after how many had broken into my place. I could set up for our movie night, make the popcorn, get it ready. I could put a blanket on the couch, place the candles I'd gotten, maybe even set a mood that could get things in the direction I wanted them to be. I mean, who could resist fake LED candles and microwaved popcorn?

I thought for a moment about what romance was back in my old world, when I would have expected Aaron to take me to a fancy restaurant, when I would have put on lingerie to tempt him.

I didn't have access to any of that, but I had to hope this was enough.

A sound from the bedroom made me frown. Was he here? It was a deep rumble, but I couldn't seem to make it out. It didn't sound quite like him.

Was he hurt? Was there something wrong?

I followed the sound, headed toward the room. Maybe he'd gotten sick or been attacked? Maybe he needed help?

I opened the door which sat slight ajar and froze.

Apparently, I'd arrived far too early.

Standing there was the demon I'd seen before, the one who had propositioned Knox when I'd first arrived, the one Knox had driven off and rejected. What was his name? *Pele.* That wasn't the part that got me, though. Instead, it was Knox on his knees, giving the other man a blow job. The demon's fingers were wrapped in Knox's hair, clearly directing the action, the chords in his neck standing out.

"Fuck, your mouth feels good. I told you I could feed you, that you'd be happy about it. You're just walking sex, ain't you? You need someone to take care of you, someone to give you what you need. No good reason something as delicate as you should be starving."

My stomach twisted as I watched, frozen in place. I wasn't trying to be a voyeur, yet I couldn't make my feet to move or get my brain to start working again.

Each time Knox had turned me down hit me, and the way he'd told that man he wasn't interested.

Finally, my brain seemed to catch up when Pele out another groan, one full of pleasure, one that said exactly how much he enjoyed Knox's attention.

I stepped backward, wanting to escape the room as quickly as possible, to get out of there and pretend it had never happened. As it turned out, actually witnessing it was far worse than imagining it.

Doing so, however, it seemed my grace wasn't nearly as good as I wished. I smacked my elbow against the door, the sound enough to alert the distracted men. They turned their heads my way, locking their gazes on me.

I ignored Pele—he didn't matter to me—and focused instead on Knox.

He rushed to his feet, then tore his gaze from mine, as if he could bear to look into my eyes.

"I don't mind sharing," Pele said.

Knox nailed him with a hard look, one full of anger and threat. "Shut up."

Pele stood up straighter. "You asked me to come over. Don't act like I'm in the wrong."

I shook my head and rushed from the room. They could fight all they wanted — it didn't have a damn thing to do with me.

"Wait," Knox called after me.

"You've got to be kidding me," Pele said, following Knox into the living room. "I'm not here for some weird lovers' spat."

Knox pointed a finger at him. "Get out."

Pele paused. "Fuck you, buddy. You don't get to talk to me like that."

Knox didn't wilt, even though the other man appeared far scarier than he was. "You need to go now before I decide you're better as a full meal rather than a snack."

I had no idea what that meant, but it seemed Pele did. Fear skirted across his features, but it only lasted for a breath. "Yeah, sure. You're just an easy lay, just a whore who gives it out no matter what. I can find that elsewhere."

The words were totally at odds with what he'd said earlier, but then again, people tended to be more honest when having their dick sucked, I guessed.

The demon walked out, his head held high as if he'd won something. When the door shut, it left me there with Knox and so damn much I wasn't sure how to say.

Or even what to say.

"You're early," Knox said, his gaze on the ground.

I gestured toward the bar where the bag of popcorn and the candles sat.

Knox glanced over, his expression pinching when he spotted it. "Fuck," he whispered. "You came early to set up."

I nodded, then took my writing pad. My hands shook as I wrote, as I could only manage one word. "*Why?*"

He read the horribly written question, then rubbed his hands over his face. "I was hungry. I'm *always* hungry now, ever since you showed up."

I tapped my chest, trying to make him answer me for once.

"I don't want to feed from you," he said without looking at me. "I thought I could feed, take the edge off, then I wouldn't be tempted. We could be normal."

I shook my head at his words, at how he didn't seem to understand. He had his own self-hatred, but that wasn't about me. I couldn't take that on my shoulders. I went to leave, the pain in my chest enough to make my feet move.

Knox grabbed my arm, pulling me to a stop. "Just listen to me."

My reaction felt like instinct, like I'd finally started to accept what I was. I snapped my fingers with my free hand, then reached out, shaping that sound enough to strike Knox and push him back a few feet, to release me.

His eyes widened, clearly not expecting it from me. Too bad for him.

"I didn't want to hurt you. I didn't think you'd get here until after he left."

That was the edge of my patience, where I couldn't handle him anymore. I slammed my pad on the counter and scribbled out messy letters, anger pushing me forward. *"If you want to screw anyone, it isn't my business. You just can't expect me to hang around and be fine with it."*

He narrowed his eyes. "You slept with my brother, so do you have any ground to stand on?"

I had a moment of guilt before I stopped myself. I didn't need to take that bullshit. *"So?"*

"So why do you think you get to sit here and lecture me about sleeping with other people?"

"Because I don't keep turning you down! You keep acting like you're interested, you keep making me think you care about me, you tell me you aren't interested in men even, but then I find you like this. Are you just playing with me? Is this some sick game that you play because you enjoy it? I deserve better!"

Writing it didn't make me feel better. Hell, it made me feel worse, made me acknowledge and admit to how hurt I was by his actions. It wasn't even jealousy, not really. I wouldn't have cared if he screwed every person he wanted to — monogamy didn't seem possible in this sort of place. Instead, it was the fact that he spent all his time turning me down while still acting as if there was some chance.

He chose to sleep with people he claimed he wasn't interested in while rejecting me.

That hurt. It made me feel unimportant, pushed aside. I'd felt that so many times in my life, when I hadn't been enough as myself, when I'd had to be what everyone else wanted, and to be right back in that spot again hurt so damned much. It didn't feel like a specific wound, but more like the day after a car accident, when everything ached.

Knox stared at the words, and despite the pain in his face, my hurt was too much for me to feel bad about it. "I don't want this" — he waved his hands between us —

"to be tainted by that. I don't want you to be like everyone else, just looking for what you could get from me. Don't you get that? You're the only damned person who I've felt like I wanted more with, and the idea of that changing terrifies me."

That sounded good, but it didn't fix anything. I wrote again. *"Why him? Why people you say you don't even want?"*

He ran his fingers through his hair, shoving it from his face. "Because I hate him! Because I hate myself when I give in to that! Because I couldn't ever mistake *that* for what I really want." His words started off strong, almost a yell, but as he went on, they quieted until the end was nearly a whisper.

"Do you think I like what everyone says about me? Hell, they're right—*he's* right. I am just a whore, only good for what he said. Do you have any idea how many people have seen beyond what I am? Who have given a damn about me? No one except my brother and you. Everyone else only sees what I can give them, what I can make them feel. They see me as a living, breathing sex toy and worse? They're right, and I *want* to do those things, crave them, then I hate myself afterward because it isn't me but what I am. I don't blame you for being angry, for not wanting to put up with this, but I don't think I'm strong enough to see you look at me like *they* always do. I don't think I can take it if I touch you, if I do what we both want, and you look at me like I'm a thing, like I'm just a machine to dispense orgasms." His words trembled at the end.

I wanted to walk out, to tell him to fuck himself. I wasn't a doormat, not someone for him to walk over as he wanted to. He had his own hang-ups, I got that, but I didn't need to let him use them like a club against me.

Yet, as much as I wanted to walk out, my feet wouldn't do it. I couldn't seem to get myself to leave, not when he looked so miserable, not when I could hear the pain in his voice.

I thought about how getting sent here had changed my entire life, how I'd felt so helpless. Then I thought about how many times in the past I'd been shamed as a woman, that having sex was horrible, that I wasn't worth anything because of it. It was that same pain I saw in Knox.

It was strange to see it in men, when they were usually celebrated for their conquests.

Then I recalled the demon's words, the way he'd spoken, and what Knox had said.

An orgasm dispenser.

Was sex for him only pleasing his partner?

I took my pen. At this point, I doubted we had to worry about appropriate or polite questions, and certainly not about ruining the mood anymore.

"You said you feed off sexual energy…"

He let out a breath. He took a seat on the barstool, as if his legs wouldn't hold him anymore. When he spoke, his voice was quiet, almost broken. "That's right."

"How does that work?"

"If you want the science, I can't explain that."

I shook my head. *"Do you have to have sex with them? Does it have to be intercourse?"*

The words felt clumsy, clinical, but I wasn't sure how else to phrase it.

He glanced at the paper, then his shoulders sank as he answered. "No. I feed off sexual energy from others—that means pleasure. As long as I please them, I'm fed. It doesn't have to be orgasm, but that's the best method."

"What about you?"

He offered a quick jerk of his head. "My pleasure doesn't matter. It's why masturbation doesn't work, why everything about me is tuned into the other person's enjoyment. I...lose myself when it happens. I become whatever they crave."

I lowered my gaze to the counter to let myself think, to gather the pieces of what I had heard. Knox's statements, his hatred, the fact he never referred to the people he slept with as partners.

Because it wasn't a partnership, was it? I recalled how he'd been on his knees, how the demon had spoken, and it became clearer.

Knox, since turning into what he was, hadn't enjoyed sex. He'd been used to get others off, but those others hadn't given a damn about him. He'd been a toy to them, seen as less than even a real person.

It helped me to understand him a little better. He fed off those he didn't want because it was less painful. The fact that they didn't want him back, that they didn't give a damn about him? It made it easier to bear.

I swallowed, unsure what else to say, how to explain the mess my head was in.

He lifted his gaze to meet my eyes, so many shadows there. "I don't know what this is, but I know I do want it. I won't force you, won't manipulate you, won't push. I can do that, you know, could make you want me, make you stay, but I don't want that."

I wrote one more thing, the question I really needed the answer for. *"What do you want from me?"*

He stared at the words, as if he'd never considered it. When he answered, his voice was barely above a whisper. "I want you to stay the night with me. I want to feel normal, like a real person, just for a little while. I want to pretend that things can be normal, that I can have this, that it's possible." He set his hand on the counter, palm up, and waited. "I just want for you to stay because you want to, because you think I'm worth staying for."

His palm beckoned me, the question there. What did I want? Was he worth the risk, worth continuing this?

And I knew damn well my answer before he had to finish asking. It was simple, obvious even to me. I set my hand in his, wanting that night as well, a chance to distance myself from both of our fears.

Sometimes one night was all we had, and I wouldn't lose out on that.

* * * *

Knox

I woke slowly, as if my body wasn't quite ready to rouse. It was the warmth of another body that lulled me, that made me relax. I knew who it was, which was strange.

I'd never slept beside someone, yet I somehow recognized the body against mine, even though I was still half asleep.

It was Hera's soft lips that made me wake fully, that pulled me from sleep. She pressed them against my throat, over my Adam's apple, and the sweetness of the action drew a groan from me.

Then I inhaled, and the familiar scent of arousal woke my hunger. It roared in my head, a desire to have her, to give her pleasure, to gorge myself on her reaction.

The need hit me so hard I nearly gave in. I lifted my hand, reached to roll us, to strip her down, to feast on her body.

Fuck. Before I reached her, I realized what I was doing. I yanked my hand back and bolted up, nearly smacking her in the face with my own forehead.

My breathing sawed in and out, and I couldn't seem to catch my breath no matter what I did.

Hera sat up, kneeling on the bed, facing me, her hands in her lap. She didn't come closer, didn't try to pressure me, just gave me a chance to realize that she wasn't going to jump on me.

It gave me a moment to collect myself, to calm myself. The noise in my head, the need — it didn't go away but I managed to contain it, to shove it down. The more room I made, though, the smaller an area I made that go into, the more room shame had left to grow.

What the hell was wrong with me? A woman I was damn near obsessed with had kissed my throat and I was acting like this? Why was I this way? Why couldn't I just be normal?

Worse, no matter what I did, that need was still there. Her scent filled the room, and I couldn't avoid it, couldn't ignore it. It clawed at me, refused to let me free.

"Sorry," I whispered, not sure what else to say. I'd asked her to stay, and we'd crawled into bed the night before. Through the night, she'd crept closer, pressing against me, ending up all but wrapped around me.

It had been more than I'd ever thought I'd have, and there I was, ruining it all because of my own stupid hang-ups.

She shook her head, and I was reminded again I didn't fucking deserve her. She didn't attack me, didn't make me feel like shit. She just accepted my reaction when I wouldn't have blamed her for flipping me off and walking out.

I got off the bed, needing distance, hoping being on my feet might help my head clear. "This was a mistake," I said. "Maybe I thought I was capable of something I'm not."

She shook her head again, then patted the bed beside her.

The idea of getting close to her both excited and terrified me. Still, I found myself unable to resist her request. I sat beside her, but not so close that we touched, and stared at the floor.

Her pad was on the nightstand, and it seemed neither of us wanted to move, not even to grab it.

"I don't know what you want from me," I said. It was funny, a mirror of what she'd asked me the night before.

Hera took a deep breath, then blew it out slowly as if gathering her courage. She slid off the bed to her knees in front of me but didn't touch me. Instead, she lifted her gaze to mine, a question there.

I gulped, unsure what to say. Her meaning was clear. Even without having to say a word, I understood perfectly what she was offering.

And I wasn't sure anything had ever sounded that good.

Sex had been almost a job for me, a drive to give something to someone else. I hadn't ever had anyone offer to do a damned thing for me.

Hera didn't push, didn't try to force me into deciding. Instead, she just waited, just watched me. That was what made my decision so much easier to make, the fact that there was no pressure to agree.

I nodded, ignoring the anxiety inside me, the way it rushed through me like an electrical shock.

She locked her gaze to mine as she reached slowly, giving me plenty of time to back out.

I didn't. Even as I watched her hand, as everything inside me wanted to bolt, I held still. Despite expecting it, I flinched when her hand came to rest on my thigh.

Fuck...how long had it been since anyone had touched me like this? Sometimes, when feeding, the other person would try to touch me. It was never like this, though. It was always in the heat of passion, when they touched me because it pleased them, not because it had anything to do with me.

It never had anything to do with me.

Except, it did this time. Hera wasn't staring at me like something she could use, but like I mattered, like she saw me. That was what made me breathe slowly and remain still as she shifted her hand on my thigh, moving up toward the waist of my sweats.

Even with my nerves, even with how I was unsure, my cock seemed to agree with her. It was hard and aching, a slight twitch each time her hand neared it. It didn't feel like it was my hunger, though.

Yes, I was ravenous. I wanted her more than I could formulate full thoughts, but this felt like something else, something more.

She grasped the waist of my pants, then looked at me again, her expression sweet and patient.

It was that look which got me to my feet. Hell, I was pretty sure I'd have done about anything she wanted when she looked at me like that.

No...that wasn't true. I would have, but it was the fact she gave a damn about what *I* wanted that drew me in. If I said no, she would have stopped. I had no doubt.

When I rose, she pulled the sweats down, and even the fabric dragging over my shaft drew a deep groan from me. It wasn't anywhere close to the filthiest thing I'd ever done.

Hell, it was downright tame.

Yet somehow, it sank so much deeper into me.

I didn't sit back down, and she seemed fine with that. Hera rose to her knees, and that put her level with my cock. She slid her hands up my thighs, on the outside, drawing goosebumps over my skin.

I cursed at myself, at the stupidity of having such a reaction to nothing.

Yet, the first touch of her gentle fingers against my shaft made me laugh at that statement. This wasn't nothing.

She didn't wrap her hand around me, didn't stroke me the way others had done. They'd only done so to get me hard, to make me useful to them. They'd never given a damn about whether or not I enjoyed it, whether or not I wanted them.

Hera did. She teased me, dancing fingers up my length, stroking along the head of my cock with her thumb. I could have come just from that. It was embarrassing just how close I was, as if I were a virgin being touched by a pretty girl for the first time.

Hell, if I wasn't careful, I wouldn't make it long, would leave her dissatisfied.

The thought burned away when Hera looked up at me, her dark eyes beautiful, just before she dragged her tongue up the underside of my cock. That sight alone made my knees weak, made me question how long I'd last.

She wasn't done, though. She repeated the motion on each side of my cock, the touch slow and sensual. It felt like teasing, like fun, and I couldn't recall when sex had ever been fun for me.

She offered a line of kisses up my cock, and, when she reached the top, slid her lips around me. The heat of her mouth seared me, the way she didn't close her eyes, didn't hide from me.

It felt like she still saw me, like she knew who and what I was and still wanted me. That shook me more than the softness of her mouth, the eager touches of her tongue, the tightness of her lips.

She set a hand on my hip for balance and wrapped her other hand around the base of my cock. She bobbed forward and back, using her hand so my entire dick was pleasured without taking me too deep.

Not that I gave a damn. I suspected that she could have blown air over my hip and I'd still have come from it. The girl was everything I could have wanted — sweet and tough and so damned beautiful. She didn't have to do a damn thing to wind me up, to make me fall, and yet each thing she did pushed me further.

I stopped questioning it, stopped caring, refused to miss out because I was worried about my past and what I was and what would happen. Instead, I submitted to her mouth, to her warmth, to what I really wanted.

Her mouth was heavenly. I'd pleased so many people, done this for others, but I'd never understood the appeal. At least, I hadn't until this moment, until she about took the floor out from underneath me.

I was so close, teetering on the edge, desperate for release and yet desperate for the moment to not end. I tried to hold off, wanting to stretch this out for as long as possible, to memorize each detail. Still, when she pulled back and circled the head of my cock with her tongue, I made a sound that I would have never expected to have come from me.

Incubi were seductive. We were made to draw people in, to promise them things only we could give them. That was, at least, what we showed to the world. Beneath that was a monster, a starving beast that wanted to feed and didn't much care how it got what it wanted. That monster was vicious, animalistic, but usually hidden beneath that camouflage that drew prey near.

The sound I made was the beast. It was the truth of what I was. It was feral and hungry, and a moment of fear skirted through me.

What if I hurt her? What if I couldn't stop myself? What if I entranced her?

The fear couldn't gain hold, not when Hera took me deeper, when she tightened her lips and increased the suction. It drove all the thoughts from my head—no fear could stand against that.

Any plans I had to hold off were shattered when she swallowed, the action rhythmically tightening her around my cock, and I lost the battle.

I should have warned her. I should have told her I was close, given her the chance to pull away, but I couldn't. It happened so quickly, I couldn't even have expected it before the tightness in my lower back signaled my release, when I made another one of those sounds and came hard.

I didn't close my eyes, didn't look away. Instead, I stared down at Hera, at the way her lips stretched around my cock, at the way she swallowed as I spilled. She didn't appear surprised or upset—in fact, the way her throat worked almost made her seem eager.

I was a panting, sweaty mess by the time my cock started to soften, when I pulled back, out of the wonderful heat of Hera's mouth. She licked me once more, as if she couldn't get enough, and my knees gave out. I all but fell backward, onto the bed, unable to do anything but pant and stare at her.

She didn't move, looking at me, nerves playing havoc over her expression. I could see the questions she asked herself.

Would I kick her out now? Was I going to snap and turn on her again?

Maybe those would have been better options, but I couldn't do it. Instead, I reached out, caught her by the nape of her neck and pulled her up and into my lap. She came willingly, so wonderfully giving, before I took her lips in the kiss I'd wanted from her.

I could taste myself on her tongue, a reminder of what she'd done for me, only because it would make me feel good, because she'd wanted to for me.

Her in my arms was so damned right, and even though it terrified me, even though I had no idea what any of it meant, I knew I couldn't give it up.

Hera was a hell of a drug, and I'd happily sacrifice myself to that addiction.

Chapter Twenty-One

Hera

I held my breath as I tried to open the lock to the filing room. I prayed it worked, that I didn't screw it up. I'd practiced and practiced until I could open any lock on the first try.

This was the time when it mattered. There weren't any cameras in the hallway, which meant the only way I'd get caught would be if I screwed up, if I set off an alarm by getting the sensor wrong.

They wouldn't alert anyone on the first try, since people walked by enough times, and they didn't want accidental misfires to cause problems. Still, if someone tried repeatedly, the alarm would go off, drawing guards.

Which would be bad.

Still, when the flash of green told me it had worked, I smiled and slipped into the filing room.

And was hit with an immediate reminder of what had happened the last time I'd been in this room. The place had been cleaned up after my powers had set so much askew — Deacon must have done that. Even still, the sight of the table, where he'd licked me until I'd have begged if I could have, brought warmth to my cheeks.

I shook that off, trying to focus.

I needed to pay attention, to keep my mind on task. These files had the answers I needed. They *had* to.

I hurried, rushing past the different cabinets, trying to find the one I wanted. It appeared the files were separated by level, then floor. I pulled open a drawer for my floor and level, to find far more files than there should have been given I was the only person there.

My file was there, at the front, but behind a red separator were many more with names I didn't recognize. I opened on, pulling at it without removing it from the cabinet.

Keri Hellen — Kitsune
Arrival Information: Sixteen years old, newly changed, psychological evaluation reveals passive personality, but kitsunes are known for being rebellious.

I read through the information, frowning as I learned about a shade I'd never met. It was odd, to read the file to get information about them, to see them reduced to just what was on the paper. It made me wonder what was on mine, what that would say about me, how they'd make me nothing more than a set of risks.

I pushed the thought away and flipped the page to read more about Keri.

Medical evaluation — high source levels. Recommend consideration for processing.

Disciplinary Information — multiple infractions have led to repeated punishments. Subject appears regretful, but the behavior continues. It is suspected that the infractions are due to the kitsune influence and outside of subject's control. Recommend processing as future infractions are likely to increase.

Final Note — Subject transferred to North Tower for processing. Handover completed without issue.

Follow-up — Subject's blood showed no use for Lazarus Project. Remitted to Corrander Project instead.

Much of what I read didn't make sense to me, so I went to the next file. One after another told similar stories. New shades, their designation and type, their history, and they all ended the same way.

Sent to the North Tower, failing Lazarus Project, then sent to Corrander Project. Some mentioned failure of Corrander, or death, but it seemed every person who had come here had ended up there — well, beyond the few who were killed prior to going anywhere.

Frustration ate at me as I tried to find some detail, something that made it clear what had happened. What were those projects?

Lazarus clearly had something specific they were looking for, something that none of those shades seemed to have. Corrander seemed to be a throw-away project, something they sent anyone they couldn't otherwise use to.

What exactly were they doing to those shades? What did it mean?

I had no idea.

Gerald's name caught me, and a flash of him on the top floor, just before Kit had killed him, hit me.

I pulled those papers out so I could read them fully. I skimmed over what had happened when he was at Larkwood—that wasn't important. It became clear from the files that everyone was headed for North Tower eventually. Even a few of the residents who had seemed to die in other ways had files that said they'd been sent there instead.

I flipped to the last page.

Subject not a good fit for Lazarus. Sent to North Tower for processing and entry into Corrander. Neck injury occurred during transfer, but enhanced blood healed injuries.

It didn't end there, though. This one had more notes placed there.

Corrander success. Subject kept at facility for testing and evaluation. Suggest increase in new subjects for Corrander.

That got me, as if the words were a predator I was afraid would swipe at me. They were dangerous even if I wasn't sure why.

This Corrander Project had seemed to kill countless other shades, yet Gerald had survived? What had they done to him? What did it mean?

Fear gripped my chest, because I had no answers, and I was sure they wouldn't be in here anyway. The North Tower seemed to keep details close, and since even Deacon knew little, I doubted they'd store anything specific in these files.

Even still, I had something. I had names and the fact that all shades here ended up there. I knew for sure there was no other path out of this place, that they intended for us all to be just names in those files, ones everyone would forget.

I grabbed a handful of those papers, leaving the files to avoid bulk, and folded them then tucked them into my sweater.

I'd been in that room for over thirty minutes, and I had no idea how long I had before someone might come looking for me, or worse, when someone might come into the room.

I took a deep breath by the door, shifting the papers to make sure they were tucked safely in my sweater, before slipping from the room. I pulled the door closed behind me softly, and the click of the lock made me breathe a sigh of relief.

"What are you doing?" Of all the voices I could have heard, that was hands down the worst.

I turned to find guard standing behind me, his gaze hard.

He had the expression of someone who was just looking for a reason to be angry. "What are you doing touching that door? You don't have clearance for staff areas. Were you trying to get in?"

I shook my head. If he was asking, did that mean he hadn't seen me exit? I pulled the pad from my pocket and scribbled down an excuse, trying hard to come up with something without appearing guilty.

"I got turned around and thought this was the classroom."

He peered at the words but showed no reaction to them. "You've been here this long, and you still got no idea where anything is? I can't believe you're that stupid."

I shifted, trying not to toy with my hair or bite my lip or do anything else that might out me as being nervous or guilty, then shrugged softly. I tried to play up the whole, 'I'm an idiot' thing people seemed to already believe. Why not use it for my benefit for once?

He pressed his lips together before gesturing, as if the conversation had started to bore him. "Go on, and don't get lost again. Get caught playing with the wrong door'll land you in trouble."

I nodded, then turned to leave. I couldn't believe I'd gotten away with it, that I'd done this under the warden's nose, and she had no idea.

A moment of elation hit me, at how I'd outsmarted him, at how I was one step ahead of all of Larkwood.

At least, it did until the papers slid from my sweater, when they fluttered to the ground in front of the guard.

He peered at them, easily able to see they were private files that I should have never had access to. Lines appeared in his forehead as he lifted an eyebrow.

Well, I'm fucked...

* * * *

As it turned out, solitary sucked. I should have expected that, yet nothing quite prepared a person for how isolated they could feel.

I'd always thought that being alone was nice. It was a break from the world, an ability to enjoy the quiet when no one wanted anything from me.

That wasn't what solitary was like. It wasn't some vacation. It was twenty-four hours a day of darkness, of quiet, of *nothing*. They delivered food through a slot at the bottom of the door, just pushing it in without a word once a day, along with a large jug of water. I couldn't bathe, and the toilet in the corner had no privacy.

It was hour after hour of nothing but my own thoughts. I had no idea how much time had passed,

Jayce Carter

with my food arriving my only way of tracking time. They hadn't told me how long I'd have to stay, so even though I knew it had been four days, I didn't have a clue what four days was of.

A week? Two weeks?

Without an end point, I had nothing to count.

The only positive was it gave me time to run the facts through my head, to try to work through it all.

I had a plan, but not useful enough for real steps.

I needed to figure out what Project Lazarus and Corrander were. I needed to find out how they picked what shades would be taken for them, and what happened to the successes.

All that lead to the main thing—I needed to find a way out of Larkwood, and the only path still seemed to be the North Tower. I might not know exactly how to use it, but that was still the only option I saw.

The lock clicked open on the door, and I squinted when light poured in from the hallway. It was funny how bright it could seem out there, how normal, compared to the hellish cells.

It took a moment for my vision to clear enough to identify my visitor.

Deacon.

He closed the door behind him, which plunged the room into darkness again. At least that was easier on my eyes.

He said nothing at first, but it was easy to hear when he sat on the floor beside me. His motions were slow, which was odd. He wasn't smooth, not like he usually was.

Had he gotten hurt?

I lifted my hands as if to sign before remembering how dark it was.

"I can see," he said softly, his voice different, darker, pained. "You can sign."

"How long am I here for?"

"Another week is the current count. I don't see the warden that mad that often, so she threw the book at you. Seems like breaking into staff areas is a hot button for her." Deacon sighed. "What the fuck were you thinking, Hera? What were you doing in there? How did you even get in there?"

I was careful. Sitting in a cell, thrown in here by guards, was a good reminder that Deacon was one of them. *"I wanted to understand what happened to the others, to all the shades who came before me."*

"Why? What do some dead shades matter to you?"

"Because it's where I'm going, too, isn't it? We're all headed to the North Tower, aren't we?"

"Yeah," he admitted. "But you'll end up there a lot fucking faster if you make stupid choices like that. If you act like an idiot, you'll get sent there well before you're ready."

"So you want me to be a good girl? To sit down and shut up and follow the rules?"

Even as I asked, the words felt sharp. That was exactly what I'd done before, wasn't it? I'd always worked toward being what I was supposed to, yet now the idea was unfathomable. I couldn't just shut my yes and pretend none of this was happening. I couldn't wait here, knowing I was just biding my time until Larkwood decided to throw me to the North Tower, to the horrors there.

"I want you to be smart. If there's a tiger, it might kill you, but pulling its tail won't help you. It'll just make sure it eats you quicker."

I shook my head. It was easy for him to say that,

because he wasn't part of this world. He had no idea what it felt like to be trapped, to have no choices, and to tell me to just wait it out was too far. *I just had to know,* I told him. It was true, even if it didn't tell him why.

"Do you feel better now? Did knowing help you at all? You're stuck in solitary, on the warden's radar, and all you've gotten out of it is knowing that every person who came before you died in these walls. So, Hera, was it worth it?"

I thought about the names I'd seen, how nearly all of them were marked as deceased, and how my own file had been in there as well. Those shades had died because they didn't know what they faced, because they weren't prepared.

I knew what was coming for me, knew the risks, and I'd do whatever I had to do.

"It was worth it," I signed.

Deacon let out a frustrated sound before he got to his feet, his motions still halted and slow. "Well, we'll see if another four days doesn't change that for you. If we're lucky, you'll see what a stupid idea this was, and you'll smarten up." He paused by the door, when he opened it and was illuminated by the hallway light. "Please, Hera, smarten up. I don't want to see them add Project Lazarus or Corrander to your file."

He didn't look back, even as my hands moved, as I tried to ask questions. He closed the door, leaving me alone in the cell with more questions and only one answer.

Deacon knew about the two projects. Without me naming them, he knew exactly what had been on those papers.

What else did Deacon know exactly?

Whatever it was, I knew I couldn't trust him.

Chapter Twenty-Two

A bath was beyond orgasmic after what turned out to be fourteen days in solitary. A layer of dirt covered me, and the ring of brown left in the tub after the water drained said I'd needed the bath.

Deacon hadn't escorted me back to my room, which had surprised me. Where was he?

I recalled the way he'd moved, slow and pained, but tried not to let the worry settle. After what he'd said, after realizing he was keeping secrets from me, I didn't believe he deserved my concern.

So instead of checking on him, I'd pulled myself to my own room after they'd released me, my legs tired and my eyes so sensitive to the light I had trouble even opening them. Mostly, I'd made the trip by sound and memory alone.

Still, washing off the filth made me feel alive again, and less like an animal.

The heat of the bathroom made me sit on the closed toilet, my body so tired that the walk to my bed seemed too far away to be possible.

Eventually, though, I grasped the counter and pulled myself to my feet. I opened the door, ready to collapse into my covers and sleep for the eighteen hours before my next class.

Except, I didn't find my room nearly as empty as I'd expected it to be.

Instead, Knox, Brax and Wade were there. Brax paced, while Wade read one of my books as he leaned against the bookshelf and Knox had stretched out on my bed.

It took me by surprise, made me pause there in the doorway of the bathroom. The men took up far too much space in my room, making it feel smaller than it ever had before.

Brax noticed me first, stopping his pacing to land a heavy look on me. He moved his gaze over me, head to foot, as if checking if I was okay.

It was strange, because it almost felt like he gave a damn.

I lifted my hands and signed, *"What are you doing here?"*

Wade translated, since it seemed Brax didn't know any sign language.

"You got out of solitary," Knox said, not moving from his place on my bed. His arm was up and behind his head, looking far too comfortable and tempting. "Wanted to check up on you."

I frowned. *"You all know each other?"*

Wade let out a soft laugh. "The world is pretty small here at Larkwood. We didn't plan this, though. I came and Knox was already here. Brax showed up a few minutes later. Seems you have more friends than you thought."

Brax made a dismissive sound, as if friends wasn't even close to an accurate description but didn't speak.

"I don't understand."

Knox turned his head to look at me. "You were caught in a filing room."

I shrugged.

"That's why you wanted the sensor, wasn't it?" Wade asked.

Brax turned toward Wade, his eyes narrowing. "*You* gave her a sensor to practice that trick on? What the fuck were you thinking? If a guard caught her with that—"

"Would it have been better to have her trying to practice on real locks? Where she could get caught trying to break into something? Contraband is miles less trouble than breaking into restricted areas."

Brax didn't appear any less angry at the answer, even though he nodded as if admitting Wade might be right.

Knox, however, ignored their fight. He sat up and met my gaze. "You keep telling me that you just want to get along, that you don't want trouble. Clearly, that's not true. You're watching guards, you're practicing opening locks, you're asking questions. All that points to you having some sort of plan."

He didn't ask me to tell him my plan, but the point was clear.

Still, it didn't come. I'd learned over and over again that trust was bad, that I couldn't rely on others, that they'd turn their backs on me the moment they could.

"For fuck's sake," Brax all but snarled, advancing on me until I had to stare up at his angry face. "You got yourself caught because you're doing whatever this is on your own. You want the reality of Larkwood? The guards and the warden work really fucking hard to keep us separate and at each other's throats, and do you know why? Because shades are scary on our own but when we stop fighting each other and work together? We're fucking terrifying. I've watched people here, waiting for an opening, seeing where they went wrong, and it's always the same. They get fucked over because they're one person against an entire organization."

I swallowed, then stepped past him so I had enough space to sign a response. "*I don't know what you're talking about.*"

Wade closed my book and set it back on the shelf. "You're looking to escape. You wouldn't be the first, but you know what? You might be the first who has a shot. At least, you might if you stop trying to do it all on your own."

I frowned. "*You want to escape?*"

Knox gave me a sarcastic look. "*Everyone* who is here wants to escape. I doubt there's a single person — well, maybe Kit — who's actually happy here. It's just a matter of deciding if it's possible, and so far? It hasn't been. What were you doing in the filing room, songbird?"

The nickname, spoken sweetly like he tended to do, pulled me in. They weren't wrong. What I'd found out over and over again was that ignoring the fact that others here knew more, that they'd been here longer, that they had information I lacked had screwed me over. It had been Deacon's knowledge of the North Tower that had clued me in on details there, and Wade who had given me the sensory to practice on, and Kit who had given me the book. Knox had warned me about the ambush and Brax had...well, mostly he'd insulted me, but I'd bet he still had uses. The reality was that these three men could help.

I just had to risk it, had to let them in, had to trust them.

Which wasn't so easy a thing.

"If you want out of here," Knox said, "then you need to start trusting us. You want to get out? You want some shot at a real life? Well, there's no reward without risk."

I looked between the three men, reminded of what Deacon had told me — *No one has ever escaped Larkwood before.*

Still, I had the first real moment of hope, the first time I thought it might be possible, that I wasn't totally alone in it all.

My hands moved, and after Wade translated my statement, the others nodded in agreement.

"Let's escape Larkwood Academy."

Want to see more from this author?
Here's a taster for you to enjoy!

Larkwood Academy: Whispers
Jayce Carter

Excerpt

I never missed my voice more than when Deacon touched me, when I opened my mouth and wanted to moan his name.

Sure, there were other times it annoyed me, when I wanted to tell someone off, when I wanted to explain myself, when I just wanted to *be heard*. Those times irked, but the loss never bothered me as much as when Deacon teased his lips over my breast, when the lack of noise from me made it feel incomplete.

Not that Deacon seemed to mind — or perhaps it was better to say he could make up for it easily. He might not have been the most vocal man usually, but that all changed in bed.

I looked around for a moment, noting the quiet corner of a shed in the yard where we'd tucked ourselves away. *Maybe bed is a stretch…*

We couldn't risk people catching on to us, which had left us finding out-of-the-way spots like this for these little rendezvous. Neither of us wanted to turn into a weakness for the other.

"I missed you," Deacon whispered in his low voice against my skin, his breath warm and rapid.

I loved these moments, how he lost that composure he usually had, how he seemed like anyone else. Normally Deacon was bigger than life, a guard at Larkwood Academy who even the other guards feared and distrusted.

In these moments, though, he wasn't any of that. He was just *mine*.

I set my hand on the back of his neck and brought him closer, pulled him to my body until I could try to tell him the things I couldn't say with my kiss.

He groaned against my lips, then grabbed my thigh to pull it around him. My ass pressed against the small table I sat on, but I didn't care about anything. Not splinters, not discomfort, nothing but drowning myself in these rare moments of happiness.

I'd lived at Larkwood for months, had mostly accepted the brutality that made up my world now, but that made these moments even more important. When Deacon touched me, when he growled into my ear, it made the rest of the ugliness of my life drift away.

He sank his cock into me, and I dug my nails into his back. It was always this wonderful burn when he took me, when I could feel entirely filled by him.

So I lost myself in him, in his strength, in the rough, whispered praise he offered. Too soon, it ended. Too quickly, I wiped off and pulled my sweats back on, brushing my hair with my fingers to appear presentable. We never had much time, never got to indulge in the quiet happiness when normal people could enjoy languid motions and gentle kisses through the night.

Deacon buttoned his pants, his expression having shifted back to the usual closed off one he showed to everyone else. No doubt that was one reason I so cherished the times we had, because it was the only chance I got to really see him.

"You need to be more careful," he muttered.

I turned toward him, furrowing my brows.

The zipper of his pants was loud in the quiet shed. "You've got guards watching you. Warden put out a memo to keep a close eye on you. You think they don't know you've been meeting up with those delinquents you seem to think are friends?"

I pressed my lips together and narrowed my eyes. Of course Deacon didn't care for the other connections I'd made—he considered all the shades dangerous, so he saw any other resident a risk to me.

What he didn't get was that *everything* was a risk to me. The whole damned world seemed to want to take me apart, to pull me to pieces until nothing was left.

He came forward and set his hand on the back of my neck, angling my face so I looked right into those bright purple eyes of his. Those eyes had ushered me into my new life at one time, but they meant so much more to me now. "I don't want to lose you, Hera. You can't trust anyone, can't let your guard down. Whatever they're talking you into, it'll get you killed."

I set my hand on his chest and pushed. He didn't move because of the pressure, but on his own. I could have used my powers, my ability to control sound waves, but I tried my hardest to keep that hidden. I'd finally gotten to where I didn't do it on accident, so I kept it on a tight leash.

"Nothing to say?" Anger flashed across his features, but I didn't fear him. I knew him too well already, knew he'd never hurt me, at least not on purpose. Sure, he was a guard at the very place holding me captive, but he did all he could to keep me safe.

"No one makes me do anything," I signed to him.

"You're too naïve," he snapped. "You think I don't know they're trouble? That they're looking for some magical way out? Look, this place has stood for a long-damned time, and no level one shade has ever escaped. A lot of them have died trying, though. I don't care how good a *friend* you think they are, they'll let you take the fall if it benefits them at all."

Deacon's words were callous but not unexpected.

We'd done this for weeks, ever since I'd left solitary after being caught breaking into that file room. Deacon was smart enough to know I was up to something, but pushing too much might just end up making me a bigger target. It had driven a wedge between us, one that hurt more than I liked to admit.

I hated having to separate my life, to keep things from all the people around me, but I didn't have a choice.

Deacon couldn't find out about the plans I had with Wade, Knox and Brax, and the three of them couldn't know the extent of my relationship with Deacon.

Though I had a feeling all the men in my life had made wrong guesses about each other. It was in the looks, in the aggression they all showed when talking about each other. No doubt each of them assumed I was sleeping with all the others in my life.

Which wasn't true.

Though not because of lack of effort on my side.

It just turned out romance was as foreign a concept to me as the economics of other countries and how football worked. Getting people into bed was much more difficult than I'd have ever imagined. I recalled all the times I'd heard as a teenager how boys were animals who only wanted one thing, how I had to be careful as a woman or I'd get taken advantage of.

Yet most of these men were not taking advantage of me in the way I wanted them to, no matter how I tried to tempt them.

Not that telling them that would matter. Deception was a way of life here at Larkwood, and we *all* had our secrets.

"Don't fight with me. We don't have long."

"I'm not trying to fight," he assured me, despite the aggressive tone of voice that he used almost exclusively for fighting. "I just worry about you. I'm afraid I'll open my email and see your name on the North Tower list. I don't want that."

Which, to be fair, neither did I. Despite the fact The North Tower seemed my only real escape option, I wasn't ready to face that horror just yet. I needed a better plan, more information, anything to give me an edge.

But it wasn't as if I could admit any of that to Deacon. If he discovered any plan for escape I had, he'd just ruin it to protect me.

So I had to keep that all close to my chest. *"You don't need to worry about me."*

He made a soft sound low in his throat, as if he couldn't believe what an idiot I was. "Of course I do. You're trouble, Hera, and you attract trouble like a fucking magnet. Don't forget, I was the one who saved you that night when you changed. I saw it all. I know exactly how much you need someone worrying about you."

I dropped my gaze at the painful reminder, at the fact he was right. If it wasn't for him, I'd have died on that parking structure floor. I'd have bled out from the man who had slit my throat, the one who had taken my voice.

Instead, Deacon had heard my scream, had come and saved me.

Then he'd brought me to Larkwood.

It was a complicated relationship.

He reached forward again, but he didn't touch my cheek. Instead, he touched the scar at my throat, the whole reason I couldn't speak. "You almost died. *This* happened because the world didn't like what you were. I saved you that time, but I'm terrified I won't be able to the next, that you'll do something stupid and end up in a situation I can't do anything about." His words were so soft, so sad that they took me back.

I forced myself to stare into his eyes, to witness the pain and fear there. For all Deacon's faults — and there were a lot of them — he wasn't a bad man. He wanted the best for me.

The problem?

We didn't agree what was best. He wanted me alive even if it meant losing everything else. I wanted freedom, even if it meant risking my life for it.

It was an impasse I didn't know how to fix.

"I don't want to see you get finished off because you want to escape," he whispered.

I forced my hand up so I could sign back. *"I'm not planning anything."*

* * * *

"So, what's the plan for our escape?"

Knox let out a laugh as he read what I had signed. "You really don't beat around the bush, do you?"

I shrugged before reaching into his fridge for a water. It was odd to think that weeks before, I'd been so nervous in his place, so afraid of doing anything wrong, of upsetting him.

Now I treated his space as if it were my own, and each time I did? He seemed to smile a little wider.

I held one water out to him, but he shook his head. It gave me the chance to look at him for a moment, surprised as ever by just how handsome he was.

He had a body that could have tempted me even if he weren't the kind man he was. He was lean but strong, and he kept his hair so short it was basically buzzed off. He had on a T-shirt, and while that wasn't normally the type of outfit to swoon over, he made even it look amazing.

Then again, that was partly due to the general sensuality he had, all thanks to his incubus side. He was a walking billboard offering sex, and while he and I had never fully gone there, it didn't make me immune to noticing.

"How's Deacon?"

I let out an obvious sigh along with an eye roll for good measure. *"Why do you ask?"*

"You're way too casual with him." Knox shook his head, the same argument I'd had with him a few times. I'd had the same fight with Brax as well, though my fights with him were more yelling—at least from him—and always ended up with us having angry sex. Wade didn't bitch, but his snarky comments had suggested he didn't approve.

Knox at least acted nice when we argued.

"It's nothing to worry about."

"You say that because you don't know the real him. If he gets wind of anything, he'll turn you in right away."

"He wouldn't do that."

Knox didn't know Deacon like I did. Sure, I wasn't rushing to tell Deacon everything—that would have been stupid. But I was fully capable of spending time with him without blurting out everything on my mind.

The fact I can't speak helps.

Knox set a hand on my cheek, his palm warm and teasing. He stroked his thumb against my skin. "The fact you can still have some of that innocence after being here is amazing. I just don't want to see it get your killed because you trusted the wrong person."

His words melted some of my annoyance. I understood his worry, especially because if I made the wrong choice, if I trusted the wrong person, if we got caught, Knox and his brother could easily pay the price for it.

Even with that, though, I couldn't just *not* spend time with Deacon. Sure, things would end when I escaped, because what sort of future was there? That should have made it easier to let go now, before I got too attached, but the opposite seemed true.

I just couldn't imagine ending it sooner than I had to.

Knox offered a half-hearted smile, as if I were an idiot climbing too high into a tree and he knew I'd fall and break something. "You are impossible." He leaned in and brushed his warm lips against mine, the touch gentle and sweet.

And it did what his innocent touches *always* did to me. A rush of sensation, like drowning and suddenly being able to breathe all at once. It was his power, that incubus part of him hungry and wanting to feed.

But he'd refused to feed from me or to touch me beyond the bare minimum. I'd been able to touch him, to focus on him, but he never reciprocated. It wasn't selfishness but fear.

As soon as it happened, however, he pulled back and shook his head hard, as though to clear it.

"It's okay," I told him the way I always did, even when his rejection hurt, even when it didn't feel okay at all.

"It's not."

I missed the warmth of his hand when he took it away, when we stood there with this distance between us that I had no idea how to fix. Understanding the reason for it didn't change the hurt. No matter what I did, he didn't trust himself, didn't trust that other part of himself, didn't want it near me.

And there wasn't a thing I could do about that.

Instead of letting him see just how much it hurt, I turned away and brought the water bottle to my lips, trying to let the cold liquid cool my flushed cheeks and slow my racing heart.

Why the hell was my libido like this, anyway? I'd never given a damn about sex before coming to Larkwood, before finding myself tied to a few different men. It hadn't been bad at all, but I'd never cared one way or the other about it. I had to guess my new desires had to do with changing into a shade.

"Hera," Knox started to say, but the opening of his door front saved me.

Sort of.

I wasn't sure if the angry face of a berserker who I felt certain hated me counted as being saved.

"Have you found anything yet?" Brax asked, his tone annoyed.

Was he ever *not* annoyed, though? Maybe, when around others. I had no idea if it was just me or if he was always unpleasant.

Judging from his glare my way, I'd say it was a mixture.

"Nothing yet."

Knox translated for me, since Brax seemed the only person unable—or more likely unwilling—to learn American Sign Language. When it was just the two of us, I used my writing pad, but when others were around, they translated.

"So what good are you? You had this big idea about wanting to escape but then you get nothing over the last month? Fuck, I hate people who are all talk."

And, as usual, I rose to the occasion when it came to his anger. Funny that back when I'd first met him, he'd terrified me. Now? Now I didn't give a fuck about his little hissy fits. If he hadn't killed me yet, he probably wouldn't.

Most likely…

I was pretty sure…

"I'm sorry that I'm not doing enough for you. What exactly was it you've done? Because I figured out about the North Tower and the two projects they're doing there."

Brax narrowed his blue eyes into a murderous glare as Knox translated. At the end, he let out a huff. "Well, don't get sloppy. If you fuck up, we all go down, and I'm not about to let that happen."

I lifted my eyebrow to stare back. What was the point in arguing? Brax only heard what he wanted to hear, and having Knox translate everything made it all take longer.

"Be careful," Knox offered, his voice even gentler than before, as if trying to make up for the attitude of his twin.

Then again, the two were always looking out for each other. Brax tried to protect Knox and Knox made excuses for Brax's horrible behavior.

When I didn't respond, Knox went on. "After getting thrown in solitary, you're bound to get watched more closely. I know Brax is pushing you, but don't do anything risky."

Brax opened his mouth as if to argue that point but snapped his lips together before he could. He let out an angry sound and the edges of his face sharpened the way they always did when his temper got away from him. Berserkers weren't known for their control and calm. Instead of saying anything else, he turned on his heel and stormed out, slamming the door behind him, his exit as dramatic and quick as his entrance had been.

Knox sighed, his gaze pinned to the door as if he could still watch his brother through it. "I swear, his temper is worse than ever."

It seemed the same to me. The only reason he was annoyed there was because he wanted me to do whatever it took, no matter the danger to me, and the fact it was a dick-thing to say frustrated him.

"You don't understand him," Knox said.

"Stop defending him."

"That's never going to happen." Knox gave me a sad smile. "He's not the easiest to get along with, but there's more to him than anyone realizes. Don't take the things he says at face value."

I took another drink of water, mostly to give us a way to end the conversation. I knew what Brax was like, had experienced his brand of asshole behavior plenty of times. The last thing I needed was for Brax's bad behavior to sour my relationship with Knox.

It was already all rather precarious.

Knox glanced behind him at the clock on the wall. "You already had your work detail this morning, right?"

"I have an evaluation in about an hour."

He pressed his lips together, and I knew he was getting ready to lecture me yet again. This time, about Kit.

But what did all these warnings matter? I couldn't just not see Kit since the adjunct professor handled not only teaching lessons but also most of the evaluations. It wasn't like I had an option to not go.

Besides, we hadn't had one since solitary, since I'd gotten caught with files from a restricted room. After spending the time in isolation, I'd had my work details increased for two weeks after. That made this the first eval since that had all happened.

Which meant I'd probably get an earful from him as well.

Why was it that everyone thought I needed their advice? That everyone saw me as a helpless creature who others had to tell how to behave?

Well, I did get caught when I tried stuff on my own.

I cut off his lecture by tossing the now empty water bottle into the recycling bin under Knox's sink. *"I'll be careful, I promise."*

Knox let out a long breath, catching my arm before I walked out. When he tugged me back and pressed his lips to mine in a kiss that stole all my annoyance away, I worried I'd lose myself. Kissing him was like looking over a cliff and down at a body of water. It tempted me to jump, made me want to dive in no matter how deep or dangerous.

As quickly as it happened, however, he let me go, stealing away that warmth. It was like shoving me away from the edge of that cliff. He swallowed hard, his green eyes bright as he stared at me, as if he wanted me to understand something.

What, though?

Maybe he didn't know, either. Maybe it was just hopeless, pointless desire, a drive to have something that wasn't possible.

Whatever it was, he stepped backward, fleeing as he so often did to his room, leaving me there confused and surprisingly cold.

Which felt like a good representation of whatever I had with Knox.

About the Author

Jayce Carter lives in Southern California with her husband and two spawns. She originally wanted to take over the world but realized that would require wearing pants. This led her to choosing writing, a completely pants-free occupation. She has a fear of heights yet rock climbs for fun and enjoys making up excuses for not going out and socializing.

Jayce loves to hear from readers. You can find her contact information, website details and author profile page at https://www.totallybound.com

Home of Erotic Romance

Sign up for our newsletter and find out about all our romance book releases, eBook sales and promotions, sneak peeks and FREE romance books!